# THE PATH OF THE DRAGON

## by

## GLENN RAHMAN
## &
## RICHARD L. TIERNEY



ISBN-10: 1-953215-89-0
ISBN-13: 978-1-953215-89-5

Published by Pickman's Press
Edgewood, NM, USA
www.pickmanspress.com

# TABLE OF CONTENTS

# INTRODUCTION

*WARNING: Contains mild spoilers*

Richard L. Tierney and I were collaborative writers for many years. We became friends in the 1970s as fellow Twin Cities residents. In 1980, I asked Richard to join me in writing a Simon of Gitta story, and he agreed. That same year, we completed "The Wedding of Sheila-na-gog," though it would not be published until 1985. It continued the story of Simon's adventures in the West, which begin in "The Dragons of Mons Fractus." ("Dragons" would not be published until 1984, but I had read the carbon.) The story of "Wedding" is set in Clark Ashton Smith's Averoigne and features Simon interacting with the Druids of Gaul.

Our collaboration having been a successful one, I worked up another plot, one which would lead Simon of Gitta into the Rome of Emperor Claudius. Richard endorsed the idea and we worked on it from 1981-1982. But the book companies of the day proved surprisingly uncooperative and the book, *The Gardens of Lucullus*, would not find a publisher until 2001.

In 1983, I devised a story for a magazine seeking stories inspired by Viking mythology. I crafted a plot based on the material found in 19th-century Swedish scholar Viktor Rydberg's work Teutonic Mythology (1891). Richard agreed to collaborate, and the resultant story, "The Swordmaker of Jotunheim," first appeared in *Fantasy Book* in 1985.

Overall, the 1980s were a productive time for Simon of Gitta, with Richard turning out ten adventure stories. In 1990, he featured Simon in "The Pillars of Melkarth," where Simon reunites with his beloved Helena, who had died when the warrior was in his early twenties. Simon discovers Helena has been reincarnated and is serving at a temple in Tyre in 50 A.D. Richard's plan was for the couple to remain together until Simon's death at the court of Nero in 64 A.D. After that, Richard went on to write *The House of the Toad* (Fedogan and Bremer, 1993), a modern-day horror story in hardcover.

By now a decade had passed since we'd done *Lucullus*, and I was more than ready to revisit Simon's world. This time the setting would be Britain because in *Lucullus* Simon refers to his having joined with the British to resist the Roman invasion of 43 AD. I ran my plot past my collaborator, and the new story clicked with him. This was *The Path of the Dragon*, and we worked on it from 1993 to 1994. Then circumstances caused the work to stop. We didn't realize *Path* would remain in rough draft form until 2023.

In 1994, Richard surprised me when he said he was wrapping up his writing career. At 59, I thought he was too young to retire from an art that had always been important in his life. But Richard said he'd been writing for over forty years, and the Muse was no longer tapping at his window. He felt drained of inspiration and low in energy. He wanted to start taking life easy.

So Richard L. Tierney went into retirement. Even so, *The Gardens of Lucullus* would be published in 2001 (Sidecar Preservation Society of Minneapolis, MN) and *The Drums of Chaos* would go into print with Mythos Books in 2008. Many fans must have believed that the author of the Simon of Gita stories was still at work.

There was also *The Path of the Dragon*, which I could have finished alone. But I felt checkmated by the obduracy of the publishing industry, and my writing career had been a frustrating one. At that point in time, I was only being published in the "semi-pro market."

Richard and I continued to submit *Lucullus* to publishers but in vain. I began doing less fiction, concentrating on gaming projects, especially a board game called Divine Right. The original came out in 1979, but it was still popular as a cult game. I had many expansions for it in mind and wanted to do a new edition. Further, I was (slowly) writing a book of stories about the game world (*The Minarian Legends*), while my employment was sapping most of my time and energy. So many simultaneous labors amounted to a big load, and I wasn't as young as I used to be.

But my retirement age arrived, and I left the Post Office after twenty-five years. By 2020, I had completed both Divine Right and *The Minarian Legends*. (Both have since been published.)

With these distractions gone, I dived into a new sword and sorcery book project, one I had wanted to do since the 80s. I'd written two Bingor and Donalbain stories in the 70s and now wrote six more. I called the compendium *A Feast of Ambrosia: The Adventures of Bingor and Donalbain*. In 2022, I placed these adventure tales with DMR Books. Published in 2023, it is still available from Amazon.com.

In 2019, things became interesting on the Simon of Gitta front. Pickman's Press had contacted Richard L. Tierney with a plan to re-release all his Simon stories, as well as to reissue *The Drums of Chaos* and *The Gardens of Lucullus*. Richard asked me to submit the rough draft of *Path* to Pickman and the book was accepted, pending revision work. At the same time, Pickman agreed to reissue my 1989 novel, *The Heir of Darkness,* an adventure set in the Simon of Gitta universe. Pickman released *Heir* in the spring of 2024 and is now available at Amazon.com.

After revising *Heir,* I performed the necessary work on *The Path of the Dragon*. I worked alone because Richard's advanced age and ill health made it impossible to come out of retirement. Nonetheless, he very much wanted

Simon of Gitta's career to continue. To this end, he granted me permission to do future Simon works under my own byline, an opportunity that I gratefully accepted. Alas, in early 2022, Richard L. Tierney unexpectedly passed away.

My work on *The Path of the Dragon* continued until 2023. Instead of resting, I was fired up to continue the Samaritan's career promptly. In late 2023, I started working on *The City of Pillars: The New Adventures of Simon of Gitta.*

For decades, Richard had been telling me about his story ideas. He usually wrote and published these stories, but there were three plots that he'd never got around to writing before his retirement. I applied myself to these ideas and turned them into stories for my new book, citing Richard L. Tierney as my source of inspiration.

*The Path of the Dragon* was one of the most engaging fantasy adventures I have ever worked on. It began with a totally whacked-out idea: Simon of Gitta would meet, befriend, and support King Arthur!

King Arthur? The idea isn't as ridiculous as it sounds. Just hear me out.

Since at least the 19$^{th}$ century, historians and mythographers have tried to identify the historical character that presumably inspired the legend of King Arthur. They failed. No matter how well or poorly these scholars researched or wrote, they never found convincing evidence to prove their hypotheses.

But in the early 90s, I had read a book by John Whitehead entitled *Guardian of the Grail* (first edition Jan. 1, 1959). He identified King Arthur with King Caratacus, who fought the Romans in 43 A.D. His case was strongly argued in a book of 350 pages, but his theory made no impression on staid academia. The reading public reacted differently, and the book has gained a deserved following. It has had two reprint publications since 1959, and *The Guardian of the Grail* is still available at Amazon.com, reissued by Dorset.

Establishment scholars always dislike outsiders who poach their specialties, but academic scholars have little reason to boast. They traditionally rehash old ideas *ad infinum* instead of thinking outside the box and making new discoveries. As a talented and unblinkered outsider, Whitehead approached the topic of Arthur's identity with fresh eyes and an open mind. He saw what so many academics could not.

Whitehead concluded that the real King Arthur existed in antiquity, not the Dark Ages. He decided that the real Arthur had been Caratacus, the king of the Catuvellauni tribe. This is the long-remembered hero who led his country against the Roman invasion of 43 A.D.

But how is it that the deeds of Caratacus have been remembered as the deeds of Arthur? It seems that after the fall of Rome, the British suffered a new invasion by Saxons, one as terrible as the one carried out by Rome four hundred years earlier.

The Britons fought the invaders under local leaders. After the victory was temporarily won, the bards of Britain did not choose to honor any living men in their songs and stories. Instead, they evoked the heroes of an earlier war, and these were given credit for their victory. They created a Dark Age version of Caratacus, a new king who had defended his country like his original had. By a strange alchemy, the Dark Age Britons had rewritten the life of Caratacus as the life of King Arthur.

Geoffrey of Monmouth (1195 to 1155 AD) was a Welshman who took pride in his country's legends. He wrote *The History of the Kings of Britain* to celebrate the ancient, pre-Roman days of Britain. But after 1100 years, even the Welsh had forgotten the relationship between Caratacus and Arthur. Hence, Arthur and Caratacus appear in Geoffrey's book as two courageous leaders supposedly living centuries apart.

I told Richard I wanted to use Whitehead's theories, and he endorsed the idea. The way was now clear for me to bring the project to life.

In building the world of Caratacus/Arthur, I drew from Geoffrey, not much from Roman propaganda. The Classical-era writers held the British in scorn, depicting them as human-sacrificing barbarians (fine talk from people who probably enjoyed the gladiatorial games). In fact, the British had complex societies with rich cultural traditions, including impressive hill forts, coinage, roads, and trade connections with mainland Europe. Their major trade products were tin, copper, leather goods, and slaves. Their housing was not always made from sticks. Modern archaeology shows that the Britons constructed wooden and stone structures, some quite sophisticated.

As for human sacrifice, Geoffrey does not mention that the British ever practiced it. Even history has failed to uncover a pervasive system of human sacrifice in Britannica.

Were the British primitive? They indeed developed no written language, but the people were not stay-at-home simpletons. They traded with the Greeks, Romans, and other advanced people. Their leaders knew about writing systems. The Druids, too, were far-traveled and were presumably acquainted with what foreigners were doing.

So why didn't the islanders create their own writing system? Seemingly, they willfully chose not to write. The bard-rich societies of the British had a robust tradition of oral history, and the Britons must have thought that putting words on pages was a pale and inadequate way to remember their peoples' glory.

When constructing the plot of *Path*, I wanted it to feature Lovecraftian elements, like those Richard had put into his earlier stories. I had an idea of what to do on that score. H. P. Lovecraft mentioned the Druids in his story "The Rats in the Walls." I knew this story well and liked it very much. It was easy to envision that the evil Druid settlement stood on the same ground where Exham Priory would stand in later days. But to do that properly, I had to find out where Lovecraft's Exham Priory was located.

"The Rats in the Walls" gives two geographical references regarding the castle's location. First, Exham Priory stood near the English Town of Anchester. Second, Anchester was near the archaeological site of an ancient Roman fort originally garrisoned by the Third Augustus Legion. What does this tell us?

Sadly, no town in Britain has ever borne the name of Anchester. And the Third Augustan Legion was never stationed in Britain. Taken at face value, Lovecraft's story is of no help in pinpointing the whereabouts of Exham Priory.

But not so fast. As Lovecraft fans know, the lead character of the story, Delapore, was a madman who composed his terrifying memoir inside a madhouse. His deranged mind could have introduced serious errors into his narrative. What might these errors have been?

Although there was no British town called "Anchester," there was a town called Alchester, which was near Oxford. That's something to work with, but it isn't enough. To seal the deal, we need additional supportive information.

Fortunately, supporting evidence is available. Next to historic Alchester was a Roman fort, established in the early days of the Roman invasion. It housed the Second Augustan Legion. Not the Third, but the Second. Would it not have been easy for Delapore to have made a mistake? Might he not have been speaking about Alchester and the 2nd Augustan Legion? Did Lovecraft have this information, but chose to disguise it for some reason? Or had he misremembered his research reading?

So, where is Exham Priory? Alchester no longer exists, but the present-day town closest to its site is Bicester in Oxfordshire. While writing the story, I envisioned the action taking place near Bicester.

So, the new plot had a location, heroes, and villains. It also needed monsters, preferably monsters with a British flavor. I doubt anyone can argue that there is any Lovecraftian race more British than the Lloigor, who are the creation of author Colin Wilson.

What were the Lloigor? The name of Lloigor first appeared in "The Lair of the Star-Spawn" (1932), a story by August Derleth and Mark Schorer. The authors saw Lloigor as one of the Great Old Ones, who had a brother named Zhar. Together, they are referred to as the Twin Obscenities.

Wilson gave the name Lloigor to his new Lovecraftian race. His story was "The Return of the Lloigor" (1969), and he crafted creatures very different from Derleth's. The mystic power of Wilson's Lloigor waxes and wanes with the changing stars. In their natural state, they are vortices of psychic energy. But when their power cycle is high, they may manifest themselves physically as powerful monsters.

When the Lloigor infest a region, they collectively act as a subtle vampiric force, drawing psychic energy from sleeping humans. They awaken feeling enervated or ill for most of the following day. The Lloigor use this stolen power to perform strange feats, including causing mysterious explosions and slaying humans selectively.

There is no great body of work about the Lloigor to date. Their fullest description is given in *The Call of Cthulhu* fantasy role-playing game by Chaosium. The article expands on the information that Wilson provided. But where did Chaosium get these expansive ideas regarding the Lloigor? Well, it so happens that Chaosium got them from me.

In 1982, shortly after finishing the manuscript for *Heir of Darkness*, I learned that the Chaosium company was accepting manuscripts for a forthcoming compendium called *The Cthulhu Companion*. It needed brief articles about topics congenial to their monster-hunting game.

I took this opportunity to bring Wilson's Lloigor into *Call of Cthulhu*.

I filled my descriptive article with details gleaned from Wilson's story but developed ideas that the author had left vague. For example, he said that the Lloigor's manifestations were the source of the sea monster legends. Unfortunately, he didn't say what sort of sea monster was meant. Was it a squid, a sea dragon, or something else entirely?

I stated authoritatively that the Lloigor could assume the shape of sea dragons. But I pushed the idea further, adding that when the Lloigor manifest on land, they are seen as another kind of dragon, the classic dragon of legend. Further, I clarified the method used by the Lloigor to assassinate humans. I revealed that the strange and lethal phenomenon known as "spontaneous combustion" is a sign of Lloigor activity.

The material published in *The Cthulhu Companion* was soon incorporated into later editions of *The Call of Cthulhu* game. It spread far and wide and today, wherever a fan refers to the Lloigor, he repeats the ideas I established in my article in 1982.

Is it any wonder that the Lloigor have long been my favorite Lovecraftian monster race?

With all these ideas lined up, I built a concise plot. As the book was written, I established a mythic past for Britain that would do justice to the dragons who lived there!

So, please start reading. And have fun!

— Glenn Rahman, 2025

# FOREWARD

In the Simon of Gitta fiction series, this novel takes place in 43 A.D., between the short story "The Wedding of Sheila-Na-Gog" and the novel *The Gardens of Lucullus*.

# Barrows and Stones

## PROLOGUE

Every Briton learned about dragons at his mother's breast, but learning didn't mean believing. To Hywel ab Goneril, dragons were beasts of long ago, banished from the world by the brave deeds of Britannia's ancient heroes. How surprising it was that rumor was now claiming that a living dragon was spreading destruction across western Logres and Lothan.

But the idea of dragon-hunting fired Hywel's imagination. They spent days pondering amazing stories, and then four young warriors rode west, hoping for legendary fame. Encountering an actual dragon could make their names famous for centuries to come!

Riding west, they crossed over the borders of Glouchedon, where the Dobunni tribe held sway. Common people whom they encountered spoke about the destruction they had found. The youths from Logres investigated the ravaged sites; they resembled bandit plunder, yet he suspected more than simple banditry. Why would robbers leave half-devoured cattle out in the open to rot? Locals claimed a whale-sized beast caused the attacks. Many accounts sounded unreliable to the young questers.

Upon passing beyond the rule of the king of Logres, the warriors were set upon by marauding Picts, and two of their number were killed in a brief fight. The third, Hywel's friend Illtud, had been wounded by a Pictish spear. Hywel, fighting alone, suffered a bludgeoning and was kicked and beaten into submission. Afterward, both survivors were taken to a nearby village.

Imprisoned, the young man had no choice but to stand by his cell window, noting everything he could see and hear. The savages were an unruly sort, quarreling and coming to blows with their neighbors. The Briton saw madness in the tribesmen's expressions, even those of young children. Oddly, they hosted men dressed like druids, though their gray-green robes were unlike any priestly attire he knew. His jailers refused to tell him anything, least of all whether his comrade Illtud was still among the living.

Though sometimes threatened, Hywel was not assaulted while in captivity. His meals were adequate but not enjoyable, comprised of turnips with what appeared to be goat.

Then warriors burst in, seized him from his cell, and fastened him to a chariot, one of many on the green. The cars almost immediately set out for the south. His captors were sullen druids accompanied by acolytes and Pictish guards.

The chariots wound their way across a dismal countryside pocked with barrows and overgrown with gorse. Except for infrequent herds of sheep and goats, life signs were few. The bleak landscape looked empty of men, depressed, and lacking vitality.

He wondered whether even a marauding dragon could have fed itself by ravaging such depleted terrain.

The travelers camped twice during their journey. Near twilight on the third day, his captors reined up within sight of another ruin from the forgotten past—a ring of linteled sarsen stones. Hywel learned that "the Giants' Dance" was the structure's name. Logresians knew about this ancient monument. Men avoided it because of its evil reputation.

The standing stones created a majestic silhouette against the red sky. Ancient spirits imbued the stones with a faint glow, while elongated shadows were cast around its base.

Hywel expected to die here, in a ritual sacrifice by Picts and rogue druids. Two acolytes came to take him from his chariot and held him while the rest of the train resumed its approach to the Giants' Dance.

His captors left him sitting bound on the ground while the sky dome dimmed. Soon all he could see of the shunned monument was a fire kindled within its stone rings. At that point, he heard chanting and singing, a sound like evil spirits moaning.

The youth remembered that it was Beltane Day, or very close to it, the most revered fertility ritual of the year. Women were regular participants in Beltane celebrations, whereas only men had taken on this extensive trip. The absence of fertility priestesses at Beltane seemed wrong.

Hywel's two captors had meanwhile been watching the stars as they appeared. The youth himself saw nothing unusual when he glanced skyward. Of a sudden, one acolyte said to his companion, " 'Tis time," and they started removing the warrior's bindings. He tensed, ready to fight for his freedom should his arms be untied.

One acolyte cautioned the Logresian against striking out. "We intend to turn you loose."

Hywel eyed them, sensing ridicule, yet darkness hid their faces. He chose not to fight, hopeful he was being told the truth. When he was unbound, the pair ran to their chariot and drove swiftly toward the wavering Giants' Dance flames.

His release had eased none of his misgivings. He sensed the druids had something evil on their minds. Glancing about at the landscape and at the stars, Hywel felt his anxiety rising. He was on cursed ground, and men shunned burial grounds as haunts of evil spirits.

Perhaps he was still intended to be sacrificed. Wild tribes sometimes reenacted the "wild hunt," when a victim was run down and killed by hunters as an immolation to the dark gods. He needed to flee, and so Hywel set out through the knee-high grass. Fortunately, the stars afforded some light to guide his flight.

The fires of the Giant's Dance were no longer visible when Hywel entered upon a grassy tract pocked with long, low barrows. A superstitious dread caused his flesh to prickle. Though he had often walked across haunted ground by daylight before, he'd always done so with boyhood friends, making light of the grisly legends about the ghosts of the cairns. Now he felt alone and menaced.

Just then, a sound!

Hywel turned and thought he glimpsed a black shape moving behind a cairn. Trackers? A wolf? The youth was familiar with animal sounds, but he had heard something unusual. Hywel quickened his pace and changed direction, but the odd rustling grew more pronounced instead of fading. The thing was trailing him!

Anxious, he looked for any shelter, but the landscape was bare of trees. He was on the verge of shouting to startle his stalker into showing itself, but he suppressed the urge. If it was a man, a cry would reveal Hywel's location.

Skirting a small barrow, Hywel felt the drag of the vegetation slowing his tired strides. Panting, he looked and listened. There! Heavy footfalls headed his way! Straining to see by starlight, he thought he glimpsed something dark and huge flow over the barrow he'd just rounded.

Only now did he remember the dragon story, and the first shudder of genuine fear rippled through his body. The young warrior broke into a dead run, but the thundering steps behind him were gaining. Then a powerful blow knocked Hywel to the ground, unable to breathe in the grip of his pain.

A crushing weight bore down, and his ribs cracked. Then blackness took him.

The pain had vanished.

*And without pain, there was nothing left of him at all.*

# THE FLIGHT OF THE MERLIN

## CHAPTER I

Simon the Samaritan barely heard the roaring waterfall or noticed the gleaming sky dome stretching from horizon to horizon. He felt the spray of the tumbling water as no more than the lightest of Brythonic mists. In his meditative state, he existed like a free-floating wraith no longer constrained by its prison of flesh. His cramped limbs had already ceased to ache. In the embrace of his bullhide cocoon, he felt comfortable, like an infant wrapped in swaddling.

Without years of severe mental training, the ordeal might have driven a common man mad. But for Simon, a trained mystic, the experience had become very nearly euphoric.

The sewn bull-hide wrapping held him tightly; laced cables, likewise of sacred white bullhide, held him in bobbing suspension over the mountain gorge. The Samaritan could vaguely hear the chants of the Druids standing in line upon the ledge overlooking the chasm. The chanters wore blue robes, registering as an azure blur out of the corner of Simon's left eye. Blue was the color of New Beginnings, the Druids said, and so now they wore it for this, the ceremony of the Opening of the Way.

Distinct words came to him—at first softly and then louder. They arrived not as spoken speech but as received thoughts exchanged between two separate minds.

*Simon—the chant. The chant!*

The entranced man opened his bleary eyes to see a glossy black bird perched on a whitish cable. By its midnight plumage and red, downward-curving bill, he recognized the cult bird, the "chough," also called the "merlin" by the Welsh mountaineers. The feathered one had its dark pink eyes fixed on him like an accusing demon.

*Simon—the chant!* the words repeated.

His mind clearing, the Samaritan remembered that the speaker was Emrys, his druidic master, and he was urging Simon to recite what he had already committed to memory:

*All that we see or seem to see,*
*Is but a dream within a dream.*
*Bring me my wings of gleaming ebony, Oh Ceridwen,*

*Make me a spirit eternally free,*
*Arm me with talons, let the clouds bear me high,*
*Let me ride my chariot o'er the ocean of air!*

And then, suddenly—

Simon entered a different place where he felt nothing like himself. All around, the sky and mountain peaks were reeling, rising, and breaking like the sea.

*Simon! Discipline yourself! See what is truly there!* came Emrys' third call.

Simon tried to heed, but he was distracted by a sensation of falling.

*Steady, Simon, steady,* the mind-voice exhorted. The Samaritan struggled to remember his teaching, but without conscious effort, his arms were doing what he wanted them to do. His arms were wings, and their flapping was sustaining him in midair, in flight. The world ceased to spin and he could see that he was high above the hills and forests, like a butterfly over a garden. He was seeing colors—more colors; endless colors!

*He had become a bird.*

The bird could see so much, but it wanted to see much more. Simon beheld the summit of the mountain Yr Wyddfa and yearned to move closer, to merge with its majesty. The man's mind now took command of the bird's body. It was more by instinct than conscious direction that the chough moved toward the mountain, slowly and arduously at first, but then with increasing confidence.

A bird squawk made Simon's look back. There was a black bird there, sailing just behind him. He realized belatedly that the feathered creature was his teacher, Emrys, also in a bird guise.

*Good, Simon, good,* came the savant's thought-voice. *Follow me and pay heed, but say naught as we explore together. Remember, young friend: say naught.*

Simon did not at once react.

*Simon!* Said Emrys with greater firmness. *Come!*

The Samaritan heedfully endeavored to change direction but did so awkwardly. The other merlin maintained a slow glide, encouraging its pupil to catch up.

Gradually, flying became easier. Master Merlin Emrys had told Simon his theory of flight. Flying was intrinsic to a bird. One should allow it to carry out the physical actions of flight while making his human spirit a detached observer.

Simon's mentor led him back to the gorge where his human form still hung suspended in a basket of leather straps made from sacred white bullhide. The Master Druid alighted gracefully on a cable supporting the basket. Simon tried to follow his example, snatching at one of the braided ropes himself. Missing and falling, he righted himself with furious fluttering, rose, came around, and tried again. The second attempt also failed, but on the third try, he took a firm grasp of the cable with his red, clawed feet.

*But is any of this real?* Simon wondered. Was he experiencing a mere illusion induced by long meditation and sensory deprivation? Simon had been deceived by the ingenuity of Celtic priests before. He'd studied briefly with the Black Goat Druids in Gaul before arriving in Britain. But that episode had been a fraud—perhaps the longest sustained gulling the canny Samaritan had ever been subjected to. He'd learned little of druidic wisdom, though he had at least achieved enough fluency in the Gallic language to get along in the similar dialects of Britain.

Was this present experience real or an illusion? He wanted this amazing experience to be real, but his nagging doubts stirred him to anger.

*Gain control of your emotions,* Emrys exhorted the trainee.

Next, by a motion of his red beak, Emrys directed Simon's attention toward the cocoon. Simon saw his hanging body through the straps, but detachedly, as if viewing a random object in space. His lack of emotion in regard to his natural body perplexed him.

Emrys, still perching passively, gave the pupil time to orient himself. But the Samaritan's grace period was brief and the novice again heard his mentor's mind-message, saying: *Follow me, Simon. Time is short.*

With a small leap, the lead black bird quit the bullhide cord; the latter was so taut that it reacted not at all to the departure of the bird's slight weight. Simon, in imitation, flapped from his perch and, though he was still uneasy with flying, overtook his teacher in very few minutes.

*You learn aptly, Simon,* said the elder Druid. *The golden key to success is controlling one's fear. Fear is the presager of defeat.*

Simon almost sent a thought question to his master but remembered Emrys' injunction in time. The strict discipline of the Druids rankled him. He had thought that he had advanced beyond his student days, that he'd become master of his own destiny. But in the previous year, he had requested instruction from the Druids of Britannia. Since then he had worked assiduously in pursuit of that goal, though it was hard to perform as a servant after having enjoyed years of freedom. But Simon of Gitta was determined to play out his role faithfully. He had learned as a youth that ego and pride, just like fear, were pathways to failure.

The Merlin Druid led the Easterner through the sky at speed while his disciple had to push hard to keep up. Already the Samaritan had apprehended that flying—while difficult—was less difficult than anticipated. It was, in fact, the bird that was flying; his human mind did no more than choose the direction. Yet Simon suspected there was more to this lesson than mere practice in temporary transmigration.

Another mind-whisper came. *Look!*

Ahead of Simon was again the mighty mountain of Yr Wyddfa, the tallest peak on the island of Britannia. Yr Wyddfa meant "grave." Legend told of a giant named Rhita Gawr who long ago had ruled Wales, murdering human trespassers who ventured there. He was eventually slain by an ancient hero who buried him under a cairn of stones at the mountain's peak.

But the adventurer saw below more than mere rock and snow. At the summit was a ripple of light, and the longer Simon stared, the stronger the luminescence grew. Before his eyes, the glow transmogrified into a straight line running northwest to southeast.

*A bird's eyes can see more than a man's, Simon,* said Emrys. *Soon the northern line will be lost under the sea; it is the southerly path that will lead us to what I wish to show you.*

Emrys dipped and skimmed, following the light trail like a road. Simon believed he was observing a "ley line." The Brythonic Druids also referred to these as "dragon paths." Simon had burning questions to ask about their nature, but dutifully held his peace.

About two Roman *milles*—miles—farther on, the adventurer observed a second glowing line that intersected the first atop an earth formation that was obviously the work of men. From the air, the long mound displayed the shape of a squirming serpent. The intersecting ley lines drew a Latin "X" over the point where the snake's eye would have been.

Said Emrys:

*Heed this, Simon. Within this ancient land, giants sleep. In times agone, great tribes of deities made war, and the victors entrapped the vanquished in the world of spirit. It had been the fallen giants that had drawn these lines of power across the land. Because the old gods has long been empowered by these lines, the new gods broke the lines of power in the wake of their enemies' downfall, lest they return one day in great might. But over many centuries, the seals confining the fallen giants to the world of spirit have grown weak. Already, the process of their return was beginning.*

Simon recalled that his first mentor, Dositheus, had told him stories about angry and imprisoned gods. The Hebrews possessed their own legends of the arch-devil and his host of demon servants; the Greeks had many legends of the Titans in Tartarus. Did Emrys mean that those ancient tales should be taken as historical facts? He had asked Emrys that question previously without receiving a satisfactory answer.

While the Druids in bird form proceeded along the paths of light, Simon occasionally observed menhirs—standing stones—erected at many of the points of intersection. The Black Goat Druids of Gaul, he knew, had revered the menhirs, but when he came to Britannia, the Merlin Druids had warned him to shun them. Only evil men adored the ancient stones, they said, but had failed to explain what danger they posed.

*We have seen what we need to,* the arch-Druid told his pupil. He went into a wide, sailing turn and Simon followed, expecting the two of them would make the long flight back to the mountain stronghold of the Merlin Druids.

But that was not to be!

In the blink of an eye, the adventurer found himself elsewhere.

He lay on his back once more, claustrophobic and trapped within the bullhide straps of his leather cage. The Druids' chants drifted to his ears; from the corner of his eye, he caught the blue blur of their robes. He saw Mount Yr Wyddfa through the square spaces between the straps. He had lost the visual clarity that he had possessed mere seconds before; the privilege of seeing creation through the eyes of a bird was no longer his.

Simon rested back, wondering what was about to happen.

"Enough!" he heard Emrys call—using his human voice, not a thought-message. "Bring him back. The novice has passed his every test!"

Pulleys creaked and his bullhide cradle glided along its path of cables leading to the cliff where the Druids were deployed. Simon of Gitta tried hard to remember every detail of his flight experience. In fact, it had not faded away like most dreams did upon waking; he could still remember it in stark detail.

Were those memories real? He wondered. If real, he realized that he would henceforth have to look at the world in a new and different way. He would have to ask himself many questions about the very nature of Reality.

# THE EMISSARY

## CHAPTER II

With the pale-faced barber dabbing away the last shaving oil from Simon's cheek, the Samaritan touched the naked part of his scalp and grimaced. The front of his head had been shaved back to an imaginary line running between the tips of his ears and over the dome of his skull. This was the "Celtic tonsure," the cult's public announcement that he had been recognized as a new brother at the first degree of druidism. He sighed. The adventurer very well understood that a haircut amounted to a small sacrifice in exchange for the enlightenment. Even so, he would have preferred to keep his customary black bangs. Had it been politic to forego a change of hairstyle, he would gladly have done so.

The barber stepped back and the Samaritan, standing up, started to brush away the few oily hairs on his garments. He had not finished his task before a hubbub arose in the village outside.

"What's that?" Simon muttered, not really expecting the barber to know. Going to the door, he saw many Druids and village people filling the lanes, all abuzz with excitement. He stepped outside and hailed an untonsured acolyte whom he knew, asking. "What news, Seincyn?"

The youth looked up and saw Simon. "It's a terrible thing!" he said. "High King Guiderios is dead—slain on the Medway battlefield by a traitor!"

Simon gritted his teeth. This was serious. The country was under invasion but because of an assassin, the lairds of Logres would be forced to set everything else aside and gather together to name a new king for Logres, and also the next high king over the Logresian confederacy of kingdoms. The young king had left no issue, but fortunately, he did have a younger brother, Caratacos—a prince held in good regard by Logres' leaders.

Simon had by now achieved some insight into Brythonic politics. Britannia teemed with kings; there were kings everywhere. Some were independent, others held only local authority and were subject to stronger kings.

Britannia's largest power block consisted of the kingdom of Logres and its confederacy. The latter consisted of Loges and all its subject kingdoms in southern Britannica. Logres was the home of the powerful and warlike Catuvellauni tribe. The tribe started to expand its power after the Logresian king Cassivellaunus gained hero status across the face of Britannia for having defeated Julius Caesar. All the Logresian kings that had reigned since then had been Cassivellaunus' blood descendants.

"Will this assassination make Caratacos king?" Simon asked his friend.

Seincyn looked uncertain. "He's worthy but too young; who can say whether the lairds will risk advancing a man of only eighteen summers while the country is in the grip of deadly war?"

"Who brought word?"

"A courier from the court. An embassy from Logres will arrive soon to meet with the Merlins."

"Why do they need to take counsel with the Merlins?" asked Simon. "Are not the Eagles and the Ravens already the trusted counselors of the high kings?"

Seincyn shrugged.


At twilight a day later, the conclave of the Merlin Druids sat assembled within a large log-built meeting hall. It was a simple structure that provided only stools, benches, and plank tables. Yet, because the Britons were an artistic race, many of the wall boards had been cut with cursive carvings. Additionally, many wooden idols decorated the chamber's sundry shelves and shadowy niches.

Wherever Simon looked, unfriendly Merlin faces glowered back at him. He had grown used to their coldness. Inciting jealous rejection was the price to be paid for having quickly gained Master Merlin Emrys' favor. The only smile that came his way from the crowd beamed not from a Merlin's face, but from a Wren's—the arch-Druid Mog Ruith from Ireland.

The Wrens and the Merlins had long-established ties and Ruith had dwelled at the Merlin stronghold all summer engaging in study. Ruith was a man of powerful intellect housed in an imposing body. Large and muscular, he carried little excess fat. In fact, except for his attire, one might have taken Mog Ruith for a warrior. Not being a slave to tradition, the Wren had forgone wearing formal attire for this important conclave and wore instead comfortable traveling clothes—a brown, hooded shoulder piece trimmed with bearskin over a plain tunic. His simple britches were voluminous while his boots, like his shoulders, had bearskin trimmings. A sardonic good humor usually animated the gold-flecked eyes of his round, good-natured countenance.

The royal envoys, who had arrived the evening before, were seated near the head of the main table. According to Seincyn, each would be a man of distinction from the royal court at Camelos. Their mission leader was Kai ab Ectyr, a rather young man.

Kai was the foster brother to Prince Caratacos himself, fosterage being an honored institution among the Brythonic aristocracy. Kai, it was said, had stronger ties with Caratacos than did the late King Guiderios, his brother by blood. The two Catuvellaunian princes had been fostered at different noble homes and had seen little of one another during their childhood.

Kai was of average stature, broad-faced, and wearing a short beard with no trace of gray. Though youthful, the warrior had already made a name for himself. According to the story buzzing about the town, Kai had leaped astride the king's assassinated body to keep the lairds of Logres away from it—not in pious vigil, but to protect the fallen king's sword. This ceremonial weapon was held to be the most sacred item included with the Catuvellaunian royal regalia. Kai had aptly realized that should a credible heir to the now-vacated throne physically claim the sword, that man's pretension to the kingship would have been markedly magnified.

Kai, risking his life, had held back the mightiest and most ambitious lairds of the land until Caratacos arrived personally to claim the honored blade. Interestingly, as soon as the prince lifted the sword from the earth, he immediately passed it to Kai, saying: "A sword should not be used to choose a king. I say, let the warriors of Logres acclaim a leader of their own liking. Let them choose the man they will most eagerly follow at the forefront of battle."

A politic move, if true, Simon mused. The warriors on the battlefield had supposedly shouted back, "Arto! You are king! Arto of Cornwall! Arto of Camelos! You are the new high king!"

"Arto" was a nickname meaning "bear." Most notable Britons bore a plethora of aliases, most of them being honorifics and titles. The warriors, especially, addressed the prince as "Arto" more frequently than they used any of his more formal names, such as Caratacos, Carados, Arwiragus, and Karadeg. Similarly, his late brother had been known as Guideros, Gwydr, and Togodumnos. Their father had accumulated even more cognomens, most famously Cunobelinos, Cymberline, Gynvelyn, and Uther.

Even so, an acclamation from the warriors was not enough to seal a royal succession—unlike the rowdy and illegal way that the Praetorian Guard had elevated Emperor Claudius after the assassination of Emperor Caligula. That accession had been a naked military usurpation and the intimidated Senate had little choice but to affirm it. By contrast, the crowning of a British king was a sacred trust involving many rites, tests, oaths, and omens taken. The Romans called the Britons barbarians, yet they scrupulously obeyed their own laws, while lawlessness ruled Rome.

Even so, Brythonic tradition mattered and Kai's impromptu drama had made Arto Pendragon the all but unassailable royal contender.

Simon considered "pendragon" to be an odd term. It meant "chief dragon" and it referred to any chieftain entrusted to lead a major war band. But after Cassivellaunus had ousted Julius Caesar from Britannia, the lairds of the Catuvellauni offered Cassivellaunus the tribe's kingship, replacing a failed leader who had been so ineffectual during the war. Because Cassivellaunus had won his victory under the title of pendragon, he had adopted the title as his dynasty's name.

Simon noticed Master Merlin Emrys enter the hall. The arch-Druid's heavy burden of years had reduced him to a mere wisp of a man, thin of limb and stooped over. Even so, the Samaritan knew how sharp his mind still was. Acolytes ushered him to the table of honor, to sit next to Caratacos' foster brother, Kai.

The much younger man suddenly shifted uneasily, possibly feeling out of place next to the esteemed arch-Druid. Though Kai's garments reflected the pomp of the occasion, Simon suspected that the youthful warrior—brave in war and awkward in peace—would have preferred to be doing sentry duty right now, wearing stained leather and homespun.

"Brothers," began the Master Merlin. "Laird Kai has been dispatched by the king to discuss matters of the gravest importance. Be silent and pay heed."

Following that introduction, Kai stood up. "I-I thank you, Master Merlin," he stammered. "Arto...." Kai realized his error and cleared his throat. "I ask your pardon, worthies of Britannia, I should say 'King Caratacos' needs the support of every druidic order during these days of peril, and among the greatest of all the orders of Britannia are the Merlins of Gwynedd."

Simon frowned, noting that Kai was already speaking of Caratacos' as the king of Logres. Was the succession settled? Or was the young chieftain simply an enthusiastic partisan supporting his foster brother's claim? The Samaritan continued to listen in silence.

But in the boisterous, outspoken Celtic way, most of the others who were present did not. Despite Emrys' request for quiet, a seated Druid asked, "Why does Caratacos send to the Merlins, when King Guiderios and his father had for so long held the Eagles and Ravens in much higher esteem?"

Kai looked at the man reprovingly, saying, "During his short reign, High King Guiderios served Logres well, and all that he did, he did for good reason. But Caratacos is not Guiderios, and the peaceful kingdom that Guiderios inherited is no more. The gods have seen fit to call King Guiderios unto the Western Isles and elevate Caratacos into his lofty seat of authority. A leadership change always heralds new policies, and this mission to the Merlin Druids demonstrates profoundly we have a new man leading our nation."

"That is fairly said," one priest near to Simon declared.

Kai, his voice raised, continued. "Why must Britons continually throw up old quarrels and stale resentments? I come to the Merlin Druids with tidings of the utmost importance. Hear me, for our embassy arrives with dire news! The greatest of the Eagles and Ravens have been attacked in their own stronghold and slain!"

This revelation brought shocked silence to the room, but it also incited some men of status to stand up, expressing their wish to speak. "What do you mean they are slain?" an attendee demanded without waiting to be called.

Mog Ruith, also rising, asked, "Who slew them? How? By steel? By the magic of the Roman flamens?!" Some frowned at the Irish Druid. The very idea that part-time Italian priests might sorcerously assail and destroy the Eagles in union with the Ravens reeked of impossibility.

"No! Not by the useless flamens of Rome!" Kai answered back. "If magic was performed, its enactors were persons still unknown!"

"How much is known?" a third Druid asked.

"I can only tell you what some people suspect!" Kai declared. "We are beset by a school of traitors called the Black Goat Druids!"

Simon sat up straight. Until this moment, he had believed that the Gallic school of the Black Goats had been destroyed for at least a year.

The Samaritan had been taken prisoner by the Roman proconsul Mettius Aelius Scaevola, who was engaged in plotting treason with the Black Goats. The plotters asked the Roman politician to attend a Black Goat ceremony of the greatest importance. Scaevola had accepted the invitation, but had left behind a cohort of troops in the Black Goats' main village with orders to wipe out the whole cult if he didn't return from the distant druidic ritual safely.

As it turned out, none of this Roman-Druid party ever returned. The Samaritan had witnessed the ritual party being attacked and massacred by a wild tribe of Averonean mountaineers.

In the press of events occurring since then, Simon had lost track of the matter, assuming that the druidic order had been destroyed by Gaul's Roman garrison.

"The Black Goats are hunted outlaws," a Druid protested.

"That used to be so," Kai nodded, once more in control of his temper. "They were being hunted by the Romans and many of their common supporters were slain or taken as slaves. But Goddeu, the cult's highest-ranking arch-druid, contacted the Romans through intermediaries and provided evidence of Scaevola's treasonous conspiracies. This new information cooled the anger of the Roman government. After negotiation, the proscription against the Black Goats was withdrawn and the cult pledged to aid the Romans against their own kin in Britannia!

"These intrigues," Kai went on, "have recently become known to the king of Logres. Now we know that the Black Goats, infamous for siding with the Romans during Caesar's invasion, are now betraying the people of Britannia! With their powerful sorcery serving the Empire, Rome will gain an important advantage it has lacked. And these same plotting wretches might very well have something to do with the destruction of the Eagles and Ravens!"

To Kai's frustration, the room became loud and rowdy. "Brothers! Stop shouting and talking over one another!" he bawled.

The chamber quieted and the young leader started to speak again, holding their attention with a tale of disastrous loss. He told his listeners how the two druidic orders had gathered in a conclave at their stronghold outside the village of Rathtyen in Logres. The local villagers reported that the Druids had gathered unexpectedly and without explanation. They had remained secluded at their assembly hall, saying very little to the people of the village. Witnesses said they displayed troubled expressions as if the matters to be debated must have been of grave concern to all. They outwardly claimed their aim was to discuss the war against the Romans. Even so, there were hints that something else weighed even heavier upon their minds. It was as if a menace more grave than the Roman invasion had come upon Britannia.

"At eventide on the day of the disaster," said Kai, "most of the Eagles and Ravens were convened inside a hall like this one. They had not been gathered long when the villagers heard sinister sounds like rumbling thunder, though the sky was clear and lit by stars. Suddenly, some country people came into Rathtyen crying out that the Druids were under attack.

"The town-dwellers rushed out to man their stockade but when no assault came, the bravest of them went to see what had befallen the Druids. They brought back alarming reports that caused Rathtyen's headman to send runners to the closest warrior camp asking for aid. When the armed men arrived, they found a meeting hall that had been torn to pieces, its beams shattered like kindling sticks. Worse, the bodies of the Druids lay all around, burned and torn, as if assailed by the claws and breath of fire-giants. To the great wonder of all, the bodies of some of the fallen had been reduced to mere patches of ash."

Mutterings filled the hall. Simon continued to listen avidly.

The young war chief continued. "The baffled soldiers sent riders to alert King Guiderios. These arrived at the Medway battle site just after the king's great victory. Guiderios went out to meet the messengers when a traitor attacked him with a dagger. As soon as Caratacos arrived, he ended the confusion and met with Rathtyen's messengers. They reported the fate of the Eagles and the Ravens.

"By nightfall, the new king summoned me and others he trusted with the task of bearing the news unto the Merlin Druids, whose help the kingdom now needed more than ever. Because the Eagles and Ravens have been rendered leaderless, because their greatest spell-weavers were slain, King Caratacos enjoined me to offer the Merlins the place of honor formerly held by the Eagles and Ravens. As many will recall, the new king has long held the Merlin Druids in the highest regard. On sundry occasions, he has consulted with Master Merlin Emrys, both in Cornwall and Gwynedd."

"Did the enemy use sorcery?" a Druid inquired.

"Yes," said Kai. "There were no signs of any attack by soldiers or assassins. Whoever the slayers were, they must not have feared the wizards' defenses. Caratacos is rallying the leadership of all the druidic colleges for consultation."

"Will the king also be calling the Wyrms to his presence?" a priest asked sardonically.

Kai frowned. "Nay! King Caratacos has heard too many stories about untoward doings among the Wyrms. His call goes out to true and proven men only. The king has pledged that he will deal with Brythonic traitors as severely as he will treat any foreign invader who is captured!"

With the conclusion of Kai's address, a flood of questions poured forth. Kai left the matter to his colleagues and left the hall accompanied by Emrys. With all the clamor, Simon couldn't hear anything worth listening to. Secluded in his corner, he sighed. The Brythonic standard of leadership was always too quick to argue and too slow in making decisions.

With the procedure having been reduced to noise and wrangling, the Levantine wanderer left the hall. Despite Britannia's recent victory, he knew the country was still periled. He hoped that the inexperienced Arto, the as-yet uncrowned king of a boisterous and balky realm, would measure up to the great burden of his responsibilities. But Simon felt glum. How could so young a man prove capable of bringing order to such a war-torn, disunited, and uproarious country?

# THE FOUNTAIN OF NIMUE

## CHAPTER III

The road to Camelos brought Simon of Gitta and the Merlin Druids into the independent kingdom of Sorestan, where the Cornovii tribe held sway. Even in November, Britannia presented the traveler with a fragile beauty, unlike the Easterner's harshly angled homeland. But the two countries were alike in one way: both were troubled lands under the shadow of the Roman Empire.

Before he had seen Albion for himself, Simon had anticipated finding a primitive land where—the Romans insisted—dark magic and human sacrifice held sway. What he discovered instead was a civilization to be admired. Its main faults were that it did not have its own written language and had lagged behind in the art of architecture. The people were industrious and vital, neither ignorant nor backward. Simon had heard his druidic acquaintances state that what their island lacked, it lacked because it was unimportant.

Indeed, the Samaritan reasoned, a civilization should be admired not only for what it possessed but for what it refused to accept. Trained thinkers, the Druids, held that where too many foreign ideas were tolerated, the character of a people would change, and rarely for the better. Simon had seen the truth of that across the water in Gaul. After ninety years of Roman exploitation, the old ways and the old wisdom were very nearly extinguished, while banditry, vice, and corruption were everywhere.

Above all, the Britons excelled in the arts. Their songs, poetry, and oral literature ranked among the best in the world. In crafts and science, the people also excelled. The man of Gitta had seen Brythonic physicians healing patients who would have died if their ailments had been treated in any of the Empire's great cities. Far from being illiterate, the Brythonic aristocracy was commonly schooled in Greek and Latin. Arto's father, King Cunobelinos, had been educated in Rome. Having rejected Roman vice, he had returned home laden with ideas for improving the material standards of the Logresian kingdom. In fact, the corrugated road that Simon and his companions were now following had been laid down using Roman engineering principles that would not have been held to scorn even in Italy.

Seeing the lead chariots turning off the road brought Simon out of his reverie. The train was veering off upon a more rustic track.

"Where are we going?" Simon called back to Kai, whose car was just behind his. Simon had bettered his opinion about the young man's character.

Though he had shown rough edges as a diplomat, Kai ab Ectyr was a good-natured man of common sense.

"We go to the sacred Fountain of Nimue, Simon," the Catuvellaunian answered, "for prayer, rest, and refreshment."

The train entered the shade of a woodland with baring trees overhead and heavy autumnal litter across the roadway. After traveling a mile beyond the turnoff, they saw a row of well-made round huts. Simon supposed these would be occupied by cult priests—or, as this was a goddess shrine, priestesses—along with any mates, children, servants, guards, and retainers dwelling around the fountain.

The druids' party was not the shrine's only visitors. Many chariots were lined up just off the roadway, attesting to the shrine's popularity. The visitors they observed were garbed in a wealthy, even princely, manner, and their company included aristocratic-looking ladies.

A few of the men moved hospitably toward the druids. Big, imposing, fair-haired and fair-eyed fellows, they looked like doughty fighters—as they had better be, Simon knew. The safety of the roads had declined quickly since the recent fighting had started, and deserters, defeated soldiers, emboldened bandits, and malingering opportunists had filled the countryside. The ostentatious possessions these travelers were loaded down with would surely tempt such rogues.

"Hail, Fathers," one of the visitors called out. He was a fellow whose mustache was stiffened with beeswax at both ends.

"Greetings, friends. Where do you hail from?" responded Master Merlin Emrys, who was riding in a car of honor near the head of the train.

"We come from Estrangore," called out a lady with a strong voice that sounded youthful, if not very melodic. Tall and athletic-looking, she was probably less than twenty. The maid had on a green-dyed tunic partially covered by a tartan shoulder cloak of red and green. This mantle was pinned at the shoulder with a large brooch of polished bronze. The maid's ankle-length woolen skirt was also tartan. Yet what set her apart was the sunlight that imparted a remarkable luster to her fair hair. The sheath at her waist held a dagger encrusted with gold and semi-precious stones. The weapon caught Simon's eye, as he had seldom seen Brythonic ladies going about armed in friendly company.

But the girl's carriage communicated her rank more clearly than her garments.

The maiden, noticing Simon's studying glance, met his stare with her own—bold and challenging. Yet her fine features did not register offense. Her expression was neither friendly nor unfriendly.

Simon glanced ahead toward Emrys, who had already dismounted and was walking toward the sacred spring, there to pay his courtesies to the "queen of the fountain." The Easterner saw that the shrine's chief priestess was a young matron attended by a lightly-armored man bearing polished arms. No doubt, this impressive fellow was the traditional "warrior of the lady," a sacred personage commonly found at goddess shrines. In practice, such men served as a priestess's bodyguard commander. These wealthy and popular shrines needed to be defended against thieves and bandits.

According to what Simon knew, the warrior would rank as the sacred husband of the "queen." Oddly, British custom allowed any daring male of social status to challenge the lady's warrior for his place of honor. This duel was, of course, a reenactment of the ancient king-sacrifice rite. Dismayingly, the victor was allowed to slay the vanquished one. If the upstart won, he would be considered the new sacred husband of the "queen."

Simon thought this to be a barbarous tradition. What if the priestess had wifely feelings toward her slain warrior? What if the couple already had children? A real goddess would have accepted the bloody ritual as a matter of course, but this fountain lady was not a goddess but a young woman. How was a youthful wife expected to cope with seeing her consort die before her eyes and, worse, being obligated to accept into her bed the very man who had killed her mate? The Samaritan shook his head. Everywhere in his travels, he'd seen ugly and cruel customs being observed. How had these rituals come to be, and why had people tolerated them for centuries?

Mog Ruith advanced to stand beside Emrys. "We are the Druids from the Merlin sanctuary at Yr Wyddfa," he informed the fountain goddess. "We are accompanied by Laird Kai, foster brother of King Caratacos. Also with us are many distinguished men from the court of Camelos."

The priestess responded to his greeting with bland courtesies. Just then, a handsomely caparisoned laird approached the Irish Druid:

"I am Cubert," he said. "We comprise the wedding party of Princess Voada, daughter of Calladan, late high king of the Brigantians. She is the sister of Venut, the reigning high king of Estrangore, and we are escorting our lady to the court of King Antedios of Eastland. Lady Voada is to be wed to Prince Prasutagos, his heir."

Simon wondered whether Voada's sober mood indicated that the prospective bride was not enthusiastic about her betrothal. As the sister of the Brigantian high king, she would have had almost no say in choosing her own husband. Royal marriages were customarily arranged. But every princess was also a woman, and women wanted a voice in selecting a husband.

Moreover, Simon knew that the convention sometimes led to epic mismatching. In this case, however, Prince Prasutagos shouldn't be too old for the girl, as his father was still the reigning monarch. On the other hand, the prince might very well be a prepubescent child unable to act the role of a real husband for several years. And there were times when two families, long hostile, would marry their sons and daughters as a gesture of reconciliation. In such circumstances, not every young person would be happy to wed with one who had lately been perceived as an enemy. And then, there were cases when a forced marriage would separate two people who would otherwise very much wish to wed.

The Samaritan shrugged. There was no reason to speculate on such matters. The princess's mood might reflect some passing and unimportant inconvenience, such as a spot of wine sloshing upon one of her favorite garments.

"Fathers, you are welcome to share in our repast," the Brigantian Cubert said. "We are tarrying at this god-sanctioned location in anticipation of the arrival of the Iceanian delegation. In fact, we have just received a message informing us that the Eastlanders are drawing near."

Mog Ruith nodded genially. "If our master finds no objection, we should be pleased to break bread with your august company."

With the customary greetings completed, the Druids—including Simon—proceeded to the fountain. There, they spoke the customary prayers and made a donation to Nimue. At the ritual's culmination, the Divine Lady—acting through her earthly priestess, of course—gifted the new arrivals with dippers so that they might drink from the holy well.

The parties subsequently withdrew to the dining tables. Though the people of Estrangore were reputedly less polished than the Catuvellauni of Logres, the wedding party had arrived well-supplied with good Caecuban wine from Italy. Finding an exotic wine in a remote location no longer surprised Simon, who had learned that Brythonic sailors regularly visited the most distant ports of the Mediterranean and ventured down the western coasts of Africa.

The Brigantian males drank their wine neat, though their women preferred to dilute it with fountain water. Additionally, the merry-makers had brought plentiful flasks filled with a favorite native drink, a wheaten beer called *corma*. Simon knew this was prepared with honey and, by custom, was poured into a *krater*—a large drinking vessel—to be passed around for every male to sip from.

The travelers had brought ample fare—salted pork and smoked fish being the staple. Additionally, cheese slabs and loaves baked with honey were on offer. Guests were also given portions of fresh red deer meat, Britons being accomplished huntsmen.

While they dined, the feasters heard chariot wheels rattling along the unpaved track. They saw cars approaching, each holding two men—a driver and a dignitary. Simon noticed that one of the vehicles carried a youth of about nineteen years, wearing cheap but festive-looking garments. Brown of hair, even-featured, and fair-complexioned, he looked more like a servant than a member of the aristocracy. Instead of sporting a weapon, he carried a harp tucked under his arm. This detail explained his presence. Music-makers were a fixture at any Brythonic festival or feast.

The diners rose as a welcoming gesture toward the newcomers. A tall young Eastlandian warrior dismounted from his car and waited beside it for some of his companions to join him, including the presumed bard.

"Am I addressing the wedding party of the Princess Voada?" the Icenian laird asked.

The bride-to-be raised her head. "I am Voada of the Brigantians."

The warrior smiled. "I am Lemovic ab Seithenyn of Eastland, foster brother to Prince Prasutagos. Greetings, Lady."

Voada nodded. "I bid welcome to Laird Lemovic and also to his companions."

The nobleman bowed slightly.

"Has the prince himself accompanied your delegation?" asked the princess.

"Alas, the Romans are encamped in Cantia, which is uncomfortably close to our borders. The prince has military obligations that require him to stay near our capital at Caer Venta.

"On behalf of Estrangore, we extend our greetings," said another of Voada's male companions. "I am Daldav, commander of our lady's guard. Come, join our repast. We have already been joined by the Merlin Druids from the Gwynedd district of Norgales. They are accompanied by several distinguished emissaries representing Prince Caratacos of Cornwall."

Simon took note of the "Cornwall" reference. Estrangore and Logres were rivals, and partisans of the former deigned not to acknowledge a new high king of the Logresian confederacy until Caratacos' elevation became an accomplished fact. The Brigantians of Estrangore were technically allies of Logres in the war against the Romans. But its leaders had been grumbling that the northern kingdom was not supporting the war in any notable way.

Lemovic, meanwhile, was exchanging courtesies with Kai. "What news of the war?" Kai asked.

The Icenian grinned. "I have heard that Laird Kai was at the Medway. You know the Romans were well bloodied and retreated south of the river." Then, with a small smile, he added, "It appears that these new invaders are finding Brythonic hospitality just as overwhelming as Julius Caesar did in his day!"

Simon smiled at the quip. The Brythonic tradition held that Gaius Julius Caesar was defeated in Britannia and forced to evacuate. Caesar's memoirs, on the other hand, endlessly boasted about his victories in Britannia and told the Roman people that the Britons were now a client people under tribute to the Empire.

Every claim Caesar made had been nonsensical. Britannia had been one of the tyrant's least successful campaigns. He had arrived late in the season—the same error that General Plautius had recently made—and then marched up and down the coastlands for several weeks, unable to deliver a solid blow against the islanders. Moreover, Caesar had a faulty supply situation. Not wanting to sail too far from his Gallic bases, he had debarked just across the channel. But that was an area where there were no useful ports to capture. With no bases, the supply ships were at a loss to find the invading army.

With September almost gone and October bearing down on him, Caesar knew the autumn weather would worsen his situation. He also knew that Roman tactics were ineffective in snowy weather. Facing disaster, he offered the Britons a generous, patched-together peace in exchange for a safe withdrawal. Once back in Gaul, Caesar passed the winter writing dispatches to Rome describing his fictional Brythonic victories. Simon sighed. Everything that Simon had ever heard about Julius Caesar sounded so depressingly Roman.

Lemovic and Kai were still talking about the Medway battle. "Where is the Boar now?" asked the man of Camelos.

The Boar referred to General Plautius. The nickname was satiric, of course, but not wholly disrespectful. While the Britons disliked the Romans, they regarded wild pigs highly.

"Plautius keeps his men inside their fortified camps. They are so hemmed in that they're scarcely able to forage. The warriors of Logres have been stopping most of the Roman provisions being sent out from River's Mouth. The legionaries will be on short rations until spring. Hopefully, they will be rendered sick and weak by then.

"And Plautius' supply problem was bound to worsen. With no new ships arriving, River Mouth would become an empty bin before winter, when nearly all shipping would have to cease."

"Do the Catuvellaunians plan to attack the invaders in their forts when the Romans are most wretched?" asked Kai.

"I can't say what the war chiefs intend. The Romans are deadly fighters when hiding behind their fortifications. Spies report that the Romans are not telling their people about their failures in Britain. Even Caesar's Praetorians might turn against Claudius if the truth were known. There have only been three Caesars. One of them was murdered by his wife, and the other two were murdered by Praetorians. May that noble tradition continue!"

Kai nodded, pleased that Plautius had accomplished nothing since his defeat on the Medway River. Now the invaders were nursing their wounds in territory they already conquered, and probably trying to keep the Britons from massing against them by stirring up the island's vermin—mostly Pictish tribesmen—to raid the hinterland.

"Please, Laird Lemovic," urged Daldav from afar, "come to our table."

"That we will do, and with gratitude," the Eastlandian warrior shouted back. "But first, let us present the prince's soon-to-be bride with a token of his very high regard."

The Icenian gestured to an attendant holding a silver krater, one much better than the one the Brigantians had brought. It had two vertical silver handles with handsome designs beaten into its gleaming surface. The serving man placed this work of art into Lemovic's hands, and the laird, in turn, handed the vessel over to Daldav, who bore it to the princess's table.

"A tidy bauble," Voada remarked with a nod. "But why should Prasutagos choose to send me a drinking cup?"

Simon blinked, thinking that the reply had sounded ungracious.

"It may be because the prince is almost as fond of wine as he is of beautiful damsels," offered the young man behind Lemovic, the one with the harp.

Simon regarded the youth. In such an aristocratic company, fellows of his ilk were not allowed to speak out of turn. Voada glared at the boy and then looked toward Lemovic as if waiting for the noble warrior to rebuke the musician.

But the Eastlandian continued to smile, saying, "This is Broch, Prince Prasutagos' bard and gleeman. I trust the lady will find him an amusing fellow. He plays, sings, and is especially apt at spreading court gossip."

Broch meant "badger."

Simon wondered at Lemovic's careless attitude. A merryman was customarily given a bit of leeway when making inappropriate jests, but Broch had been excessively forward.

"If this person is to be a servant of my Eastlandian house, should I not regard him as a servant of my own?" asked the princess.

"As the lady pleases," said Lemovic.

Her tone had chilled the careless banter. Servants got to work, ushering the newcomers to their places and bringing additional food and wine. While this happened, Emrys approached the princess' table and sat across from her. Except for the Master Merlin's age and eminence, this would have been a bold move.

"My lady," he said, "our brotherhood thanks you again for your hospitality. In return, I would grant our lady a boon. Scathach, the Far-Seeing, occasionally endows me with second sight. Should you permit it, it would be my privilege to read your fortune as the gods have written it in the lines of your left hand—the hand closest to your heart and soul."

The princess searched the Druid's face before extending her open palm. "What do you see, Father?"

The Master Merlin cupped the hand lightly and pondered the lines lightly traced upon it. Voada thought she noticed some consternation in his expression.

"What do you see, Father?" she repeated.

"You are at a crossroads, Lady," he said slowly.

"What kind of crossroads?"

"Very soon, you will be presented with choices. Important choices. I hesitate to say more."

"What choices? Between danger and safety? Good and evil?" she asked.

"Something will transpire that will change the direction of your life."

"Will the change be my choice, or will it be dictated by fate?" she prompted.

"Sometimes what seems to be a choice is not a choice at all."

"Your prognostication sounds ominous, Revered One. Please say something to put my mind at ease, or else I will not sleep well this night."

The Master Merlin nodded resignedly. "When I peer through the obscuring mists, I perceive you standing at a crossroads. I foresee a future life full of happiness and reward, but it shall not be a long life, and it will end in despair and anguish."

"T-That hardly seems to be a desirable fate," the girl replied nervously. "What is the other road?"

"It is a longer road, and it betokens a longer life. But it is a dry, dusty path. The spring and summer of your life will flow away with regret, sadness, and longing. Yet perseverance will end your journey at a pleasant arbor. Your autumnal sky will be bright, and your last harvests shall be bountiful. The winters that come will be visions of crystal beauty."

"In the winter of my life, I doubt that anyone shall consider me beautiful," she said with a painful smile.

"That is so, but is it not possible to find beauty in some place other than a lady's mirror?"

He released her hand, and Voada drew it back. "I find both of your predictions very daunting, Father. When will I be forced to make this fateful choice?"

"Soon."

"Wise One, might you tell me which road I should follow?"

"I have no answer," said Emrys. "But when the time for choosing comes, your heart shall decide, not your mind."

Silence prevailed around the tables until Cubert spoke with forced heartiness:

"If the master sees such bleakness in our lady's future, I would not care to hear of my own destiny!"

Emrys regarded him gravely.

"Cubert, your fate isn't one to daunt you. I think you would gladly choose it over many another."

"Where does that place me, Father?" the nobleman asked. "I have many preferences, many wishes—more than I could enumerate on two hands. Should you not look at my palm before you contemplate my fate?"

"Your fate is written in stone. It is like a bird singing loudly on your shoulder," the arch-Druid informed him. Then he regarded the other feasters. "I have no more auguries worth telling," began Emrys. Those gathered there breathed an audible sigh of relief until the old man glanced sharply toward the harper lad, saying, "Except I bespeak a destiny that involves you, young man."

Broch stared at him abashedly. "Me?"

The prognosticator nodded. "Show me your hand."

Broch glanced at his left palm. "Whatever you tell me, I will probably not understand it, my wits being so dull."

"Would you prefer that I remain silent?" the Druid asked.

The youth wrinkled his brow. "No, Father, I will hear it. The sooner words are spoken, the sooner they are forgotten." He extended his hand.

The Master Merlin scanned the palm and then let it fall away. Instead of speaking, the savant rose and made to leave.

"Wait, Revered One, what have you read?" the young man asked.

Emrys looked back. "It is a fate you might not wish me to reveal."

The harper frowned perplexedly. "I understand, Father. If doom besets me, I might not want to hear it. But is there nothing you can foresee that I should be happy to hear?"

"And what news might you receive with happiness?" inquired the Master Merlin.

The youth seemed to consider the question seriously. "Knowing I might live for some good while in health might make me cheerful."

Emrys smiled ruefully. "Your life shall be vigorous and healthy. I foresee that you shall live longer than any other man here, be he either Icenian or Brigantian."

Simon took pause. These words struck him as more ominous than the other two prophecies. But why should that be? Emrys had said nothing very weighty. The adventurer could only suppose something disturbing was conveyed in the savant's inscrutable expression and the odd flicker in his eyes.

The musician chuckled nervously. "Well, living long is a good thing, isn't it, Father?"

"If it is good, be cheerful!" replied the Druid. "But remember all you who dine here—a worthwhile life is not to be measured by its length. A life's value derives from the thoughts and deeds that have collectively comprised it until the moment of death."

The arch-druid withdrew from the tables and shuffled away toward the fountain, not to say another word for the remainder of the evening.

# THE BATTLE AT THE BRIDGE

## CHAPTER IV

The groups parted in the morning. The Druids withdrew to the highway, bound for Camelos. The Brigantians and Icenians, now a united party, took a more northerly and direct route toward Eastland.

After an hour's ride, Princess Voada directed her charioteer to slow down, allowing Broch's car to catch up with hers. She shouted, "Harper, do you know how to drive a team?"

"I can, My Lady. Why?" he shouted back.

"Because I would have you act as my driver for the day."

That statement—the command—surprised the musician, but he could not properly refuse it. Both cars slowed and stopped to allow the exchange of drivers. The harper crossed over to the princess' chariot while her driver became a passenger in the other vehicle. When standing next to the young woman, Broch was no taller than she was. The youth started the ponies moving with a light slap of the reigns. Though he expected to be criticized for his driving skill, the Estrangorean maid said no word for the next several minutes. From her manner, he guessed that she had something to say but was uncomfortable saying it.

"Broch," she said suddenly, "Laird Lemovic remarked that you were a useful source—for court gossip, I mean. Is that so?"

Broch shrugged. "I suppose I know most of what is said around the court, Princess."

"Fine. I've so far been dependent on my kingdom's diplomats and Eastland's diplomats to inform me on matters concerning your home court. But it's always frustrating expecting diplomats to speak plainly. I've also questioned Laird Lemovic, but he's remained coy."

Broch nodded. "The Laird is not well versed in royal gossip. His duties often take him away from the king's house. Also," the youth added in a lowered tone, "he is the prince's foster brother, and it behooves him to be discrete on matters involving his sovereign's family."

"And you are not so discrete as he is?"

"There are few who would call me discrete, My Lady," the harper replied with a smile.

Expecting a question about the court, Broch was taken off guard when she asked, "Is your singing competent?"

"I do not sing so well as I should like to, Lady."

"If you are not a capable singer, why has the prince chosen you to be his musician?"

"It's sad to say, but the prince has no ear for songs or music," the young man replied. "If I sang accompanied by a frog he would be hard put to say which voice was the better. But I have other talents that meet his approval."

"What other talents?"

"There *are* some matters I would prefer to be discrete about!"

"So, you are his nance?"

The youth almost fell out of the car.

"No! By no means! By the gods! Who has said that Prince Prasutagos behaves like a Greek?"

"If you do not wish to be misunderstood, do not couch your words so mysteriously. I would like to know more about the man to whom I am betrothed. I feel no urgency to wed, and I agreed to the marriage only because my kingly brothers saw it as politically advantageous. If your association with your prince is honorable, please brief me on his character. Remember, if I am to marry your master, all the secrets that the two of you share will soon be laid open to me."

"I am not trying to be mysterious, Lady. It is only that my low station behooves me to… choose my words carefully."

"In that case, you should not so readily boast about how indiscreet you are," Voada observed.

"I would only refrain from imparting information that might give my masters good cause to remove my head."

"Then, I will begin with an easier question. Tell me the songs that you sing best."

"There are many songs, Lady. The list is long. What type of song do you enjoy most? Songs of love, I might guess?"

She shook her head. "Love is a lonely wolf that has never howled at my door. While love is rare game, warfare is everywhere. I feel in the mood for a battle song."

The boy looked straight ahead, frowning.

"Well, gleeman, you have a few songs memorized, do you not?!"

"I have! Here's one I've learned recently:

*Here's to the chieftains*
*Of the Catuvellauni tribe,*
*Who fought the fight that gave Rome flight!*
*And they'll do it all again.*

*The pipers' horns are sounding*
*Ripple, ripple go the drums,*
*Bring out the sword and shake the spear,*
*The battle's on again!*

*Here's to our brave master,*
*Let laurels crown his brow!*
*Shame to every craven dog*
*Who will not fight again!*

*Let ev'ry warrior soul be stout,*
*Its courage burnished bright,*
*Our heroes won the day before,*
*And they'll do the deed again!"*

The singer, pausing, awaited the maid's reaction.

"Fair…" Voada finally said.

"Only fair?" Broch asked.

"Oh, it will do as a song, I suppose. But I am glad that you possess other talents. It would be sad if a failed merryman were cast out to starve."

The youth returned a hard smile, preferring to take her statement as a joke. "Are you a singer also, Lady?"

"No. I am told that my voice is not a tuneful one."

"That is regrettable, but the princess is undoubtedly blessed with many another talents," the boy replied.

"Do not be a sycophant; flatterers annoy me."

Broch regarded her anew. "Would the lady prefer that I converse plainly with her, as would a robust harvester, or should I cut my capers as a polished and courtly man?"

"Speak as you prefer. I am not easy to mislead. If you know the prince Prasutagos so very well, describe to me the mettle of the man."

Broch, glowering thoughtfully, replied, "He is most admired by the women of the court."

"Why is that? Is he well-graced and charming?"

"Oh, not at all, My Lady! And in such a court he does not need to be. The minxes at the king's house are predisposed to admire a man for his wealth and rank only. They seem not to care how he looks or how he speaks."

"What say you? That he is ill-favored?"

The young man nodded. "Our heir has taken to fat, alas. Strong spirits, indulged in for too long, leaches away a man's good looks. In truth, they call him 'the Roman,' not so much because he likes Romans, but because he is as pot-bellied and gluttonous as the worst of them."

"He is not old, I hope," Voada stated, frowning.

"He is your age, I think, but he looks older. The loss of a man's hair adds ghost years to his appearance. Too, pox scars suffered in childhood have taken away any good looks that Nature might have graced him with. Lamentably, too, Prasutagos is an angry man. Roiling rage, held within for too long, harms the body no less it does the character."

"How does he conduct himself when this anger is upon him?"

"Oh, Princess! I would hesitate to describe such wild behavior to one hopeful of a happy wedlock!"

"Tell me simply, does he truly want this marriage?"

Broch, taking a deep breath, answered cautiously. "I do not think he cares either way. He will accept whatever wife would please his mother."

"His mother? Does he not pay better heed to the will of his kingly father?"

"At times. If his mother does not object he will seek to please the king. It is his nature to be obsequious with all those mightier than he is, even if he despises them."

Voada scowled. "You are indeed far from discreet! But I suspect that your words are scurrilous and spoken in malice!"

Broch shook his head. "Not so! For what cause would I slander a man who has been so generous with me? I am one of the fortunate few who he has not cheated or threshed. But if he treats you rudely, My Lady, it is not out of personal enmity. He rails against all and sundry. He will abuse persons of rank as readily as he will rail against the base."

Her expression hardened. "Why should I believe anything you say?" Voada asked sternly. "Clearly, you do not care for the prince. I think you may be seeking to harm him by making a suspicious wife of me. Can you say nothing complimentary about the royal family that sustains you?"

"Well, Lady, that is a hard question. Old families tend to decay. The prince's two brothers were born mad. They still live but are kept far from court, watched by warriors."

"I never heard that the prince had brothers."

"The queen, especially, would be pleased to hear they are forgotten. In plain truth, violent lunacy has been the family's curse. People say that the brothers take after their uncle."

"An uncle on their mother's side? No one has said that King Antedios had a brother."

"Oh, yes, the pathetic one exists. He was disowned long ago by his father for committing an outrageous murder. The prince was kept locked away in comfort until he wantonly murdered one of his own jailors. For that, the king ordered him to be kept shackled night and day. None at court are permitted to speak his name!"

"But you are speaking about him now!"

"Aye, Lady, but I have not spoken his name!"

"What of the present king? Does he possess a fit mind?"

Broch bit his lower lip. "Would that he were stronger in spirit. His court has forever been ruled by his wife and her favorites. All the important posts are filled by the queen's sufferance. The king's servants have learned who truly rules and know tenure depends on keeping the queen fond of them."

Voada balled her fists. "Phaff! Either my brothers are marrying me into a dynasty of swine, or you are a cold villain who slanders his patrons. I do not doubt that in due course, you will pleasurably disparage my character, also!"

"Blame me not, My Lady. I am speaking with honesty for a worthy purpose! I seek to fortify my queen, lest she be scandalized at what she soon shall see and hear at court and flee away. My tribe is in dire need of Your Ladyship. We pray by every god that your pristine bloodline will improve our royal dynasty."

"*Hruh!*" she said scornfully, showing him her back and crossing her arms.

The harper continued to speak, assuming a conspiratorial tone. "If the princess wishes to thrive at our court, she must be wary of her husband's mother. If the lady dislikes you, she may seek your death. Take care to defer to the queen in all things. If she tells you to do something against what the king prefers, your own safety depends upon heeding the words of the queen."

Voada struck the rim of the chariot with her fist. "I think you are a liar. How could one so gallant-seeming as Lord Lemovic adhere faithfully to a family rift with depravity?"

"The noble Lemovic does what he does because he is the finest of the Icenians," Broch declared. "He is also blessed to have no strong blood link to the royal family. That accounts for his good character. I am advised that loyalty compels him to be silent about matters that render his honest heart. Do you not see it as strange that he has bidden that you seek *my* advice on matters pertaining to affairs at court?"

"If you have such a high opinion of Lemovic's honor, I shall ask him to confirm what you have told me. Do you suppose such a man will support your calumnies, or will he beat you to within an inch of your scurrilous life?"

Broch maintained a confident smile. "Yea, Lady, do tell him. I trust you will see no change in his kind regard for me. And when you know I continue in his favor, should that not serve for testimony regarding the truthfulness of my information?"

The princess met his glance and said, "We shall see what we shall see!"

*     *     *

Just a couple of miles farther along, Lemovic, at the head of the train, held up his right arm and shouted, "Hold!" Just ahead, a wagon loaded with cut wood was blocking the way, half on and half off a bridge. The small gorge it spanned was steep-sided and uncrossable.

"Our oxen broke loose," called one of the cart men in a thick accent. "We have sent to the village for help. Be patient, my lord." He was a small, wiry man with very dark hair and beard. Lemovic knew him at once for a Pict.

Britons, as a whole, had no liking for Picts. Before the Brythonic people had come from the continent, the island had been divided into several Pictish kingdoms. They were poor warriors compared to the Britons and were driven into the cold and unproductive northlands. Their dispossessed descendants degenerated into a savage breed bent on invading the South for pillage and slaughter.

In each war, the surviving raiders were given to the aristocracy as slave laborers. Some ran away from their bondage, but many grudgingly stayed. Not even the runaways chose to return to Pictland, preferring to live as beggars or bandits. Additional Pictish vagabonds continually drifted south into the Brythonic kingdoms to settle amongst the bondmen. They willingly became serving men and women for the privilege of living in a land better than theirs.

The frustrated Lemovic took stock. The forest encroached from every side, and his party had no choice but to cross the span. "Throw that piece of junk into the ditch," the Icenian laird finally instructed the wagon men, "and make way for Princess Voada!"

"Laird!" replied the Pict. "Will you deal with poor men so harshly?"

"Do as told!" the Lemovic shouted. His patience being exhausted, he signaled to his warriors, and several strong Britons leaped from their vehicles and approached the bridge with swords drawn. Those in the train behind them watched intently. The distraction caused them to miss the furtive movements that rustled the leafy growth.

Then came a Pictish shout and a flight of whispering arrows. Britons cried out, several of them wounded. The thickets burst open as lean, tattooed spearmen crashed through them.

"Brigands! Ambush!" Lemovic shouted.

Pictish war cries echoed, and the Celtic warriors bellowed back with rage. The tribesmen's swift rush gave the travelers no chance to circle their chariots for defense. The swarming attackers concentrated on destroying the swordsmen. But the latter were supported by their servants, using stones and dead limbs as makeshift weapons. Other menials dragged frightened women away from the fighting. Voada, springing from her chariot, ran fleetly to join a knot of warriors. She brandished her dagger against the onrushing Picts, but watchful warriors thrust her deeper into their ranks for protection.

More tribesmen came crowding over the bridge, reinforcing the ambushers. Briton and Pict fought with equal frenzy.

Voada armed herself by taking a dropped sword from a helpless wounded warrior, but her guards pushed her back lest she attack the enemy.

"We can't hold them!" Daldav shouted. "Help the princess away!" But a sudden surge of tribesmen tore the warriors' line apart, leaving no one between Voada and the oncoming savages.

"Here she is!" a Pictish club man cried out in his own language. Voada braced herself, expecting to die, but the wild-looking brute groped for the maid as if to take her captive. The princess, slashing, scored a blood wound on her opponent, who sought then to hit her with his club. The weapons-trained maid ducked his blow and cut at his groin. With this second wound, the Pict twisted away, barely able to remain on his feet.

Voada made for the bushes but a savage lurched in front of her, his double-bladed ax uplifted for a kill. Abruptly, the Pict yowled in agony, and the princess saw a spearhead barbing from his chest. She dodged around the tribesman and made for the tree growth, but a pair of hands from nowhere clutched her from behind.

Voada swung her sword blindly, but the assailant captured her wrist. "Lady!" Broch exclaimed. "It's you they seek. You must get away!"

"I won't run!"

"Do as I say!"

"Let me go!"

The lad slammed the heel of his hand against the side of the girl's head, stunning her. Then, appropriating her sword for his own use, he dragged the princess behind him, looking for a way across the gorge. At its edge, their combined weight caused the moist ground to crumple beneath their feet and sent them rolling down the steep-sided ravine. They only stopped when they felt the cold swash of the stream at its bottom.

"We must reach the other shore," the gasping youth told the maid, urgently trying to help her rise.

The pair stepped into the stream to wade across it, but the current's force threw them down. Half submerged, sometimes with their heads underwater, Broch guided them along as best he could, drawing his companion along. Voada, realizing that she could drown, stopped resisting and attempted to swim.

The rushing current bore them downstream, out of sight of the combatants. The harper regained his footing and drew the princess out of the water.

Voada, shaking off his grip, struggled higher up the bank and dropped to her knees. "You left them to die…" she accused her rescuer.

Broch shouted back: "They fought for *you!* Honor their deaths by saving yourself!"

Again, he seized Voada's arm and compelled her to follow him to drier ground. Pointing at the steep slope ahead, he panted, "We'll climb to the top… and hide in the woods."

They made a slippery ascent, needing to make headway by grabbing onto handfuls of rooted weeds and ivy. Having attained the lip of the ravine, they struggled to their feet and made a stumbling flight into the forest.

The brush dragged at them, inflicted many a scratch. The princess, despite the heat of her emotions, was tiring. Broch, not much better off, gasped, "It's no good, Voada! You have to hide. I'll let them see me and draw them away!"

She reacted with surprise. "All right!" she huffed. "Thank you!"

"I hope you get away."

"What about you?"

"I'll probably be killed!"

They pressed on, looking for a hiding place. They stayed behind the autumnal growth as much as possible.

"There!" huffed the harper, pointing to a backwater gully beneath a grassy overhang. "Hide in there, but don't make any tracks!"

"How can I do that?"

"Think of something!"

Broch pushed away and dragged himself off alone.

Voada went to the edge of the rude sanctuary and jumped to the other side of it, landing on her hands and knees. Then, the girl ducked beneath the overhang and waded into the brown pool that filled it. With the force of will, she lowered herself beneath the muddy, chill water and lay on her back. She was nearly submerged but used her elbows as props to keep her nose and mouth above the surface.

Shocked, wet, and cold, she had never felt such fear. But even in that state, she didn't like that a boy she didn't know was sacrificing his life to save hers….

# Caratacos the King

## CHAPTER V

Broch heard rustling in the litter behind him—running feet! Expecting to die, he intended to use the last minutes of his life to lead the savages as far away from Voada as possible. Besides, he had little hope of escape, no matter what he did. If he had to die this day, he preferred to do it while accomplishing something.

"There he is!" came a yell. Broch knew enough Pictish to understand the words.

"Go to the Death Queen!" Broch swore back over his shoulder. He and his friends had been tossing around that Pictish curse since childhood.

He couldn't run rapidly over the slippery mud under the mat of leaves. The enemy gained on him swiftly, and a war club struck his shoulder from behind. He pitched to the ground with the breath knocked out of him, and his assailants kicked and stomped on him.

"No more!" barked the hunters' headman. "Let the dog tell us where the princess hides!"

They turned him over, and one Pict dropped to his knees to shove a bloody dagger up against his throat.

"Speak, swine, or be cut to pieces," his captor demanded in heavily accented Brythonic.

"I don't know where the princess is!" he snarled.

"Cut off one ear," the headman ordered.

"Stop!" came a woman's command.

The hunters looked back to see a dripping mass of slime and mud standing erect.

"Are you the Princess Voada?" the headman demanded.

"I am! Release my servant. The coward abandoned me to die! His base blood can only befoul a true warrior's blade."

The brigands started to laugh, either at her appearance or at her words.

"Voada, run!" the youth shouted, only to receive another kick in the ribs.

"Do the Picts torment the helpless?" Voada challenged the three warriors.

"Yes," replied the headman, "we do. Helpless enemies make for an easy kill."

"What do we do with this wretch?" asked one of the hunters.

Voada addressed the one speaking Brythonic. "He's a trained bard, his prince's favorite. His ransom will be a high one. Also, he is timid and without true manhood. He will obey you like a craven dog."

"Take him with us," the headmen told his warriors. "The chief will decide."

They seized both Broch and Voada, forcing them to maintain a stumbling walk back to the battlefield.


The night after leaving the Fountain of Nimue, Simon dared ask his mentor about the baleful prophecies that he'd given.

The Master Merlin was seated on the leaf-strewn grass within the firelight of their night camp, looking up at the stars. Simon, standing over him, asked, "May we speak?" He waited, but when his teacher held silent, the Easterner stepped back and began to turn away.

"Stay, pupil," the old man said. "What is on your mind?"

Simon looked back. "The prophecies you gave back at the fountain sounded ominous. I sensed that you were foreseeing danger for those people, yet you did not explain the danger."

Emrys sighed. "Alas, Simon, when I looked across the tables, I saw all those men showed the gray faces of corpses. All but one."

"Corpses, Master?"

Emrys nodded. "Every marked man was doomed to perish very soon, and from violence."

"Why didn't you let them know that?" the younger man asked—almost accused.

"Warn them of what?" asked the savant. "Is it not the fate of all men to die? No warning would have changed the wyrd that Fate has placed upon them. Had I tried, the gods might have taken away my voice, or perhaps even my life. For whatever Fate decrees, there is a reason. If we are to grant due honor to the gods, we must defer to their plans. That is regrettable, but yet is it not better that we allow death to come upon carefree people suddenly rather than have them anguish over a destiny that cannot be averted?"

Simon saw the man's point, but he did not believe that any fate was truly unavoidable. Many a time he had challenged evil circumstances that had seemed irresistible and yet had managed to thwart them. "I must respect your decision, Mentor," he said uneasily and started to draw back.

"Wait, Simon, my son. One question has been answered, but are you not burdened with more questions than one?"

The younger man returned a troubled grimace. "I do, Mentor."

"So ask."

"Master Emrys, most of the Druids are resentful of the favors you have so far shown me. Though they have protested this to you many times, your generosity has continued unabated. I need to ask you why. Have you seen some merit in me that justifies it?"

Emrys' flame-lit eyes flashed. "Simon, are you so very certain that you know what your own merits are?"

"Perhaps not. The gods have never taken me into their confidence."

"On my oath, this is what the far-seeing Scathach has told me: You are a destiny-driven man. Our people have a word for it. They call such a one an *uchel-enaid.*"

"I do not know the term, Mentor."

"The name bespeaks one who is god-touched. Usually, an uchel-enaid appears when the world draws nigh to a nexus point. Usually, Fate offers a bifurcated path. One path leads into darkness and the other into light. The uchel-enaid is sent by heaven's will into the world when lost mankind needs to be led into the light. Am I the first of your masters to have cited such a quality in you?"

Simon looked away. "No, Master. Some have called me a chosen man, but their prognostications have been so vague that I could make nothing of them. I have always taken care not to repeat what they've told me, lest I sound like a deranged boaster. Tell me, are the uchel-enaids blessed, or are they cursed?"

The wizard shifted his glance toward the flickering fire. "The name betokens a high soul, one whose fortune cannot be foretold."

"Why is that so?"

"Because the uchel-enaids are one of the bricks from which fortune itself is created."

"Is that why you have never given me any inevitable prophecy such as those you gave to those random strangers?"

"I am giving you your prophecy *now*, young friend, to the extent that I am empowered to do so."

"But if the fortune of a high soul cannot be foretold, are you not speaking in contradictions, Mentor?" asked Simon.

"Let me be more clear. The destiny of an uchel-enaid is continually renewed, so long as Fate wills that he should walk the earth. He is a chosen High One whom the gods cloak in flesh and cast astride the careening mare of Destiny. The beast is not guided by him, but by the gods, carrying him into those places where he must go. It is the mission of such a rare man to accomplish great deeds, but when his mission runs out, his life ends suddenly and tragically. In a way, he is born to be the true king-sacrifice that the universe is forever demanding."

"I have never asked to become anyone's sacrifice," the novice replied.

"No you have not; an onerous burden has been placed upon your shoulders without your consent, Simon. Chosen ones like yourself live by instinct, never knowing when their work is done. That work is only finished when the gods deem that it is.

"Alas, not every uchel-enid is successful," Emrys continued. "When darkness comes, when the All-Night falls, that is a sign that the uchel-enid of the appointed hour has failed."

"I have heard the term 'All-Night' before. I gather that it is to be an age of evil magic and chaos that overwhelms the world."

Emrys chuckled softly. "That describes the topic fairly enough. Evil is a banal thing and it is unprofitable to make a serious study of it."

"I hear your words, Mentor, but they do not carry the ring of truth for me. I hope I am not truly a kind of demigod," Simon confessed. "I do not see how my life has differed so much from that of other men, even admitting that the road I've walked has been strange."

"You carry one blessing, Simon: You do not need to ponder your destiny. Fate will take you where you need to be taken and bring you before the problem you are fated to solve. Do not hesitate at any crossroad; the uchel-enaid goes wherever a silent and hidden voice commands him."

"If I accepted this as true, how should I live? By being a rudderless man acting on mere whim?"

"No. Even if you tried hard to be rudderless, you never would accomplish it."

"I do not follow."

"That is so. You were not sent into this world to be a follower, Simon of Gitta. Your destiny is to lead. Even when no one stands behind you, never doubt that you are a leader."

After that, the wise one resumed his star-gazing, and Simon was not inclined to press the discussion.


After more than a week on the road, the group led by Kai and Emrys at last saw Camelos through a tumble of dropping leaves. The city itself was a hill fort, a caer like many others. Nonetheless, it represented what was probably the most modern town in all of Britannia.

More than a century previously, the settlement had been established by the Catuvellaunian war chief Beli to serve as the base of his warrior band. Beli had been recruited in Gaul and tasked with defending the confederated people of southeastern Britannia from barbarians and northern enemies. As the pendragon serving the confederated kings, the warrior and his followers thrived in their adopted homeland. Beli wed a

Brythonic princess and became the father of Cassivellaunus, the worthy son who would succeed him.

During Cassivellaunus' maturity, a new and greater menace encroached upon southeastern Britannia. The native kings trembled to hear that Julius Caesar had come. Many considered surrender. In disdain of such weak leadership, the lairds of the land offered a throne to Cassivellaunus should he overcome the Roman invaders. Using caution and delaying tactics, he forced Caesar out of Britannia, and the proffered crown became his.

The new monarch reorganized the confederacy into an organic kingdom he named "Logres," meaning "the southeast." The new line of Pendragon kings, sometimes by bribery, sometimes by intimidation, brought several additional kingdoms into a new and expanded confederacy. Whenever a throne became vacant, a member of the high king's circle was usually appointed, strengthening the high king's sovereignty over the whole. Arto had been reigning as the vassal king of Cornwall when Guiderios was assassinated.

Simon was pleased to notice that Brythonic life flourished in Camelos despite the mild Roman influence introduced by King Cunobelinos. Sheep and goats were tethered close to the king's villa, awaiting the kitchen master's attention. Horses nickered in nearby corrals, and pasturing cattle lowed in the fields beyond the town. Kai had sent messengers ahead of the train, informing his foster brother of his imminent return. His heralds had brought back news that Caratacos had been formally awarded the throne by the collective lairds of Logres, which cheered the young laird. As the chariots drew up before the high king's residence, servants came to attend the travel-weary dignitaries.

The palace of King Caratacos looked like a Roman villa. Along its covered walkways men and women had already formed a welcoming party. Simon picked Caratacos out of the crowd, having briefly met him before. Now, as the new high king, he came forth from the assembly to greet the Master Merlin, with whom he was already acquainted.

"Father," the king said to Emrys, "it cheers my heart that you have so swiftly arrived."

"I come as my sovereign commands, King Caratacos," replied the arch-Druid.

Kai walked boldly up to his brother and slapped him on the shoulder as if they were no more than young brothers roughhousing. Arto, seizing Kai's neck in the crook of his elbow, pulled him up against himself.

"Is your elevation absolutely settled, Brother?" Simon heard Kai ask.

Arto laughed. "Ah, yes! I was crowned in wondrous haste. The great men of the land acted with dispatch, embarrassed at having an empty throne while an enemy was encamped on their soil. I have not had a peaceful moment since this golden burden was placed upon my brow."

This new king was a long-boned and compactly muscled youth. Though tall, he wasn't the tallest man there. His hair was thick and dark-honey-colored, as was his short beard, which he had undoubtedly decided to grow to lend himself a more mature appearance.

King Arto welcomed each member of Kai's Brythonic entourage singularly. He stood in place to receive the senior Druids one at a time. Diverse ladies were also permitted to greet the Merlins, including the king's mother, Igraine—a notably attractive matron. One of her daughters, Arto's sister Margawse, a little older than her brother, was married to one of Logres' significant vassals, Arawn Rheged, king of Lothan.

This Rheged, Simon knew, had become notorious in political circles. Cunobelinos had elevated him to occupy the vacant throne of Celidoine—a vassal kingdom known as Lothan by most of its own population. Once installed, he adopted the name of Loth, a popular name among Lothanian kings. Many conquered Picts had been settled inside the kingdom to perform labor, and many said Loth treated these unruly and disloyal people unnecessarily well.

Interestingly, most of Loth's opposition came not from within his kingdom, but from the Catuvellaunians of neighboring kingdoms. King Loth's western borders were harried by Pictish raiders and dragon attacks, yet his army seemed inactive. Worse, the king had lately been active in the succession debate in Logres and, in the course of that, had shown himself to be excessively ambitious.

As twilight approached, the king's guests were ushered into the *triclinium* of Arto's house for a welcoming feast. Unlike its Roman prototype, this triclinium presented an open space amenable to Brythonic-style feasting and carousing. From a central fire blazing within a stone circle, smoke rose straight up and escaped through a sooty vent in the ceiling. The fuel being burned was not commonplace peat, which tended to smoke profusely, but was dry oak kindling, a wood widely favored for its hot, slow, and clean burn.

Attentive servants kept the visitors' kraters full. As at the Brigantean wedding party, multiple guests shared these large vessels. By the time the meat portions were brought out, the waxing conversation had already grown loud and hearty. Kai caught peoples' attention when he said, "Caratacos, who is the scoundrel reviving that time-worn slander? Was it—?" He caught himself. Loth of Lothan's queen was sitting near at hand, overhearing his disparaging statement.

"I have not personally heard anyone citing that damnable calumny," said the king. "We may hope that its author will accept the judgment of Britannia's lairds and lay all that discredited nonsense to rest."

Simon guessed that Kai must have been referring to a lingering slander holding that Arto was illegitimate. In Loth's mind, that allegation made his youngest son Modred—his child by his second wife Margawse—the eldest male heir to Guiderios.

"Is the king satisfied with his northern vassal?" asked Balin, one of the kingdom's significant war chiefs. He also meant this as a barb aimed at Loth.

Caratacos glanced amiably at the one he appreciated for being an outspoken supporter. "For the present, I am," he replied.

"Yea, for the *present*," said Kai, laughing scornfully.

Despite the rowdiness, the feasters were content to set aside the discordant topic.

One laird, a man named Brastias, brought up another issue. "Is the king considering any choice for a queen as yet?"

"Not thus far," said Caratacos. "By the gods, do not hurry me. My crown is so new that it still feels strange on my scalp!"

"I have a candidate to offer!" Kai burst out. "At the Fountain of Nimue, we took a feast with Voada of Estrangore. She's a fine figure of a girl— even if she's a little tall, and her voice is scarcely melodic. The lady is the sister of Charatak of Clarants and Vanet of Estrangore. To make her your consort would be a powerful political move!"

Arto grinned tolerantly toward his foster brother. "Have I not heard that the maiden is already betrothed to Prince Prasutagos of Eastland? Unless my memory deceives me, that match was affirmed by Guiderios' blessing."

"Hah!" laughed the war chief Sacramore. "Prasutagos will have a hard time with her if I know damsels! Most tall women are bitter shrews! Moreover, people say that Voada has been trained with the sword and would make a better shieldmaid than she would a bride!"

"The Briganteans have a tradition of training warrior-women," King Pellinor added, his tone neither approving nor disapproving.

Simon had heard that this laird Pellinor was a friend and mainstay of the much younger Arto. The hair and beard of the King of Avalon were heavily streaked with gray. Pellinor looked to be in his fifties, elderly for a battlefield warrior. Despite his age, he was a muscular man with little fat, though the strength of his arms must have diminished from the prime of his life. The man's sun-browned, weathered face evidenced a vigorous life lived outdoors. Though a vassal king of Logres, he was reputedly too restless to stay home dealing with commonplace matters. Instead, his entire adult life had been dedicated to military issues. Avalon's affairs were being managed by a senior steward since Pellinor visited his home only irregularly.

"Whomever I choose to wed, I will take pains to see that she will be a gentle sort of wife," the broadly smiling Caratacos informed the men and women around him.

"What news of the Romans?" Kai impatiently asked the king. "We heard some talk along the way, but little that was said sounded trustworthy, Brother."

Caratacos gestured toward Pellinor, stating, "Our worthy retainer is famous for his bold commentaries on warlike actions. What say you, King of Avalon?"

"Aye, tell us!" urged Kai. "I wager that many seated here have not heard the story of our victory told as well as it should be!"

Pellinor surveyed the many faces looking his way and took a deep breath. "There has been little that's new worth telling since the battle at the Medway River—where you performed so notably, Laird Kai," the old warrior said. "All I can say is that the Boar has kept his head down. Maybe he thinks we'll forget about his sty if he wallows quietly and makes no trouble. Ah, that's one choice pig that most of us would dearly like to stick!"

Laughter passed around the triclinium.

"Then tell us about the Medway, warrior, the way you saw it happen," said Sadok of Clarants. "Did the Romans blunder so badly, as so many are saying? Stand up, old friend. Let us hear it all!"

Pellinor glanced toward Arto, who gave back an encouraging smile and a nod.

# The Road to Ruin

## CHAPTER VI

The war chief Pellinor pushed up from his bench and took a deep breath before beginning his narration.

"As all here must know, the Romans landed at the best port harbor of the land, River's Mouth, near the Isle of Vecta. They at least didn't make Julius Caesar's mistake of invading an area where ports were few and bad. Plautius captured the best port closest to Gaul, but was most interested in controlling the mouth of the river Tamesa. He made a hurried march east along the southeast coast. Unfortunately, he'd started his war late in the summer, having been delayed by troop mutinies in Gaul. Plautius had committed Julius Caesar's worst blunder all over again.

"We always knew that the Tamesa would make a superior port, but our kings had never allowed it. They knew the Romans would want to seize a good port close to Gaul once they got up the nerve to invade us again. I think Plautius planned to take the mouth of the Tamesa and build a port there over the winter. That wasn't a bad idea if he could have brought it off.

"But the farther the old Boar advanced from River's Mouth, the harder we fought him. He couldn't spare the troops he needed to protect the supply trains behind him. The farther he advanced from River's Mouth, the easier it became to plunder his supplies. We should thank old Emperor Claudius for keeping our warriors well-fed and equipped.

"But Plautius couldn't reach the Tamesa unless he forced a crossing of the River Medway. But the gods were with us, and he was pinned down by the early fall rains, giving Guiderios time to build up his strength on the north side of the Medway. The season was so late that the old Boar had to attack, though the flood waters were still rising. If he failed to cross the Medway, his army would spend the winter on short rations. He knew very well that the fear of starvation had ended Caesar's little romp in Britannia. The Romans tried to cross the flooded Medway when the rains let up, even though Guiderios was opposite to him with a full muster."

Laughter came from Pellinor's listeners. They knew that the best part of the story lay just ahead.

"I've never seen pigs hurrying to the slaughter as eagerly as the hungry legionaries did that day. But what do you expect? Any Brythonic pig is wiser than a Roman soldier!

"I watched those damned fools trying to cross from the shore near Orynko Wood. The Boar must have believed that the flash of Roman steel would make our boys run away! Guiderios actually told his warriors to act afraid when the legionaries could see them, to encourage the Romans to make the crossing. The king had already seen the enemy making every mistake an army could make, so why shouldn't he expect them to make the biggest mistake of all?

"The poor fellows came at us, even though they didn't know where the Medway's best fords were. You should have seen those men wearing heavy armor wallowing neck-deep in mud! Their chins were barely above water. Brythonic warriors would have turned back when faced with drowning. But the Romans will decimate their men if they disobey even the most cracked-brain order. We're free people, but the Roman soldiers are nothing but slaves with swords. They're more afraid of their officers than they are of death!

"Our young pups made a good show of sheer terror to entice the Romans to plunge ahead. When enough Romans had staggered out of the muck looking exhausted, our men came from behind the trees, like butchers coming at a herd of pigs!

"Gods alive! How those Roman pigs squealed! We only spared those who threw down their weapons and dropped to their knees! Those still in the dirty water stopped in midstream, afraid of us but too scared to turn around and go back.

"To help them decide, we sent plenty of javelins and arrows their way! Our men couldn't hear their own shouting over the pitiful noise that the Romans were making. A good share of them lost their place on the fords and were swept away by the strong currents.

"That's when Guiderios ordered his chariots to cross the high-water fords we knew about. They attacked the demoralized Romans on the south side. The poor sots must have thought that our Druids had launched demons at them from the gates of Tartarus!

"Ah, the broken pilums, the thrown-away shields! Those Latin screams were like music to our ears. They started running south, back to their fort. But they had to endure our charioteers stabbing them in their asses all along the way. Now that the river line was safe, Guiderios sent his warriors across the river to join in the chase after the Romans.

"When overtaken, they yelled for mercy, but our boys were in no mood for any of that nonsense. If any Romans among them had wanted to grow old, they should have assassinated their emperor and stayed in Italy!

"My oldest son, Aglovale, saw it all from his chariot. Our men were spearing those Romans like boatmen spear carp. The fishing didn't stop until the last Romans ran into their fort at Pevensey."

Pellinor had put his listeners into a state of hilarity. For most of a century, Britons had been laughing at the old stories about how Julius Caesar had fled back to Gaul in humiliation. But now those good old days were back again! "What glory King Guiderios brought to Logres that day!" the king of Avalon declared. "What a worthy successor he was to his ancestor Cassivellaunus!"

When the noise settled down, Pellinor continued. "After their losses, the Roman officers doubted they could hold their fort against a storm. They had sheltered boats in an inlet and ordered the fort evacuated by sea. When we broke in, we only spared those Romans lying on their faces, begging for mercy. Our only stroke of bad luck was that the Romans had abandoned so much valuable material that our army stopped killing and started looting while the enemy got away.

"When the Boar arrived the next day, leading reinforcements, he found no army at Pevensey to reinforce. He turned tail and drove his little swine herd back to the fortifications at Caer Perys. Our men had nothing better to do, so they gave chase. A good share of Plautius' Romans never reached Caer Perys alive. Any day now, we expect to hear that Emperor Claudius has ordered Plautius to commit suicide and decimate all four legions of the invasion!"

The booming laughter continued until a Druid spoke up. "Should not the Raven and Eagle Druids be given some credit for the victory? Did they not cause the rains that flooded the Medway? Did the Romans have no battle wizards that were the match of ours?"

The young king answered for Pellinor. "The Romans do not take wizards to war. We are their masters in the practice of magical warfare!"

Mog Ruith stood up next. "Truly, magic has decided victory in many a desperate fight. But take care, men of Logres; when the enemy realizes he needs magic to prevail against Britannia, their emperor will scour his empire to find recruitable wizards. The Romans were probably behind the massacre at Rathtyen."

Neither Caratacos nor the war chiefs present could gainsay that.


After the feast, Arthur spoke with his war chiefs and the Merlin Druids. He had been very concerned about the Rathtyen affair, but only now, with the succession issue settled, had he gained the freedom of action to solve the mystery.

At dawn, the king and the Master Merlin rode out to the town of Rathtyen accompanied by their warriors and Druids. Simon had been asked to attend Emrys while he and King Arto searched the ruins. The slain had long since been removed, but the physical wreckage was appalling.

From appearances, something too large to gain entry by the main door had forced its way through, ripping out the surrounding wall.

They saw evidence of burning, though the assembly hall had, incomprehensibly, not caught fire.

Arto was beside Emrys when the latter stooped to pinch a bit of dried mud. He scrutinized it before letting it drop.

"What sort of magic has been at play here, Master Merlin?" Arto asked.

"It's nothing like anything I have ever seen," the old man replied, "but the dark magic was powerful. Were there any witnesses?"

"Yes," responded the king, "but only one. The warriors found a man hiding in the forest nearby, scarcely in his right mind. Because he insisted that his life was in danger, I commanded that the fellow be taken to a hiding place."

"What did he say?" asked Emrys.

"He made little sense. If you wish to speak with him, I have a warrior who knows his place of concealment."

"Yes, we must speak to an eyewitness," said Emrys.

"Do you suppose that the man might truly be in danger?" Arto asked.

"Possibly. If a creature—" The old wizard suddenly broke off.

"What sort of creature are you referring to?" the king urged.

"Majesty, I believe the damage was done by… a dragon!"

The party of stumbling captives following behind slaver wagons would scarcely have been noticed by anyone along the rutted roadway. But with the two-score slaves in the coffle were more than a dozen Brythonic survivors from the bridge ambush. These included seven male servants and nine women, all shackled two by two.

Having stolen the prisoners' good shoes, the Picts had provided them with humble Pictish footwear. Likewise, the wedding party's fine clothing had been purloined, leaving the captives with only shirts or shifts. Blankets for their warmth and sleeping had been provided, but the Picts never did anything in the spirit of compassion.

The barbarians wanted to deliver fit and healthy slaves to the market. Sick or lame slaves would have slowed down the coffle. Coughing or prostrate captives would bring poor bids. People with sickness would spread illness to those with them, guards included.

After the bridge battle, the Picts had put the Brythonic wounded and the captured warriors to death. Fighters were slain outright out of fear for their superior strength and propensity for violence.

But one slave had special value. Voada of Estrangore was a political prize worth a ransom. The chief to whom she had been delivered had given special orders regarding her. He had ordered her shackled to the young man with whom she had been captured. While other slaves could be beaten into submission, he wanted to sell Voada to the Romans in good condition. Instead of punishing her directly, he instructed the slavers' chief to flog the boy she had been protecting. If she truly cared about his welfare, she would behave.

Even the people of her home court would have had difficulty recognizing Voada as she now appeared. After her mud bath, she had been denied any opportunity to clean up. Her master preferred to keep her unrecognizable while on the road to the market. The princess had done her best to scrape her face free of dirt with her own—and now very broken—fingernails.

The slavers' chief was never addressed by name. His underlings called him *coku*, a Pictish word for "chief." He had a strangely shaped beard, and a shaved pate.

The slavers were dressed in the Pictish way, in baggy trousers and rude sheepskin shirts. To keep the chilly wind off their backs, they wore shapeless knit caps and fleecy cloaks. Under their ample clothing, they were colorfully tattooed.

Unlike the Britons, the Picts did not care to wear full beards. They shaved their faces eccentrically, treating hair remnants as adornments. Most Britons considered the Picts to be brutish primitives. The way they treated the captives proved that they deserved their evil reputations.

And in no way did the coku respect the princess's dignity. When Voada offered a ransom for her release, the man only scoffed, saying, "The Romans at River's Mouth will pay us much better." For her indignant reply, he knocked her to the ground with a back-handed slap.

Broch, chained to her, barely restrained himself. Yet he refrained from reacting. The Picts were notorious for beating, mutilating, and executing slaves. His intention was a successful escape, not a show of vain courage. The guards would be watchful of a balky prisoner but largely ignore an assumed coward.

Sometimes Broch felt guilty for surviving the battle when so many of his friends hadn't, including Lemovic. Thankfully, the latter had died from honorable wounds instead of being put down like a crippled horse after the battle.

But Broch could not stop wondering why Voada had given herself up for his sake. Royals were not expected to hazard themselves to save the lives of commoners. Because the guards prevented them from conversing, he could only wonder what sort of person Voada was down deep. He hoped he would have the chance to answer that question.

*      *      *

During their second morning on the road, shouted alarms awakened Broch. A slaver scout ran into camp shouting that a Belgae war band was approaching.

The frightened coku seized a weapon and strode into the view of his captives. "I will stand behind your precious princess with this knife," he told them, "and if anyone asks for help, she shall be the first to die. And if any of my men survive the fight, I'm giving them leave to put the whole of you to death! Understand?"

The Picts started kicking people to get them to their feet. The guards drove all of them off the road, except Broch and Voada. They stayed beside the coku, whose knife was hidden behind Voada's back. Three chariots rattled into view, each conveying a single warrior with his charioteer. The harper's heart sank; if there were a fight, the mob of Picts would have the better of it. Broch hoped these few warriors represented the vanguard of a large party of approaching warriors.

The Picts stood in place, awaiting orders from the coku. Meanwhile, their chief acted quickly, directing his drivers to take the wagons off the road to allow the chariots to pass by.

The lead car drew up before the chief, and a solidly built spearman surveyed the array of savages with disdain. "Who is your leader, and whence do you fare?" the chariot rider asked gruffly.

The coku replied: "I am the wagon chief. We travel to Erwain with a consignment of captured rebels."

"These are rebels?" the Belgae observed with a scowl. "Few of these men are young, and there are so many women. It could not have been much of a rebellion."

"I was not at the fight, warrior," said the coku. "I am a merchant only."

"You need leave from the king of Glouchedon to drive slaves through his domain," said the Belgae.

"Aye, Master," the coku replied obsequiously. He drew a piece of leather from his scrip and handed it to the man beside him. The underling stepped forward and passed it to the chariot warrior, who glowered at the symbols it displayed before handing it back.

This affair was not going well. Broch could not shout an alarm with Voada's life under threat. And these few Belgae warriors could not overcome the large mob of Picts. If his life had to be spent, Broch preferred to spend it profitably.

The chariot warrior spoke again, saying, "We're gathering information about the raider problem. What do you men know about lawlessness along these roads?"

"All the countryside we've passed through has been peaceful," the coku replied. "I saw nothing except good people going about their proper business."

Broch wondered whether he saw a look of suspicion on the Brythonic leader's face. The Belgae leader raised his arm and waved the chariots behind him forward. Their rapid gait soon took them out of view. No other Belgae band would be seen for the rest of the day.


The following day, the coffle veered off the road to follow a dirt track roughened by washed-out runnels. In less than an hour, they entered a forest village whose inhabitants wore Pictish garments and tattoos.

These curious denizens came and clustered around the slaves to gawk. The Pictish guards behaved as though they were already familiar with these village people. Broch could not follow their rapid Pictish speech, but something one said started women and old folks laughing. Had the scoundrel been mocking the muddy and forlorn young woman who was a princess from Estrangore? That might have been so, for many of the primitives started glancing Voada's way.

Broch winced. Becoming a laughingstock for low savages had to have been a bitter morsel for the girl standing at his side.

The coku commanded that the slaves be separated into their shackled pairs, some of these being chained to posts or trees, while the people taken at the bridge were segregated and confined inside small sheds. Broch and Voada were pushed into an ill-smelling hut that must have lately housed goats. Its windows had wicker grates. They saw that slaver guards had been posted, one in front and one in back.

Broch encouraged his companion with a weak and hopeful smile, but Voada looked away. He wished to ease her despondency, but could think of nothing to say that wouldn't sound foolish.

While they were standing on that foul floor, he remembered the Master Merlin's prophecy—that he would outlive all the Brigantean and Icenian men in the wedding party. Small comfort that! Most of those men were already dead, and the lives of the male survivors hung by a thread. No wonder the old Druid had avoided telling him how dire his fate would be!

The captive pair used their feet to scrape a corner of the floor bare of the still-soft animal droppings to make a decent place to sit down. Sunlight became twilight, and, before long, Voada was fitfully dozing against Broch's side. With so many bitter thoughts afflicting him, the youth couldn't help but stay awake. With twilight upon them, he heard music outside—deep-voiced drums and dull-toned flutes. Not wishing to awaken the girl, he resisted his urge to go to the window.

A short time later, Broch started hearing a raucous song. But even louder than the Pictish singing was the screaming they heard. Broch lurched, and his sudden movement jarred Voada awake.

"What is it?" she gasped.

"Something's happening outside. Let's look," the harper whispered. He rose and helped the girl to her feet. They peered through the window and looked at the fire-lit center of the village.

Voada trembled, and Broch's teeth clenched. The Picts, in what had to be festive raiment, danced around a blaze, both men and women together. Some villagers were carrying a giant, worm-like figure mounted on poles—an effigy of a dragon constructed from cloth and matting. Heart-rending screams rived the night. By the flames' dancing light, they saw men tied to stakes with flaming faggots piled next to them.

The young people in the hut had known some of these men personally. Broch's rage blazed hotter than the holocaust fire that was consuming them.

# Dragon Breath

## CHAPTER VII

This was no way for a decent human sacrifice to be carried out! Only in primitive regions were the rites of the Wicker Man still performed. But even in such places, custom mandated that the victims were assisted to die in dignity—not in a spectacle of torture and blood-lust. Officiating druids were scrupulous in advising the selected ones that they should inhale of the smoke deeply, to render them stupefied and unconscious before any flame touched their flesh. But this Pictish fire was smokeless—a barbaric flourish that could have been calculated by nothing else but malevolence.

Broch and Voada were unable to see who the victims were, except that they were men. But would the Picts spare even the women?

While the youth watched in horror, a whisper came from beneath the grated window: "Broch!"

He looked down, seeing nothing because the fire had left him night blinded. "Who is it?"

"Synhwyrol, Master!" said the speaker. "Is the princess there?"

Synhwyrol was the name of the surviving Eastland servant. "It's not safe!" the harper said hushedly. "Watch out for the guards!"

"They're dead," said the servant.

Broch had no reply to that.

Synhwyrol and the Brigantean manservant with him set to work, prying out the laths of the wall while making as little noise as possible. Their tool very soon poked through the wall. It was a piece of iron. The servants were working the tool to make the breach larger. They stopped when the gap was wide enough for a man to crawl through....

Gawyn, son of Loth, the stepson of King Arto's sister Annwyn, led the druidic delegation along the forest trail. Of those present, only Emrys was traveling by chariot. His advanced age had made horseback riding something to avoid. The poor quality of the track made the going rough for a wheeled vehicle, and that was making everyone's progress slow. Finally, the riders entered a small clearing and saw a humble trapper's hut shaded by bare trees. Its thatched roof sloped steeply, almost touching the earth on either side. Gawyn reined in next to it and swung from his saddle.

The less apt horsemen with the party were also dismounting, some needing to wait until the young acolytes came to assist them.

"Who is out there?" demanded a rough voice. Gawyn looked up to glimpse a middle-aged man peering out through the door crack, his face no more than a pale spot against the hut's interior gloom.

"We are sent by King Arto Pendragon. I am Gawyn, prince of Lothan," the young warrior shouted back. "You will remember me, Brute. I was with the warriors who escorted you here. Emrys, the arch-druid of the Merlins, and his lieutenants are with me now."

"The Master Merlin? He is here?" asked a second, broken, voice from out of the darkness. "Let me see!"

The door watcher opened the portal fully. "Master Merlin! Come in!" urged the other, still invisible, man. "Quickly, quietly! The sky has eyes!"

The druids started their approach all together, but Emrys halted them with a shout. "Hold! That is a small hut. I will go in and speak to Brute, along with Master Ruith and Brother Simon."

Simon winced. Yet more favoritism would only stoke the fires of resentment higher. Nonetheless, he heedfully followed the two arch-druids over the threshold.

The hut had little in the way of comfort. On the back wall their hung two sleeping platforms, one above the other, each covered with ragged blankets. For furnishing, there was only a small table and two stools. The open door and a single lamp provided all the light to be had in the windowless room.

"Is it you, Brute of Blorens?" Emrys asked, speaking to the still barely seen figure.

"It is!" declared the man.

"It has been a long time, friend," stated Emrys. "Why are you in hiding? What strangeness has befallen you?"

The Raven Druid's answer came out rasping and tremulous: "I stepped upon the road to doom only last winter, Revered One. My Raven master appointed me to spy upon the Wyrm Druids due to the continuing evil talk about them. He chose me because I am half-Pictish and have the Pictish look. Further, I am able to speak my mother's tongue as well as a tribesman. The Wyrms are wary of spies and, at times, I thought they might waylay and slay me at any moment. But, by the grace of Llew, I was spared."

"Why were you at Rathtyen, the stronghold of the Eagles?" the old Merlin asked.

Brute shook his head. "I fled from Caer Draig when I had much to report to my master. Wise One, strange things are afoot. Though I never found it safe to ask my questions directly to any Wyrm Druid, I was watchful and heedful and, by increments, I became privy to many matters that were of grave importance."

"You appear unsteady, Brute. Please, sit," coaxed the Master Merlin. "I will give us a bit of light."

Emrys raised his right hand and made it radiate a cold glow. This simple form of wizard-light allowed the three visitors to behold Brute of the Ravens. He had a worried and haggard expression on his Pictish-looking face. His druidic tonsure was very much in need of renewal. The man's servant, an elderly Briton, looked even older than his master while being just as shabbily dressed. He appeared to be almost as agitated as the Raven.

The Raven walked like an old man to one of the two stools and the arch-druid stepped up to occupy the other. "What secrets did you learn?" Emrys asked the half-Pict.

Drawing a shaky breath, Brute gave answer: "The Wyrm Druids have been obsessively studying the stories from the ancient past—stories going back to the almost forgotten era when the world groaned under the rule of the dragons."

"I am familiar with such legends," said Emrys. "Why are these legends of so much interest to the Wyrms?"

The witness shook his head. "The Picts have lived in this land for thousands of years. Once they were a race of conquerors who invaded even the mainland and, in hatred for cited cultures, they burned every habitation that was larger than a village. Wherever they walked, high civilization was put to violent death. But, at last, the gods deemed that their mad empire must be banished, and then the very earth revolted beneath their feet. Vast portions of dry ground sank rapidly into the sea, drowning the conquered and conqueror alike.

"Only remnants of their evil race survived on these islands of ours. During the age that followed, the Picts held fast to these isles, putting to death all others who were there with them, and also putting to death all non-Picts who ventured hither by boat. Their civilization was one without cities, very much as in their ancient days. In time, cults of wizards grew up amongst them to be the servants of petty kings. But these wizards came to be proudly resentful of their inferior status and, little by little, their wicked hearts led them into treachery.

"They ceased to worship their people's time-honored gods, choosing instead to adore invisible spirits that had long been haunting the land. These unseeable wraiths spoke to them through dreams, dreams that carried with them the power of evil. They incrementally maddened and corrupted the minds of the dreamers. The Great Ones, as these ghost-beings called themselves, demanded that the wizards do their bidding and the wizards obeyed. They were given certain tasks to perform, tasks aimed at restoring the primacy of the Great Ones in the material world. Long before, even before the days of Atlantis's sway, the Great Ones had ruled. The wizards came to call these immaterial beings the Dragon Spirits. But the spirits were empowered to manifest themselves in the material realm wearing a fabulous shape, the shape that is remembered in our lore as the dragons of old.

"With time passing, the Dragon kind began to work through the spell-casters to extend their rule over all the humans of the islands. They whispered their demands into the sleeping minds of common men, especially those in roles of leadership. Little by little, the spirits instilled madness and moral sickness into the many, sapping them of their will to resist even the most vile and depraved demands placed upon them. Progressively, whole tribes of Picts abandoned their old gods and cleaved instead to the Dragon Spirits. This was the beginning of a new age of the All-Night!"

Brute's shoulders began to quake, as if terrified by his own words. The Merlin touched one of his. "What else do you know?" he asked soothingly.

The furtive Raven shook his head. "The Dragon Spirits appointed their most wicked servants to be their intermediaries in the world, making them chieftains over all their neighbors. Any who resisted the will of the Great Ones were destroyed by various means, including the mighty weapon of the Dragon Breath! The captives taken in mass through endless tribal warfare were forced to perform quarry labor, and the rocks they shaped from certain types of bedrock were raised up as Standing Stones.

"The placing of these stones was done with precision at locations that the Great Ones deemed to be in resonance with the earth's energy flow. The spirits sought to harness all of this immense power for their own ends—their main aim being the bringing of more physical dragons into the world to spread their empire of the stones far and wide. They were altering the earth's natural energy flow as they needed to, channeling it like the men of today channel rivers. And these rivers of power are what are still referred to as 'the dragon paths.'

"The Dragon kind demanded that the wizards construct countless stone circles. The menhir formations were, in truth, great poles of power. The spirits fed from these pools, like men drink from wells of water.

"According to the Dragon Spirits, this Age of the Dragons was by no means their first ascendancy. In Elder Days, their rule had been much more extensive. Their potential fluctuated with the changing formations of the stars in Heaven, which were very different so long ago. Eventually, due to the slow progression of change in the firmament, the patterns in the skies entered into a long cycle of catastrophic unfavorability. The Great Ones progressively weakened until the entire race fell into a sleep of ages. This unnatural slumber held them in the chains of inert oblivion, until the continual revolution of the stars achieved new patterns that enabled them to awaken.

"Eventually, the Great Ones deemed themselves ready to return to the physical world and create a new Age of the Dragons. This time the reborn dragons would stride the earth, served by compliant men whose free thought had been taken from them. The Great Ones enlarged their unnatural domain until it ruled all the islands.

"Later, when the Dragons had harnessed all the energy potential of the isles, they endeavored to overwhelm the adjacent continent, also. Their dragons reduced the civilizations they found to broken wreckage and subdued the survivors as they had the Picts. Wherever stone formations were erected, the Great Ones were empowered to rule. They gradually seized the dominion of Gaul, Spain, and every land around the Middle Sea. At the far end of the sea they entered into a land where the earth energy waxed more intensely than elsewhere, a true treasure box for the Great Ones. Better for the spirits, the men dwelling there were lacking in inner strength. They lacked the fortitude to resist debasement, corruption, and domination. These far-away ones became the favorite servitors of the Dragon kind, being even more depraved and cruel than even the Picts had been."

Simon frowned. Could Brute be referring to the ancient Canaanites? The story of their destruction was carefully told in the Scripture. It was a story of the unrelenting hatred of the Israelites against the Canaanites of all tribes, declaring them to be the most evil people in the world. The war they had carried on against them was a war like no other. It was not a war to seize land, but a war of annihilation. They believed that their god was ordering them to slay the Canaanites' women and children along with the men, and even to slay their domestic beasts.

Brute continued: "But the ruin and misery that the Dragon Spirits had unleashed across the face of the world finally led to their overthrow. They had nurtured in mankind a spirit of greed, covetousness, hate, and envy. Poison emotions built up by accretion in the hearts of the men they ruled, like flood waters rising behind a dam. In time the dams broke and released a flood of hate and vice to wash away the loyalty of many who had been servants of the Great Ones. The evil that was nurtured to serve the ends of the Dragon kind had by then so hardened the hearts and minds of their subjects that no further oppression by the dragons was able to tame them.

"As the disobedience spread, dragon-serving warriors abandoned their masters and formed into warrior brotherhoods sworn to making endless war against the Dragon kind. Malcontent wizards usurped spells taught to their ancestors and used them to empower the insurrections. From these cults of rebel wizards came the first true druids."

This surprised Simon. How was it possible that the wise and civilizing druids had emerged from an age of madness, vice, and violence?

As Brute continued speaking, his voice was sharpened by hysteria. "The factions working against the dragons contrived cunning plans," he said, "until all was right to commit to open warfare! The rebels suddenly seized hundreds of dragon-cult strongholds at once. Their armies methodically overturned the standing stones and the rebel wizards placed magical locks upon these centers to curtail the flow of energy so vital for maintaining the dragons' power. Wherever draconic energy was inhibited, the domination of the dragons ebbed. In those regions where the spirits' control lapsed entirely, almost all of the population became rebels. Hordes infuriated by generations of continuous suffering made cause with the existing rebels, and for long years contrary hosts did battle across a thousand fields of blood. The rebels were aided by the fact that the positions in the stars were becoming detrimental to the dragons' power."

Abruptly, Brute fell into trembling. To calm and cozen him, Emrys said, "You have revealed much that is affirmed in the secret lore that we also know."

Brute, steadying himself somewhat, nodded wearily. "As the war continued, few important stone arrays were left unvandalized. Deprived of the free-flowing energy, fewer of the Great Ones were able to manifest themselves into mighty draconic forms, and less often were they able to unleash the fearsome Dragon Breath. At last, the Great Ones began retiring from the world, awaiting some future time when mankind would forget the effective means of resistance that had taken them so long to learn.

"With passing time, men wrongly assumed that the draconic menace was ended. Alas, here and there, small cults preserved the ideas of the dragon faithful and jealously protected the remnant of stones that were still properly aligned. These debased devotees continued to glory in the dreams sent to them by the spirits that were lurking just beyond the pale.

"Though the rebels' victory had been great, it was never as complete as men supposed it was. Who, truly, can destroy spirits in the spirit world? And, in reality, there never was a time when even earthy dragons were not still occasionally seen in Britannia. With passing centuries, men grew forgetful of the terrible Age of the Dragons and the lessons learned from it. But the Dragon Spirits themselves never forgot, and never did they cease to understand that the days of their earthly glory might return again."

Now Mog Ruith spoke up: "Before the outbreak of these new dragon attacks, the only dragons we heard of were those that were seen swimming in lakes. Is this because dragons are able to manifest more easily in water than on land? Or is that because there are still well-aligned standing stones hidden on lake bottoms?"

Brute glanced up bemusedly. "I cannot say. Lake monsters were hardly mentioned in the stories recounted by the Wyrms."

Emrys asked another question. "What, exactly, was the message that you carried to the Eagles and the Ravens, Brute? What news was so urgent that the most accomplished of the Ravens and the Eagles suddenly left the scene of war to meet at their fatal conclave?"

The Brute wrung his thin hands. "As you may know, Wise One, there have always been cults pretending to worship the good and benign gods—and these have included the Wyrms. My pivotal discovery was that they still practice the age-old rites of dragon adoration. No doubt the Dragon Spirits still seduce these wicked ones while they slumber. Since the last Age of the Dragons there have always remained areas of anomalous earth energy that have been hospitable to haunting spirits. In the heart of the worst of these locations the stronghold of the Wyrm Druids, Caer Draig, has been deliberately located.

"Listen friends, I have heard cult members speaking of plans that mimic what was carried out in ancient days to bring about the previous Age of the Dragons. The stars' present alignments greatly favor the empowerment of the dragons. The Dragon Spirits are excited, anticipating their return to the world in physical dragon form."

Simon frowned with incredulity. So much of what Brute was saying came across as raving. His heart was not accepting this man as a reliable informant. Emrys and Mog Ruith, however, appeared to be hanging on to his every word with rapt attention.

Brute's voice was becoming ever more brittle. "I know that the Wyrm Druids have been repairing and realigning the standing stones. They are continually recruiting others into their foul cult. There are even some lairds and kings that are partially or wholly corrupted by the Dragon Spirits. It is no coincidence that many of the readjusted stones stand in the kingdom of Lothan.

"And, yea, I have heard talk of new sorceries rising, but I do fear that these are merely the old sorceries emerging from long concealment. The evil prevalent in days of yore is all around us at the present time. Do you not feel it? It is palpable! I can myself sense it like ants crawling over my skin. I urge you, Wise Ones, do not dismiss the stories that men tell of dragons ravaging the hinterlands! They are true!"

The Master Merlin nodded. "Yes, we do believe that they are true, friend Brute. But above all else, we need to know the names of those who are supporting the dragon-worshipers. Are the Romans knowingly helping the servants of the Great Ones? Does Rome actively seek to restore the All-Night?"

Simon grimaced. The divine bird Kephri had spoken to him about the All-Night, believing that the next All-Night was imminent. The unearthly creature had prophesied that it would be marked by the fall of Rome. For a thousand years after that event, he warned, demons would be worshiped and empowered.

Suddenly Brute shouted: "*Eeeyahh!* Save me! Save my mind and soul!"

"What are you saying?" Emrys asked urgently.

"A-At Rathtyen I fell into a feverish slumber. In that darkness of the night before destruction I once again became the plaything of the invisible! I awoke and told what I saw and heard to my master, but he doubted my sanity. My master, and others also, told me not to appear at the conclave, not until I had put to rest whatever demons had risen to torment me.

"On the night of the conclave, while I lay awake shivering with terror inside a nearby hut, I suddenly *saw* it! I saw the moving thing—*the dragon!*"

The crazed man twisted away his companions and covered his feverish eyes with his palms. "I cannot speak of it! I cannot speak of it!"

The Master Merlin pushed up from his stool, stepped around the table, and took Brute's hands, like a parent comforting a child lost in nightmare. The power of this contact seemingly fed a calming energy into the excited witness.

"I-I do not remember what happened after the dragon came," babbled Brute. "I may have fainted. But when I awoke, all was in ruin. The Eagles and Ravens were all destroyed, and I knew to my eternal shame that I was responsible!"

"What do you mean?" asked Mog Ruith. "How were *you* responsible?"

Brute sent the Wren a crazed stare. "I had entered the dreaming state and they found me there. From my sleeping mind they took my deepest secrets and became fully aware of my treason. From me they learned who their active enemies were! By that discovery, the spirits were incited to draw together and attack! One of them found earth energy enough to manifest itself as a dragon and the others pooled their power of mind to support him with the Dragon Breath! They destroyed the Eagles and the Ravens! Oh, if only they had ended my torment, too, on that awful night!"

Still holding Brute's hands, Emrys asked, "What is the most vital thing that you wish to impart to us, dear friend?"

"I k-know many things!" the hysterical man said shakily. "I know the Wyrms have found a new ally."

"Who is it?" asked Mog Ruith. "The Romans?"

"N-no. Not the Romans. They have lured the Black Goats into their circle of darkness," he stammered. "There is a rottenness at Caer Draig; you can smell it in the air! That rottenness entered into me, also, and I was destroyed! But it was not by my own will! I was deceived! Deceived!"

"Deceived how?" asked the Master Merlin.

"I did not know what I was doing!" Brute shouted. "Oh, may the gods purify me!"

"Purify you of what?" Emrys pressed.

"I ate—I *ate!*" Brute cried out.

Of a sudden, the half-Pict threw himself on the floor and thrashed about like an animal endeavoring to escape a cage. Simon sprang to his feet, primed to restrain the miserable wretch, but Emrys raised a hand to hold him in check.

"What are you trying to say, Brother Brute?" the Master Merlin urged.

The wretched one cried out: "The All-Night! The All-Night!"

"Please, Brute," the Master Merlin pressed. "Calm yourself and tell us exactly what you know!"

"I wish to die! I cannot bear living in foulness!" Brute shouted.

"Tell us how to help you!" Emrys entreated.

"Cauterize me! Burn the sin from me!" the Raven howled. "Tell the king! Tell the king!"

Then, suddenly, the man seemed to lose the power of speech. Brute lay still on the dirt floor like a grotesque that was carved from wood. His stare had become amazingly strange, as if he was gazing elsewhere—or Otherwhere—like one beholding a horror that no one else could see. Suddenly, another shriek came from him—not the wail of a madman this time, but a cry of physical pain.

"I burn! I burn!" he yowled.

And Simon, in fact, thought that he could smell something burning in the hut's close air.

"Brute, what's happening?" cried Mog Ruith.

"Douse me!" Brute croaked. "I burn!"

Simon's skin prickled; there was something wrong inside that hut; the hairs on his arms and scalp were standing up. The air was full of energy.

The Master Merlin gave a shout: "The Dragon Breath! Flee or die!"

As he spoke, Brute's servant also began to cry out with shrieks of torment.

Both Mog Ruith and Simon moved to Emrys' aid, but the old man shoved the former away. "Carry Brute from here! Hurry!" Simon saw in the savant's eyes wild urgency.

Emrys backed away, shouting "The Dragon Breath! Help Brute! Outside, quickly!" But the old man caught his heel on the rough footing and fell backwards on the floor planks.

Mog Ruith went to the aid of the half-Pict while Simon swept his stunned mentor's age-wasted body into his arms and ran with him through the still-open door. They plunged into the chill autumn air while screams rived the shadows behind them.

The other druids came hurrying up and took their stunned master from Simon. The Samaritan, spinning about, went to the open door of the hut, but saw that the hut was filled with dancing blue light. Against that unearthly backdrop, Mog Ruith burst from within, and in his wake there was only one more ejaculation of unbearable pain followed by silence.

Simon stood wavering at the threshold in shock at what he thought he saw.

He remembered Emrys evoking a term—"Dragon Breath." Was this aberrant play of light the manifestation of the Dragon Breath? He couldn't know, but he did know that the hut had suddenly been overwhelmed by sorcery of the darkest hue.

What astonished him was that the weird cerulean light was casting its glow not upon the bodies of men, but upon piles of ash on the floor.

# Travelers on a Troubled Trail

## CHAPTER VIII

"Bring your blankets, if you still have them," the Iceni servant whispered urgently, "else the nights will be cold for sleeping."

Broch and Voada, freed from the hut, looked down at a dead guard, his head crushed—killed, no doubt, with the same iron bar that had enabled their escape. In the faint light of the distant fires, the two servants were each seen to be holding multiple blankets.

"What's your plan, Synhwyrol?" Broch asked the Icenian.

"To get far away!" the man said.

With Synhwyrol leading, the four escapees made for the thickets. A wild boar might have run more stealthily, but no Pict stepped up to block their way. The slavers and the villagers were all occupied with shouting and dancing, night-blinded by the holocaust fire.

After fighting through a mass of scrub, the quartet discovered a footpath, a winding track disappearing into the forest. None of them knew where to go, or even which direction was north. All they wanted was to build up a long start before the inevitable pursuit began.

It was hard to stay on the path guided by nothing more than the crescent moon's light, but they made haste until they were tired and staggering.

"Rest here," Voada ordered breathlessly, reasserting her royal prerogatives. She selected a moss-covered boulder for her chair and, panting, sat with her head hung low.

Broch asked Synhwyrol in a whisper. "How did you escape?"

The man gave a weary shrug. "We did nothing clever. Four others from the wedding party were put in with us, but the coku's guards entered and took them to the stakes. Gwenabui and I realized then that it was better to be killed in flight than to be burned alive. We began kicking at a rotten portion of the hut wall until we broke through. The guard who should have been watching must have gone off to watch the sacrifice."

"You've brought plenty of blankets," Broch observed.

"We have six; four of them belonged to the men who were taken to die."

"How did you come by that iron bar?"

"We found it leaning against a tree, sire. It's a grubbing tool, I think. It's served us well."

"It certainly has," Broch agreed. "But don't call me sire! I'm a plain man, just like you." Despite the rebuke, the youth silently admired the pair—house servants with grit enough to kill two armed savages. Brock regarded Voada on his right.

"The Picts are huntsmen and trackers," Voada reminded them with a tired voice. "Our… Our best hope is to find a stream and escape by boat."

"There's never a boat—or a stream—around when you need one," said Broch.

"Lady," Synhwyrol interjected, "may I speak?"

"Do so!"

"Gwenabui and I are worthless, lowly men. Our lives are pledged to assist those of high birth. We should separate, lest we be surrounded and captured all together. Gwenabui and I will make a careless trail to lead our pursuers after us. You and the harper must hasten in a different direction. Try to hide your tracks."

"Is there no way for us to save all our lives?" the young woman asked.

"That would be a miracle," said Broch. "But these men's lives may be saved if the Picts follow our tracks instead of theirs."

Voada dejectedly nodded.

The four fugitives continued resting in such complete silence that the night birds grew calm enough to resume their night cries. Synhwyrol and Gwenabui exchanged inaudible whispers before grimly getting to their feet. "We must be away, lady," said the man of Eastland.

"Do not go too far on a careless trail," Broch advised the pair. "Avoid making it obvious that you want to be followed, lest it arouse the Picts' suspicion. We both want you to get away. And before you protest our good regards, remember that the longer you remain at liberty, many of the Picts will look for you instead of the princess."

"May the gods have mercy upon you," he added.

"Yes, go with the gods," the princess affirmed.

"We have six blankets," said Synhwyrol. "Take two of them, Your Ladyship. We know court people have thinner skins than common folks do."

Broch accepted the blankets. Wasting no time, the serving men hurried away down the path and were almost immediately lost in the darkness.

"If I survive, I will never forget those brave ones," said Voada.

"Nor I. But we have to be gone from here, lady."

"Where do we go? Are you able to take the lead, or should I?"

"I'll lead. I'm familiar with woodland travel. I've ridden with huntsmen many a time."

"You?"

"Hunters like to hear music at their night camp. The young lairds and I became friendly, and they showed me how to hunt with the spear and the bow."

"I only hope you've learned something useful," said Voada. "We must leave this path as soon as possible because the Picts will surely search its entire length. But what are our chances of avoiding experienced huntsmen?"

"It all depends on the gods. As long as it's dark, we can't be tracked," he said. "Once we leave the path, it'll be possible to use leafy branches to sweep away the prints that we're making. If we walk on fallen leaves as much as possible, they can be easily brushed."

"All right," said the girl. "Now let's find a place where we can leave the footpath without it being noticeable."

"Agreed," said her companion.


When the path crossed a rocky area, they continued their flight over the stones. Broch suggested they ought to walk from rock to rock as a check against leaving tracks. The actual direction they took was not important, just so long as they didn't end up back in the village.

The harper had noted the position of the crescent moon during their departure from the village, but decided not to chase after the moon directly. That was something that any tracker might expect human prey to do. The princess agreed, and they went off on a bearing that kept the moon on their left side.

But all too soon, they heard distant thunder and noted that the clouds were edging close to the moon. All skylights would soon be blotted out.

"We have to stop traveling," Broch said.

"We don't dare to!"

"People walking blindly through the woods almost always go in circles. It's the trickery of the forest spirits. And we'll need to find shelter since I smell rain in the air."

They were still crossing over the rocky ground when they saw what might be a rock overhang. They approached and explored it, mostly by touch. It was a jutting ledge with a thick mat of dry autumn leaves under it, blown there by the wind.

It was the best bedding they could hope for in the wild. Ducking down, they explored the short cavity up the back wall. At that point, she knelt to pray in subdued whispers. Broch appealed to the gods, as well.

Afterward, they lay close together, each wrapped in two blankets, waiting for the rain to come. "If you get too cold, I'll give you one of my blankets," the boy offered. The princess did not reply. Only then did Broch realize that Voada was breathing rhythmically, as if in slumber. As he lay on his back, there came the loudest peal of thunder yet. The girl, stirring, awakened and looked his way. Within moments, the pitch of the wind rose to a howl and blew dead leaves from the forest floor into their sleeping place. Between the barren treetops, lightning flashed.

"A lot of rain could come!" the harper muttered.

"Do you think we can stay dry?"

"The ground we're lying on slopes downhill," he said. "We shouldn't get wet, not unless the wind blows the rain in on us."

"And the rain may do us some good," Voada ventured. "It might wash away our scent if they're depending on hunting dogs. It could also wash away more of the tracks we've been leaving."

"Maybe so," Broch agreed.

"But does it matter?" asked the maid. "Doesn't our escape depend upon what fate the gods intend for us?"

"If it does, I hope that only kind gods know where we are," the harper answered.

Suddenly, the storm struck with fury, shaking the trees and snapping boughs. The cloudburst produced slapping sounds on the rocks outside.

"What a night this would be without shelter!" said Broch.

"The Picts can't search for us while the storm lasts," Voada suggested.

"No, but as soon as they're able, they'll be after us again. Even if we avoid capture, we'll be facing days of hunger and cold. As long as we're in this terrain, finding water should be no problem. Rocky areas usually have rock puddles full of clean runoff."

"I only pray that I can get back to sleep," Voada said, shivering. "That wind is cold!"

"True," sighed the lad.

"I have an idea," said the girl.

"What?"

"Let's share our blankets. Four blankets are better than two, and we'll also benefit from one another's body heat."

Broch was surprised to hear such a suggestion coming from a court lady. But the idea was a sound one, providing they both behaved properly in so awkward a situation. The alternative was to lie shivering and sleepless all night.

On that score, there was no choice at all.


The skies raged like the gods were doing battle. Streaks of lightning flared from one horizon to the other, and ear-splitting crashes were frightening the animals. The weather's fury had driven the Romans away from their tentless beds to seek the meager shelter of the leaf-poor trees.

The Roman legate, Decimus Valerius Asiaticus, now sat leaning back against the bark of a lime tree, watching the sheets of rain glitter, illuminated by flashing thunderbolts.

Though he hated getting wet, Asiaticus had always appreciated the grandeur of a thunderstorm. As a child, the Gallo-Roman officer had savored every thunderstorm that passed over his town in Provincia. The boy would push his bed next to an open window to breathe in the cool, sweet air, to be thrilled by the forked lightning, and listen to the booms of the thunder. He even liked the specks of rain that the wind blew in his face.

But his boyhood had been lost long ago. And many years had passed since he'd last campaigned in such violent, raw weather. He remembered the many times he'd been lashed by wind-driven rain when his legion was overtaken by the elements. But Nature's fury had taught him that mankind's war-making ability was paltry compared to the world-shattering power wielded by the Gallic gods in Heaven.

Between thunder rolls, Asiaticus heard shouting coming from men crouching under a different tree. A Latin voice called to him explicitly, saying that a man with them had been injured—one of the druidic servants traveling with them. The panicked horses, the shouter explained, had trampled the fellow and broken his back. Asiaticus looked to the Master Druid sheltering beside him.

"He's your man, Goddeu," the legate said. "What do you want done with him?"

Goddeu rubbed his goat-like chin beard. The flashing lighting made the black-robed man look especially sinister. Asiaticus didn't care for the Druid, even though circumstances forced them to be allies.

Only the year before, the legionaries in Gaul had been hunting for the Black Goat Druids to kill them, believing that they had abducted and murdered a proconsul—Aelius Scaevola. The Romans at first disregarded the Druids' plea that both the proconsul and the Master Druid Ferchobar had been killed in an ambush set by rebellious mountain men called the Averoni.

But the army's investigation eventually turned up letters in Scaevola's effects. These had revealed the man's treasonous dealings with enemies of the emperor. The Roman government no longer felt much vitriol against the Black Goats and became less skeptical of the story the Druids were telling.

Emperor Claudius canceled his order for the cult's destruction. He still thought that magicians so powerful as the Druids were dangerous, but Claudius also realized that the Black Goats had served Julius Caesar usefully a hundred years earlier during his war against the Gauls. The emperor was just then preparing for war against Britannia and thought that having his army supported by friendly Druids might be an asset. He had accordingly spread the word that Rome would offer the Black Goats pardon, provided they assist the Romans in subduing the people of Britannia.

"What do you want done with your injured servant?" the legate again asked the Master Black Goat.

"With a broken back, the man cannot help but die slowly and in agony. It would be a mercy to end his suffering quickly," Goddeu replied.

Asiaticus shook his head.

"We Romans are called harsh, but we do not execute decent soldiers. We only assist the suicides of those who wish to die."

Goddeu grimaced. "We dare not abandon him because he could be found by the enemy. While our servants know very little of importance, any information the enemy receives might endanger General Plautius' plans."

Asiaticus looked away, knowing full well that their mission had been concocted by Goddeu himself and Plautius had received the idea coolly at first. But, yet, Goddeu's ruthless reasoning was sound enough in the present circumstances. "Do as you please with the fellow," the legate said. "He's your responsibility, after all." Asiaticus was glad to wash his hands of that matter. He had argued against the mission and was surprised when the general appointed him to lead it. Plautius had confided that he preferred to send a cautious man to the Wyrms, since anyone too enthusiastic about Goddeu's idea might easily be led on and deceived.

The lightning continued to crash, and the legate was left wondering whether this raging storm was a sign from Heaven to warn him he was on the wrong path. Matters involving the gods always put Asiaticus on shaky ground. He had grown up with elders who still worshiped the old Gallic deities and he'd taken for granted that the stories they told were true. But later in his youth, he had been placed in the care of Roman tutors. These men had drilled into their pupils the idea that an honorable political career required adherence to the Roman gods. This advice had come across as peculiar to one his age, since his Roman pedagogues had never made the slightest effort to convince their charges that the empire's national gods truly existed.

Contrariwise, there were many poignant family stories attesting to the reality of the gods of Gaul and citing many miracles to that effect.

Now, as Asiaticus stood under the tree, wet and cold, there was one belief left in him—that Fate had put him on a strange road in a strange land that led to nothing but trouble. Sitting there, clammy and wet, he felt no optimism about the days ahead.

# THE HILL OF THE DEAD

## CHAPTER IX

At dawn, the storm having abated, the party of Romans and Druids re-organized, mounted, and rode north.

Since leaving River's Mouth, they had mainly traveled through enemy-held country. At the advice of their Pictish guides, they had looped far to the west to avoid the alert and dangerous kingdom of Logres. This morning, they rode north and crossed the borders of Glouchedon, which was neither a strong nor aggressive kingdom. Their goal, Caer Draig, lay to the north-northeast, near the borders of the Logresian vassal kingdom of Lothan.

Every Roman officer needed to be an alert military observer. Asiaticus paid close attention to the lands through which his unit passed. Herding was more prevalent in Glouchedon than in the highly cultivated south. Their northward progress took them into a variously forested and marshy landscape, more suitable for hunting and lumbering than for farming. The grain fields the riders passed had been recently harvested.

The most impressive sight along the way was the herds of pure-white bovines. Asiaticus has seen such splendid beasts before in Gaul. In that unhappy country, the scarce cattle could only be found on rich people's estates, where their lineage was respected as a tradition.

The stock represented an ancient strain bred for ceremonial sacrifice, but the herds in Gaul had been slaughtered by foraging legionaries. The soldiers always stripped bare the lands they passed through. Starving Gauls left behind had butchered the white cattle the Romans missed to feed their families. Britannia alone saw the sacred cattle as more than an oddity.

Asiaticus avoided contemplating Gaul's lost traditions. Even Asiaticus, incompletely taught, understood the old ways. The younger generation couldn't read about their ancestors' greatness even in books, because the Gauls had scorned the use of a written language.

The Gallo-Roman's grandfather had been a young druid when the Romans came with fire and sword. For the rest of his life, he lamented the death of his country's civilization. The learned druids, who could have saved much lore, were still hunted men unless they were Roman collaborators. The best of them had fled the land, mostly to Britannia.

Asiaticus had come from a stricken countryside whose population was diminished by the effects of the last century's war. Depopulation by slave capture surpassed war, famine, and disease in its devastation. Caesar had invited slavers into Gaul so he could sell off the inhabitants for profit and fill his war chests.

Asiaticus' grandfather was saddened when he heard Gallic children speaking bad Latin and becoming too comfortable with foreign ideas. The old druid shared with his grandson a hope that the old Gaul still thrived in Paradise, as it seemed to have vanished from everywhere on earth except Britannia.

Asiaticus gritted his teeth. The islands faced the same fate as Gaul, to be conquered by the empire with fire and sword.

The legate's morose reflections were suddenly interrupted by the Master Black Goat's strong voice.

"Soon, Decimus Valerius," Goddeu said, "we shall arrive at the hill called Brynymeir, the site of Caer Draig. The guides tell me we will see the stronghold when we surmount yonder ridge."

"Master Druid, have you visited that place previously?" the legate asked.

"No, I have not. We are both equally unacquainted with this land."

Asiaticus nodded, glad the journey was nearing its end. But he thought Brynymeir was a strange name. "Brynymeir," a Gallic term, signifies "Hill of the Dead." He refrained from querying Goddeu, since any conversation with the Black Goat was distasteful.

Even though Goddeu seemed to be a schemer, he was neither insulting nor foul-tempered. The officer's grudge was founded in the history of his people. The Black Goat Druids had been one of the first to collaborate with Julius Caesar during his invasion of Gaul.

Asiaticus always felt torn between his Roman and Gaulish loyalties. The Roman part of his nature was stony and cynical, but his Gallic ached. Every descendant of the original Gauls carried with them deep scars going back to the destruction of their country.

After an additional half-hour of riding, the party topped the ride and beheld a distant hill fort surrounded by harvested fields and brown, almost leafless forests. Ahead of them lay "Caer Draig," which meant "Fort of the Dragon." Undoubtedly, the Wyrm Druids had named it to honor the mythical beast that they claimed as their totem animal. Even though they were sore and slouching, the travelers picked up their pace upon seeing the promise of shelter.

Asiaticus deemed the nearby timber to be second growth, suggesting that Caer Draig was an old town. Had it been newer, the woodland would be younger. Stockaded towns always made heavy demands upon their local lumber supply.

Britannia used wood for almost all of its construction, but the Gaul in Asiaticus wished that sturdier building material had been used in his homeland. Wooden structures were short-lived and their demise eliminated the memories of those who built them.

The legate hadn't realized the extent to which the Britons had adopted Roman road-building techniques, and some of their kings had been great builders. A royal road passed by Caer Draig, skirting the turnip fields that surrounded it.

The abundance of turnip cultivation impressed the Gallo-Roman. In eastern Britannia, Asiaticus had seen few turnips. Nor had they been a popular crop in old Gaul. But the Wyrms were apparently fond of them.

Further along, runners from the hill town met the riders. The druids greeted and spoke to them, as none of the Romans could understand their jabber.

Asiaticus didn't think that they were speaking Pictish, a language that Goddeu's Druids probably didn't know. But he knew that the druidic colleges of Gaul used cult languages in the interest of secrecy. The schools also had a more general language that was widely common among druids, so that priests could readily communicate with their peers in foreign lands. This he had learned from his grandfather.

But having the Wyrms and Black Goats speaking in an unknown tongue made Asiaticus suspicious. He little trusted the Black Goats and had even less reason to trust the Wyrm Druids. What were the priests up to? What didn't they want their ostensible allies to know?

After having been briefed by the runners, Goddeu walked his horse up to the legate and informed him the town was being made ready for their welcoming.

"If they aren't ready to receive us yet, what say you we pause and give them time?" Asiaticus asked.

"That is for you to decide, Decimus Valerius. But I do not intend to go farther until we are summoned. Your men are welcome to camp alongside ours."

Asiaticus gazed up at the stockaded town. The lofty stronghold unsettled him; the bleak, uninviting place felt wrong. The officer agreed to tarry alongside the Black Goats, although the two groups were not congenial.

While they stood at the foot of the hill, the Romans drew their woolen mantles close against the chilly winds of the season. Asiaticus resumed scanning the fort's outer wall. It was a well-made stockade, protected by a ditch dug across the hillside, some hundred feet short of the fort's gatehouse.

Such a fortification would have presented an obstacle to a Brythonic enemy, but in Gaul, similar defenses had afforded poor protection against Rome's armies.

The road that led to the elevated town was a gravel-paved turnoff from the royal road. It climbed to the gatehouse of Caer Draig, passing over the intervening trench using a causeway. This would probably be constructed to allow for its easy collapse in case of an enemy attack.

The traffic traveling both up and down the hillside comprised laborers with mule-drawn carts. The majority of the horseflesh Asiaticus had seen were small native ponies. These were quite unlike the fine animals bred by the Catuvellaunian kingdom farther east, which imported excellent stock from the Continent.

The legate observed more goats on the hillside than cattle or sheep. Roman tastes dismissed goat's flesh as meat for the poor. The better-off classes preferred wild boar, suckling pig, beef, veal, lamb, deer, and hare.

With the sun hanging low above the horizon, a new squad of runners came downhill to confer with Goddeu. As before, the arch-druid conveyed their message to Asiaticus. The Black Goats had been informed that the town was ready to offer their visitors a cordial welcome.

With scant delay, the Romans and Druids gathered up their gear, mounted, rode uphill, and passed over the causeway. Asiaticus disconcertedly kept looking around, unable to fathom why he should feel so ill at ease. A threatening aura hung heavy, yet the Roman detected no visible cause. It was like the land was haunted by a gray and disquieting spirit.

A little short of the gatehouse, the legate was put off by something disagreeable carried by the chilly wind. The breeze smelled strongly of manure or worse. The Latin mutterings at his rear suggested his countrymen felt misgivings similar to his own. In contrast, Goddeu's Druids remained stoic, climbing the incline with bland, hard-set faces.

Pictish gate wardens hailed the new arrivals and, in bad Brythonic, bade them to dismount. Goddeu explained to the legate that the temple servants would stable their horses. Their group would be escorted along on foot.

Asiaticus consented and the Romans fell in behind the Gallic priests—a symbolic slight which Asiaticus disliked.

Despite this, his careful, patient nature counseled against needless conflict. If this negotiation went badly, it should be for a better reason than pride.

A druid wearing gray-green robes met the Romans and Black Goats just inside the gate. Their leader addressed Goddeu in a cult language and, once more, the Master Black Goat, again translated. The temple servants would assist the guests with their gear. Just then, the Wyrm dignitaries hailed the Romans in Greek, bidding them to accompany them to the temple. They would be greeted there by the Master Wyrm. Asiaticus showed his assent with a nod.

Following the town's narrow lanes, the Roman officer noted the Pictish look on almost everyone he saw. These people possessed meager material culture, but that didn't explain why the town reeked worse than the hillside.

Nearby, he spotted a rubbish pit. These receptacles for garbage and sewage were commonplace in Gallic villages, too, but Caer Draig had more than its share of them.

Next to the pit, servants tossed in what looked like bones. Their haste and furtiveness made Asiaticus wonder whether the locals held bones to be unseemly things, to be concealed from visitors. Asiaticus had not encountered many Picts before this. These tribesmen looked to be fond of tattooing and dressed in baggy clothing. Because of this day's chill, they went about wrapped in hooded mantles and fleecy shirts. The fashion unfortunately made the village appear to be entirely occupied by hill brigands.

Asiaticus primarily noted villagers' disapproving faces, even when observing the Black Goats. The Roman officer suspected the Picts disliked all outsiders.

The visitors' Wyrm guides brought their guests to the wooden steps of a large, board-built structure shaped like a rectangular box. This large building was assuredly the temple of the Wyrm Druids.

It did not look like a Brythonic style and the Gallo-Roman wondered whether the design displayed a Pictish influence. Traditionally, the Britons—like the old Gauls—had eschewed the use of temples and recognized the outdoor world as one grand temple for every cult group. The druids especially favored oak groves, and the gods were honored with small shrines and fountains.

The group was led up a flight of wooden steps toward the temple's double doors. A fresh delegation of green-clad druids met the Romans on the landing.

A middle-aged man, also wearing green, stood at their head. Medium in stature, he was tonsured and wearing a beard without a mustache. His face was remarkably ugly, yet Asiaticus could observe no true deformity.

At the least, the fellow was evil-looking, and his mere physical presence put the Roman on guard.

The high priest greeted Goddeu in a mannerly way, using a secret cult language. The Master Wyrm promptly shifted toward Asiaticus, introducing himself as Bhort.

The man's beard was disorderly, shaggy, and streaked with black, gray, and an unattractive yellow. He had a gaunt, narrow face with a prominent hooked nose. The man's muddy brown eyes added nothing positive to the disturbing impression he presented.

"Our college welcomes you, Legate Decimus Valerius," Bhort said.

The Briton's use of Latin, though exotically accented, was spoken correctly. Unsure about the high priest, the legate remained meticulously diplomatic.

The legate guessed that Bhort had spent his younger years in foreign travel. This was no rare thing for druids. Asiaticus' druidic great-grandfather had frequently gone abroad before the conquest.

Was the Master Wyrm a fanatic? the Roman wondered. Many priests were extreme in their beliefs. Asiaticus anticipated that Bhort was going to be a formidable negotiating opponent.

Asiaticus' mission was to make contact with the Wyrms while assessing them as potential allies. Plautius wanted him to bring back as much first-hand information as possible. If the legate presented him with a positive endorsement of the Wyrms, the major negotiations would be carried out by highly experienced Roman diplomats.

"Thank you, Master Bhort," the legate replied. "The Senate and Roman people offer their goodwill and friendship to the Wyrms."

"After such a lengthy journey, you surely need rest and a hearty meal, Decimus Valerius," proposed the Master Wyrm. "And perhaps you and your men would equally appreciate warm rooms and good beds. When visiting Rome, I observed how sensitive your countrymen are to chill weather."

"That is true," admitted the legate. "Yet we Romans manage to thrive in many different climates."

Bhort smiled with his mouth but not his eyes. Asiaticus was passing on a veiled warning—that Rome went where it pleased and almost always got what it wanted.

After the formal exchange of greetings, temple attendants guided the Romans into another part of the village, where guest houses were reserved for them.

Upon inspecting his quarters, Asiaticus decided the accommodations were unimpressive, but not offensive. Caer Draig probably had nothing better to offer.

Darkness came on swiftly and supper was brought to the Roman officers, who dined together with the legate. They were served rustic fare—blood bread, vegetables, sauces, and meat—the latter being goat. The wine provided had a good bouquet and a distinct flavor. Indeed, Britannia was said to cultivate good grapes.

Later, an Italian orderly assisted Asiaticus in preparing for bed. A fiber-stuffed mattress on a rope net, the bed was little more than a cot. Nonetheless, though not luxurious, it looked fit enough for a soldier. While a centurion, Asiaticus had made do with beds worse than this one.

The Roman officer yawned, worn out by so much rapid travel. As he lay down, he sighed. He well knew that an alliance between Romans and druids was an unnatural thing. Rome would tolerate the druids only so long as they were useful. It did not care about religions but feared skilled magicians.

While Asiaticus had a positive opinion of druids in general, he had no sympathy for traitors like the Black Goats and Wyrms. His aim was to complete this first contact swiftly and then depart speedily from Caer Draig.

That night, his slumber was difficult. At odd moments, the Roman thought he was awake and hearing voices—very unpleasant voices. At rising, he felt unrefreshed, and so uncharacteristically lingered in bed until servants arrived with his breakfast tray....

# DRAGON QUEST

## CHAPTER X

Since the ghastly death of the Raven Brute, Simon of Gitta had tried to reason out what had happened.

Both master and servant had been reduced to ashes by cremation. Surprisingly, remnants of their flesh and bone remained untouched beneath the layers of ash. Cremating a body requires intense heat and time. So why hadn't the flammable thatched roof caught fire?

Knowing of similar tragedies abroad worsened Simon's distress. The Greeks had a name for the perplexing phenomenon—*authórmētē anthrópinē kaúsē*, which translated into "spontaneous human combustion."

When it happened, a living person would suddenly cremate wherever he sat or lay. And, yes, nearby combustibles had inexplicably failed to catch fire. He was almost certain that authórmētē anthrópinē kaúsē represented a sorcerous attack.

And why did Brute believe dragons were involved in terrorizing him? Although Simon had encountered dragons before, he couldn't see the connection.

Entities witnesses called "dragons" had been sighted in the Rhaetian Alps for centuries. While traveling the region, the adventurer encountered these supposed dragons. He'd found out that they were a type of non-human being with shape-shifting powers.

Far from being animalistic destroyers, they were reasonable people who spoke articulately. Their race, they claimed, was a very ancient one, called the Serpent Men by humans. For unstated reasons, the Serpent People's population dwindled over thousands of years. As shadowy observers, they had continued going about the world disguised in assumed human shapes.

Simon and the strangers had discussed many subjects, including what they said were actual dragons, beings quite different from themselves. They told him dragons existed as invisible vortices or were occasionally seen as balls of floating light. But they could drape themselves in a type of flesh and take a monstrous form that terrified mankind. These people had a name, Lloigor, and their sightings had given rise to the legends of rampaging dragons.

The Serpent People warned Simon to never seek for the Dragon kind, neither in their spiritual nor their material forms. They were implacably hostile and dangerous. Even the Serpent People in their days of greatest power had shunned the Dragon kind.

"Spiritual minds diverge from human minds," they said. "Their thoughts are weapons and have a ruinous effect on the minds of human beings. The spirits' intruding thoughts not only maddened their victims, but overcame and dominated them. The Dragon Spirits were devoid of positivity and their thoughts corrupted the human spirit, leaving only foulness behind. These destroyed souls can afterward be manipulated by the entities."

Simon, thinking back on this, tried unsuccessfully to fit this information into the strange business unfolding before his eyes on the island of Britannia.

Following their escape, the druids had camped many miles away. Most of his companions had passed the dark hours morbidly silent. Even the Master Merlin Emrys had become remote and uncommunicative. The elder sat for hours in a deep meditative trance and the Samaritan had not disturbed him. Instead, he had gone to Mog Ruith and asked the Irish savant what he knew about dragons.

Because the Wren had at first tried to put him off, Simon turned away. But the man called him back and started speaking seriously. "The stories from our ancestors maintain that the Dragon Spirits wield a mighty weapon that Brute called the 'Dragon Breath.' When one sees the destruction wrought by Dragon Fire, the Dragon Spirits loom very near."

"Can anyone defend against these evil spirits?" Simon asked.

Mog Ruith rubbed his beard and said, "To deal with the Dragon Breath, one must know its nature and its weaknesses. According to legend, if the spirits wish to kill, they must first choose a victim and meditate evilly upon him. Once their target is selected, the spirits cannot change their focus without undoing all they have already done. I believe that Brute and his servant must have been marked for death hours before we entered their hut. The spirits had no fix on us newcomers, and we were free to escape by physical flight."

"Why did the Dragon Spirits not attack us later, after we'd fled?"

"We know very little about their ways, but either they could draw no fix upon us, or they could not attack us where we were."

"Why is that?" asked Simon.

"The Dragon Breath seems to depend upon a large draw of earth energy."

"But Brute was living in a remote hut. Why should that lonely spot be brimming with earth energy?"

"The spirits are apt at making the Earth's currents flow where they wish them to flow. But observation reveals that it takes time to prepare a Dragon Breath attack on a target. "The spirits had likely marked the man while he lived at Caer Draig. Once marked, they could follow him to Rathtyen and his forest hut at will."

"Can they go anywhere, Master? Are they uncontainable?" asked Simon.

"It is a mistake to overestimate any enemy," said Mog Ruith. "Excessive caution breeds cowardice. The Dragon Spirits do not haunt every region. An informed person may take precautions. If one leaves the spirits unchecked, their power may spread widely. In ancient days, the spirits constructed arrays of standing stone for hundreds of miles around, enabling them to dominate the entire continent."

"Can any Dragon Spirit take the deadly dragon form?"

"No. The stories suggest they cannot materialize their dragon shape except where strong earth energy enables them. Living dragons inhabit places marked by standing stones."

This was the last bold statement Mog Ruith gave. The druid displayed agitation, and his subsequent answers were short and uninformative. The Samaritan, sensing the conversation was over, politely excused himself and retired to his bedroll.

At sunup, the druids rode in file along the Camelos road until they reached the king's court. Unexpectedly, Mog Ruith appeared at Simon's barracks' door that evening and suggested the two of them ought to resume their conversation. Under night's cloak, the druid confided much important information.

"I ended our conversation last night because I sensed bellicose spirits gathering around us. Our ancestors had a saying, 'To name them is to bring them.' We are eternally spied upon by spiritual entities and must ever be careful of what we say. The safeguards I've placed upon my aura this evening should protect you also, Simon, providing our discussion is not a prolonged one.

"Knowing the hazards, my young friend, what do you say? Are you still determined to seek dangerous knowledge, or would you seek safety under a blanket of ignorance?"

Simon had an answer for that.

"Master, from childhood I have sought to find wisdom, not avoid it."

Mog Ruith grimaced thoughtfully.

"Hearken well," he said resignedly. "In their natural state, the dragons exist as evil thoughts. Each Dragon Spirit is like a different thought in a single mind. When they join as a collective mind, their unity makes them as formidable as a god. Possibly, their joining gives rise to a god. Some have supposed that Gathanothog, the god associated with the Dragon Spirits, is nothing more than the collective mind of the Dragon Spirits.

"But take note. The Dragon Spirits are not wholly restricted to feeding on earth currents. Animals, especially human beings, are to them small ponds of collected earth energy. The Dragon Spirits, like thirsty men in a desert, can replenish themselves by absorbing the energy of the living."

"What is the fate of a creature that undergoes vampirization?" Simon asked.

"If a man is tapped infrequently, he will heal. But repeated draining over many successive nights is very injurious. Soon, the victim will weaken and die. Men may attribute such deaths to some undiagnosed, yet natural, illness. Yet, such a death like that is unnatural."

"So, the Dragon Spirits may use mankind as a food source?"

Mog Ruith nodded. "A man may not only be used as a food source, but the spirits may enslave him through the process. His soul is reduced to a bitter residue, and he becomes only a husk of a man, debased and mad. If the spirits do not restrain his mad impulses, he is useless to them, a wild predator committing many violent murders for the pleasure of it.

"But a drained victim who is kept in thrall may be directed to perform useful tasks in service to the spirits' interest."

Ruith saw a question stirring in Simon's eyes. "Do you wish to speak, friend?"

"I wonder, Mentor," said the Samaritan, "what happens if a human being becomes a slave of the Dragon Spirits, but then is abandoned by them? How does he fare after that?"

The Wren shook his head. "The old stories say that undirected slaves become violent maniacs, a danger to everyone around them. But children are their most preferred victims.

"Following corruption, an individual barely possesses a soul. Someone in that state is akin to a walking corpse, devoid of moral comprehension. If a good man encounters such a person, he should eliminate the creature. Predator-slaying is a noble thing when defending the still unharmed and pure."

"There was a man," Simon drawled, "whom I tracked down in the Rhaetian Alps. I wished to end his career in crime. Pontius Pilate was his name, a rare creature of evil. But he was much worse than I expected—a demon, not a man. Could Pontius Pilate have been a corrupted one cast off by the Dragon Spirits?"

"Perhaps he was, Simon," said Mog Ruith. "Dragon Spirits may be behind more evil than currently understood."

"How do we fight a spiritual enemy striking from out of the spirit plane?" asked Simon. His angry eyes flashed like the leaping flames of twin candles.

The big druid sighed. "We must resume this discussion at a later time. I feel the spirit world encroaching on us, despite the wards of protection I have put in place."

The sky suddenly rumbled above the pair, and behind the clouds, lightning flashed.

Ruith looked up. "It's very late in the year for lightning," he observed. "I sense it portends danger."

Simon likewise gazed at the dark sky, suspicious of what he saw there.

*       *       *

On the morrow, High King Arto summoned the Merlin Druids to his villa, along with many of his most trusted war chiefs. The king directed Mog Ruith and Emrys to tell the gathering about Brute's death. As Arto listened to their strange story, determination filled him.

At the end of the discussion, the king stood up to speak. He requested that the Merlin Druids carry out an important mission. They would be the king's eyes, sent to explore the area of dragon depredations. Now secure in his kingship, Arto felt at liberty to punish those who destroyed the Eagles, Ravens, and Brute. He ordered them to discover whether humans or dragons were to blame for the destruction.

When the king requested Emrys lead the expedition, the sage refused. He avowed he was weary and unwell. He proposed a younger man should lead the druids west and recommended Mog Ruith for leadership.

Some Merlins reacted angrily. Why should a Wren lead Merlins? But cooler heads argued the contrary. After an animated discussion, the consensus endorsed Emrys' opinion. This was no time for a dispute over leadership. Besides, Ruith's appointment was very temporary. His personal and professional obligations would call him back to Ireland before winter.

Because Simon was disliked by the Merlins, he preferred to keep a low profile, but in this case, he strongly supported Emrys' proposal. He understood people and appreciated that the Wren excelled at uniting opposing viewpoints as a fit leader should.

That issue being settled, Arto interviewed each of his war chiefs separately, looking for the best man to act as the druids' escort leader. In the end, he asked Laird Pellinor to accept the appointment.

Pellinor protested, loath to withdraw from the Medway lest the battle-front become active again. But with the king pressing him, the venerable laird finally yielded to persuasion, though continuing to voice his disbelief in dragons.

Pleased, the king declared his need for a clever man to solve the West's problems. He didn't care if the man believed in dragons or not.

The king of Avalon selected his second son, Lamorak, to be his lieutenant, a choice acceptable to the great majority. For the rest of the day, Pellinor went about recruiting young blades who had a taste for adventure. He selected over a hundred and twenty hot-bloods. He preferred youthful warriors because the most seasoned fighters needed to remain faced off against the ever-dangerous Romans.

As evening came on, Pellinor ordered the recruits away to bed, to prepare for an early morning start. He ordered the palace staff to work overnight, procuring supplies for the group's long journey.

Pellinor rose before the sun and immediately became angry. Lazy efforts had characterized the overnight work, making an early departure impossible. Working diligently, the laird requisitioned horses, arms, and provisions for the druids and warriors. They would be ready to set out at midday.

Simon of Gitta had withdrawn from the assembly after Mog Ruith's appointment, seeing no special reason he should accompany the expedition. But Mog Ruith unexpectedly called at his lodgings at dusk, asking him to act as his assistant on the expedition.

Simon needed some persuading. Mog Ruith was up to the task, revealing a great number of significant Western island problems that needed addressing. Finally, because Simon wanted to explain the deaths of the Eagles, Ravens, and Brute, he finally agreed.


Given the company's late start, the Britons could not travel far before dark, and Pellinor made camp twenty miles from Camelos. Earlier that day, he'd overheard some of his young warriors laughing and discovered that some saw their mission as farcical. Pellinor, despite private doubts, rebuked them roundly, saying that every worthy warrior was enjoined by oath to obey his king's orders no matter what those orders were. The old war chief's rebukes wiped the smirks off his warriors' faces, but only so long as his glowering eyes were fixed upon them. When the old man turned his back, the bucks resumed their joking. Simon overheard them naming the supposedly imaginary creature haunting the West, "the Questing Beast."

Pellinor knew what continued to be said and vented to Mog Ruith, saying, "The Questing Beast, they call it! They think we're chasing will-o'-the-wisps. Why do young people always believe that acceptance of authority is optional? When a soldier has orders, he follows them! We have to deal with this mission before we can get back to the war front where we belong."

"I hear you, King Pellinor," the Irishman replied. 'I share your perspective."

Pellinor, his temper spent, stomped off. Simon, standing nearby, overheard his mentor mutter, "I doubt Lord Pellinor knows much more about will-o'-the-wisps than he does about dragons."

The Samaritan stepped up. "Are will-o'-the-wisps significant?" he asked.

"They can be," the Irishman ambiguously replied.

"Why? Are they are demons?"

"Aye, they are!"

"Explain that to me, Mentor."

The Wren shook his head. "That's a story for another time."

"I've heard that will-o'-the-wisps are malignant spirits," said Simon. "Could Dragon Spirits be involved?"

The druid sighed. "It's possible, my friend. But too much speculation is pointless. I'd advise you, however, to keep it in mind that reliable witnesses say that will-o'-the-wisps frequently hover above dragon pathways."

# The Harper and the Lady

## CHAPTER XI

The princess opened her eyes and saw Broch looking down at her, his upper body braced on one elbow.

She looked away. "I'm relieved the night's done."

"Uh-huh. The storm kept waking me up."

"I feel so hungry. How are we going to find food?"

"I'm not sure," the youth said. "Normally, I could kill a squirrel with a stone, but I can't throw straight using my left hand." His right was still chained.

The maid shook her head. "We have to travel. The Pictish village is still too close. Which way do we go? We can't see the moon anymore and the sky is cloudy!"

The youth pointed with his unshackled hand. "That's south!"

Voada frowned. "How do you know?"

"Hunter's lore," he answered. "The moss grows thickest on the northern side of a tree."

Voada nodded. "I suppose that's because moss doesn't like the sunlight. I wonder if any of our people are searching for us yet."

"Because of the dead bodies at the bridge, the locals will have spread the word and the local chieftains will notify their king. Even if the king does nothing else, he'll have to notify your brother in Estrangore. But even if his warriors are looking for us, we'll be hard to find in a countryside this large."

"I prayed last night for rescue. What's the use of being royal if the gods don't listen to a person's prayers?"

"I'm not confident that any of us are important to the gods," Broch declared.

Voada wrinkled her nose. "Anyway, I'm confident that Prasutagos won't much care if I don't show up! He can always ask his father for a different bride."

Broch touched her cuffed hand. "Cheer up. Remember, the Master Merlin said that even if your next two decades are the worst possible, they'll be followed by excellent years."

"I don't want to wait twenty years to be happy. There's nothing right about the world. Why do so many people fight to stay alive while enduring daily misery?"

"Many think life is preferable to the punishment awaiting evil people after death," the youth stated.

"Are you afraid to die? Do you think of yourself as evil?" Voada asked.

"I have a high opinion about myself, but I'm not sure the gods would agree with me. The gods' point of view is unpredictable."

Voada noticed her skirt was ripped. It had probably been torn while they were fighting through thorny bushes in near-darkness. Out of embarrassment, the maid pulled the edges of the tear together.

"I think you must be a very great sinner," she said to Broch.

"Why?"

"Who else but an evil wretch would have been cursed to share my misery with me?"

The youth tried to smile. "It's strange, lady, but this isn't the worst day of my life. Every time I look at your dirty face, I forget how wretched our condition is."

"Are you sure it isn't the sight of my bare legs that's keeping you cheerful?"

Her bluntness startled Broch, but also made him chuckle. "I commend you, lady, for keeping your sense of humor!"

"I wasn't trying to be funny. If someone caught sight of me now— even a poor man—would he consider me fit to be his bride?"

"You look strong enough to pull a plow and healthy enough to give him a big family. He'd absolutely marry you. But would you accept him?"

"I expect that starvation or torture can force a woman to marry almost anyone. But I couldn't respect a man who would want me looking like this."

"Why not?"

"Men who like dirty ragamuffins are contemptible."

"Please! All over the world, ill-favored women win husbands."

"So you consider me an ill-favored woman?"

"Not at all! A dip in a cold rock pool would clean you up nicely."

"You can only say that because you've seen my best garments."

"Don't be so sure. You have an irresistible charm."

"I think you're much too easily charmed, young man."

"Guilty. Being easy to please is my worst vice. But, say, I'm thirsty. We should start looking for food and water."

The shackled pair abandoned the overhang, each wrapped in two blankets.

"It's not so cold as yesterday," the young man observed. "The storm must have brought in milder air."

Ceasing their banter, they set out. Before going very far, they discovered a natural depression full of clear water.

Instead of quenching her thirst, Voada knelt to consult her reflection. She saw an unrecognizable, filthy girl with dried mud and silt caked in hair that looked like a sparrow's nest. "I look worse than any charwoman!" she said.

"There's no need to be embarrassed," said Broch.

"Why not!" she snapped.

"Because no one will recognize you. They'll think you're just a dirty, unimportant peasant wench."

"The slavers will recognize me! Do we have any real chance of getting away?"

"The odds aren't encouraging. But we can improve our odds by traveling fast. We also need luck, but we've already prayed for that."

Without answering, the princess dipped her free hand into the pool, brought up a little water, and washed her face.

"Don't let your dirty water drip back into the pool!" the harper exclaimed. "We still have to drink from there."

She looked at him. "Why should you dictate to a princess?"

"Maybe it's because I'm the only person for a hundred miles around who wants to take care of you."

She grimaced. "I suppose that's true. Nearly all my friends died at the bridge. Outside of my brothers, there's no one left who cares about me."

"I know how you feel. I lost many friends in the fight, too."

Not answering, Voada resumed washing but had become more careful about polluting the pool. Once her face was washed, she put her lips to the mirrorlike surface and sucked in a mouthful of icy water. She drank rapidly until the cold water made her teeth hurt.

Finally, she rested back on her haunches, saying, "Drink your fill. After you do, I want to bathe."

"In freezing water?" he asked.

"I'd pay any price to get clean."

"Are you going to wash your shift, too?!"

"I have to. It's crusted with mud."

"Go ahead. I promise not to look," he said with a grin.

Voada frowned.

Broch moved in and drank heavily. Suddenly, the princess tugged at the chain and he changed position to give her more slack.

Slipping into the pool without removing her shift, Voada made a terrible face against the cold. Yet, with teeth gritted, she splashed water over her dirty garments, her hair, and her upper arms, rubbing them fast with her palms. Broch watched a muddy halo surround her. The swiftness of her bathing couldn't stop her from becoming numb. Voada suddenly cried out: "Pull me out!"

Broch used their link chain to draw her from the pool and helped her wrap her two blankets around her.

Voada, still shivering, used them to dry herself before draping them around her body for warmth. Her teeth still chattering, she squeezed handfuls of wet hair hard to force out the water.

Suddenly, she shucked off the blankets.

"Don't look at me!" she said. "I need to get out of this wet shift! I can't bear it!"

Broch averted his gaze while the princess drew off her wet garment. She re-donned the blankets and then wrung out the shift as best she could. "Go ahead, look," she told the harper.

Because of their manacle chain, the best Voada could do was to wrap the shift around the chain, hoping it would dry by day's end.

Finally, she scraped the mud off her dirty shoes with a flat rock, put them on, and stood up.

"Aren't you going to bathe, too?" she asked.

He shook his head. "I never took a mud bath like you did. Besides, I can't endure the cold as easily as you can," he said.

"Oh, fine! I'm doomed to stay chained to somebody who doesn't care about smelling awful."

"Most men are alright with smelling unpleasant unless they're seeking to impress a woman."

The girl ignored him. "I hope it gets warm enough for my shift to dry," she said.

"It's strange," Broch said.

"What's strange?"

"The way you look. If I just met you, I'd assume you were only a pretty peasant girl, maybe one from the Pict village."

"All the Pict girls were ugly!" she declared.

"One or two weren't so bad," he replied.

She tossed her head. "Never mind the Pict girls. I just heard that you find me attractive."

"I do."

"I was afraid of that," Voada said.

"Why?"

"Because it will only make you miserable."

Broch didn't understand her statement. But he'd grown up with sisters and so knew that most women had twisted minds.

*     *     *

After three days of travel, Pellinor and his men reached an area of devastation. It was a lonely district of barrows and other graves. The Britons gradually ceased any cheerful conversation.

Men believed unquiet ghosts slumbered in the barrows. The grave mounds before them displayed various shapes—even the shapes of beasts— but the majority were small, round hummocks.

The passersby they met responded to their questions in low, frightened tones. The Britons learned that most of the supposed witness sightings were only hearsay. Most of these Westerners looked Pictish with a sullen and suspicious cast. Only a few of them were energetic enough to spew excited warnings. "Do not seek the dragons! Beware the punishment of the gods," they advised.

While riding past the ancient cairns, a few young men speculated about treasure inside these artificial hills. But others recounted stories of greedy diggers who had found only bones and pottery fragments inside the mounds. One warrior warned that grave loot would bring ill fortune to any house that received it.

Topping a rise, the warriors caught sight of lofty menhir stones looming in the distance, high above the surrounding sea of tall grass. This was a storied place that all had heard of, the famous Giants' Dance.

The district around the stones was uninhabited and looked unfit for cultivation. The most significant animal life in sight was small auroch herds—wild cattle grazing on heath grass and gorse. Such beasts were often taken by hunters. The creatures would have been eradicated already if the area had been more populated.

As things stood, the questers had encountered no human beings over the past couple of hours, not even hunters. The land looked desolate, as if humanity deliberately—and wisely—shunned it.

The tree coverage thereabouts was scant. What boles they espied were clusters in small groves. It was easy to imagine invisible spirits lurking everywhere, sucking all life and joy from the suffering landscape.

Simon said to Mog Ruith, "I've rarely visited a land so forlorn as this region. Up to now, I'd supposed that southern Arabia was the most forbidding country I'd ever visited."

"You saw Arabia?" asked Mog Ruith. "What is that distant land like?"

Simon shook his head. "I'd rather not remember it."

Mog Ruith didn't press him. He said, "Imagine the ghastly secrets these local ghosts must know."

"Do you believe in haunts, Mentor?" the Samaritan asked.

Mog Ruith shrugged. "Have you never encountered a ghost, Simon?"

The novice druid grimaced. "I've observed many peculiar events. There are ghostly things I've seen, but I assumed they were demons."

The arch-druid nodded. "Demons, they may have been. I am not convinced that haunts are human ghosts. I believe ghosts are evil spirits dwelling in the empty, cast off astral shells of long-dead human souls."

Simon changed the subject. "Revered One, do you believe we should ride as a group to Caer Draig, or would it be better to send a spy ahead? I doubt a show of force will do anything to reveal the treason of people who have been plotting for centuries."

"I know what you mean, Simon, but I'm against sending one man alone. Every spy should have a comrade supporting him. I intend to ride to Caer Draig myself and would appreciate having you with me. According to Master Emrys, your wizard skills, combined with your warrior training, are invaluable."

Simon shrugged. "I wasn't born with the wish to be a warrior. Left in peace, I likely would have become a scholar. But because of the Romans, I was forced to become a man-slayer. Ironically, that training has saved my life many times."

"I've long believed that the gods aptly guide us in acquiring whatever talents they want us to have," the druid said.

Simon of Gitta shook his head. "They've outdone themselves in the brutal way that they've been teaching me." When the Wren offered no comment, Simon continued. "What do you suppose awaits us within the Wyrm stronghold?"

The druid gazed thoughtfully at the Giants' Dance before answering. "Arto wants us to find traitors and expose them. Britannia cannot afford to have turncoats stabbing us in the back while invaders slash at our front. Remember, Gaul fell because so many druidic colleges surrendered to Caesar and assisted him. We cannot allow that to happen here."

"What made the Gallic Druids so corrupt?"

"All men are corrupt, Simon. The wisest way to classify people is on the strength of their corruption. Few patriots exist, though I would include King Arto as one of them. Every day, scoundrels undermine the efforts of the heroes.

"Emrys believes that the evidence against the Wyrms is considerable. I'm sure the king agrees, but he must tread lightly when dealing with the colleges. To offend a powerful school without offering overwhelming proof of crime and treachery will draw support to them—and that includes many colleges that should know better. Petty peevishness is the fuel that treason depends on. A few druidic schools in rebellion would dishearten many soldiers opposed to Rome."

"What about Brute's story? Might the Wyrms be seeking to revive the Dragon Spirits?"

"All things under the sun are possible."

"Mentor," said Simon, "I know you are a close confidant of Master Merlin Emrys. He claims he's shown me favor because he believes I'm supernaturally significant. Whether or not I believe it, what should I do?"

Mog Ruith chuckled. "The Master Merlin does indeed believe you are destiny-driven, Simon. Unfortunately, I have no advice to offer. Emrys recommended I should keep you at my side for this mission. He believes that following a god-led man will deliver his companions to a happy haven."

"I don't know about that," said the Samaritan. "Many followers of mine have perished; this grieves me."

"Death is the inevitable fate of all men, Simon. But Emrys maintains a high opinion of you. You would make a fine priest."

"A priest? I've never considered myself to be a true priest. I see myself as an acolyte following the light cast by greater men. Unfortunately, that light has led me into some peculiar situations."

"Most fate-driven men find themselves in strange circumstances."

"Fate-driven? What should a man do if he is fate-driven?"

The savant loosed a full laugh. "I advise you not to brood upon it. Go wherever you feel the urge to go. Should I travel with you, I might also learn a thing or two."

"You continually denigrate yourself, Mentor! I think you are wise and you carry your wisdom as though it were a light load. You are a powerful spirit in a powerful body. Had you wished it, I think you could have been an accomplished warrior."

Mog Ruith sighed. "Maybe, but swordsmanship doesn't appeal to me. My heart tells me to calm trouble with reason, not battle."

"I respect that," Simon said. "But you've said evil must be fought. Can reason ever be a match for the violence of evil?"

Ruith made no reply.

"Reverence," Simon continued, "Brute spoke as though he had committed some grave sin, a sin so terrible that it killed his soul before his body died. Where could his death wish have come from? What did he experience at Caer Draig to leave him so broken? What is the ugly secret of that place?"

Mog Ruith shook his head. "If I go there, that's what I aim to find out. Something at the caer singled out Brute's weaknesses and struck him at his weakest point. But weaknesses vary from man to man. Watch the ground ahead carefully as you walk, Simon."

"I am always careful," said Simon.

Mog Ruith held back a laugh. "Careful? If so, Simon of Gitta's tales, like Caesar's memoirs, ring false."

Simon, contemplating the strange appearance of the Giants' Dance, made no reply.

# The Giants' Dance

## CHAPTER XII

Under the skeletal shadows of bare trees, the princess said to Broch, "I'm so hungry. What will we do?"

"We won't have a good time of it," the young man stated, "but lack of food isn't disastrous."

"I think it would be pretty disastrous."

He shook his head. "I've heard people swear that if a person goes hungry for long enough, he loses his hunger pangs. When that happens, he ought not to eat anything at all unless he's able to eat a lot. Eating just a morsel won't sate him, but it's going to make him feel his hunger again. Even fit people can go weeks without food before reaching a point of weakness. Druids endure long periods of voluntary starvation."

"That's not starvation. That's fasting."

"I'd call it forty days and forty nights of starvation. They do it willingly to honor the gods."

"I've often wondered how not eating honors the gods."

"I've never asked a druid that question."

"After fasting, in what shape is a druid?"

"Most of them say they're very hungry."

"No surprise there!"

"Here's the best part. We have ample time—forty days—to reach Camelos. Eastland doesn't have close relations to the lairds of the West, and with a war going on it's hard to trust anyone. Are there Southeastern allies in support of Estrangore?"

"I don't know of any Southerner I'd trust with my life. But if I get hungry enough, I'm afraid I'll be on my knees begging farmers for loaves of bread," said the maid.

"Just be careful who you beg from. Anyone we meet might be an enemy. The Pict especially."

"What's the chance of finding nuts and berries?"

"Nuts, maybe. But it's late in the season for berries."

"I only wish you could give me some good news."

"Any positive news I could come up with would be false. But I can assure you that my time in the forest allows me to identify most poisonous wild foods."

"I hope it does," said Voada.

*     *     *

That afternoon, as the day warmed up, the fugitives discovered bushes hung with untouched dry raspberries and a wild lettuce patch. It wasn't a lot, but they devoured everything.

"I have a terrible thought," said Voada.

"What?"

"What if the animals didn't eat these berries because they're poison?"

"They're raspberries."

"Maybe they just look like raspberries."

"There's nothing else in the woods that looks like a raspberry, except maybe blackcaps. But blackcaps are dark purple, and they aren't poisonous either."

"If you say so."

After additional travel, they emerged from the woods overlooking a rolling down.

"I think I hear cattle," whispered the princess. "There may be a farmstead nearby!"

"Just don't be surprised if you find Picts working it. Brythonic masters hire many of them. And we've got another problem. Because we're wearing a shackle, we're going to look like escaped slaves. Even an honest countryman might capture us and turn us over to slavers."

"What a terrible world this is!" the maiden declared.

"The world has always kept slaves," said Broch, "and there will be slaves as long as slaving is profitable. Romans are the most rapacious slave raiders in the world. Julius Caesar sent about half of Gaul's population into the slave markets. The slavers actually traveled in safety under Caesar's protection. The stories say their wagons looked like a traveling marketplace."

"Why do the Romans still consider him a hero?" asked the girl.

"Many Romans recognized Caesar's true nature, yet pursuing him militarily risked civil conflict. Alas for them, when Caesar got rich enough, he started the civil war himself. Good Romans finally assassinated him, but by then, his generals held all the power in the empire. They simply chose a new tyrant for Rome."

Voada frowned. "Is it possible that what Caesar did in Gaul might happen here?"

"If the Romans win, yes. Undoubtedly, British traitors are already at work helping them."

"It's too depressing to talk about it," the Estrangorean said.

"What would you rather talk about?"

"Better things. Do you have family in Eastland?"

"No," he said after a pause. "I'm guessing that my father must have been a harper. I had to get my talent from somewhere."

The youth expected his companion to tease him with another bad harper joke, but Voada simply said, "I'm sorry."

Broch gave her a weak smile. "Don't be. If a person doesn't have family, he has fewer people to miss him when he's gone."

"It's true that people who don't exist can't feel sad. But it hurts to be alone. I have a large family."

"I didn't realize that," said Broch.

"Not much is said publicly. Most of my brothers and sisters aren't legitimate."

"Does having a big family keep you from feeling lonely?" the youth asked.

"No. Everyone, everywhere, is lonely, especially children. My mother died several years ago and my father remarried almost immediately. You've probably heard of the witch who became Estrangore's queen—Cartimandua."

"Is she truly a witch?"

"I don't know if she casts spells, but I wouldn't drink from any cup she handed to me. It seemed strange how my father became sick and died so soon after his marriage."

"Wouldn't your brother have executed her if she were a poisoner?"

"My brother said he couldn't find any proof of poisoning and told me to stop nagging him. I got so angry I advised him to employ a food taster for as long as Cartimandua is alive."

"If things are so bad in your home, I'm sorry for *you*."

"I'm getting married," she said without much emotion. "Maybe my new family will be better."

"We'd better push on," Broch urged. He'd always disliked talking about family problems, either his own or others'.


While stealing across the downs, the two young people avoided the high ground where they could be more easily seen. With dusk coming on, the pair found themselves striding across a harvested field surrounded by wheat stubble.

"I've heard that the Picts rarely plant wheat!" Voada said suddenly. "We must be back in Brythonic country!"

Broch glanced around. "Perhaps, yet caution is necessary. Pictish laborers do much of the harvesting work for Britons. Even if we avoid the Picts, evil people can be found in every tribe."

"I wish we knew exactly where we are."

"The Picts captured us in Sorestan and were taking us south toward River's Mouth. We've continued south, so we're probably well into Glouchedon by now. I wish we could go to its king, but he's unfriendly to Estrangore and is a notoriously weak leader. I wouldn't advise you to risk your life involving yourself with him. If we deal with anyone, we have to make sure it's a respectable Briton. Caratacos is our best choice; otherwise, we can contact a landowner or artisan."

"Or the wife of such a man," Voada amended.

"I suppose. Hopefully, he doesn't have a Pictish wife."

"May the gods guide us," replied Voada. This homily was not a first-time utterance from the forlorn maiden.

"I would like to meet a Brittonic iron-worker—with his tools close at hand," remarked the harper. "Getting free of this chain would be a blessing."

"I've heard that a lot of smiths make their living providing chains to slavers."

Their feet crushed an infinity of stubble but didn't leave a trail. The departed harvesters had left the field well-trampled. "It's too bad that the harvest is already over," said Broch. "A person can eat ripe grain straight from the hull."

"They've picked it bare," his companion said.

Broch spotted a sheaf of unthreshed wheat, seemingly dropped by a harvest wagon. Broch knelt and started to hull the kernels. He put a handful into his mouth and chewed. The grain became doughy between his molars and didn't taste at all bad, something like dough pinched from a kitchen bread pan. He hulled additional grain and handed it to Voada. She started chewing tentatively but soon was asking for more. The two hurriedly stripped the bundle bare and, despite the fading light, searched the area for additional gleanings. They fortunately found some.

"Mmmm," said Voada. "My life has been saved! Landholders should always leave some of their crops uncut for poor people to eat."

"Maybe when you're queen of Eastland, you can ask your husband to enact such a law!"

"Maybe I shall!"

With the light almost gone, the young people bedded down, still in the field. They scraped together enough loose straw to serve as a sleeping mat and drew their blankets over themselves. Exposed to the open sky, they hoped for continued fair weather.


While living in the Mediterranean East, Simon of Gitta had heard about the Giants' Dance. Its special stones, men said, had been brought from far away by a wizard. He had supposedly ensorcelled the stones to skip and dance and then led them a great distance, to the site of the Giants' Dance.

The troop of Britons drew up before a deep trench that posed a hazard to their horses. Simon craned in his saddle, studying the stone array from a distance. Just as the stories said, the monument comprised three concentric rings.

"So that's the marvel of ancient construction that people never stop jabbering about," remarked the king of Avalon. "What do you druids hope to discover here?"

"We were told that a dragon attacked the Eagles and Ravens," the Wren replied. "Where there are dragons, there is sorcery. For centuries, this site has been rumored to be a magnet for dark magicians. We might find traces of ritual black magic here."

Pellinor shook his head. "Are these dragons supposedly active at night, or might they show up in daytime, too?"

The Druid shrugged. "I've never seen a dragon. Our present job is to comb the grounds and find what we may. We shouldn't take our horses in; they'd trample away any trace of human activity around those stones."

"Here's where we'll make camp," the old war chief stated. "I'll send scouts in both directions to locate a safe crossing over this trench." While Pellinor was appointing his scouts, Mog Ruith dismounted and led his druids across the trench on foot.

Simon followed close behind the Merlins, counting his paces as they approached the array, getting some idea of the size of the layout.

There was an initial stone ring that started about two hundred and twenty-five feet from the trench. Upon reaching the outer ring of the monument, the Britions noticed indications of recent restoration efforts. But there were untouched areas that showed extensive decay, highlighting the Giants' Dance's age. Simon couldn't help but wonder about the purpose of such a thing. Its military design was poor; it seemed more like a temple. He expressed this opinion to the nearby Mog Ruith.

"No, Simon," replied the elder. "These stones served a greater purpose. I'm sensing a mighty flow of energy beneath our feet, one I can feel in my bones. I also smell a scent like lightning puts into the air. This place, I believe, dates back to the Age of Dragons; it must have functioned as an energy reservoir. We are standing at the edge of a lake of power. Judging from the signs of repair, living men are attempting to revive its original function."

Simon found it impossible to imagine how such large stones were quarried and transported. He had pondered similar questions regarding the pyramids in Egypt.

The largest stones occupied the outer ring, which was about thirty feet in height. And each upright was bridged to its neighbors with lintels. Amazing! Ancient tribes lacked the technology for such feats. It would have been a huge task even for the Romans.

Simon measured the outer ring; the circumference exceeded a thousand Roman feet. That would give the outer ring a diameter of well over three hundred feet.

When Simon turned his attention to the second of the three rings, he found its diameter measured about eighty feet. He noticed that many of the smaller uprights in this ring were composed of a different type of rock.

He entered the array's smallest circle, which was fifty feet across, about the size of a horse corral. But he also noted that the grass was fire-blackened. Why had a large fire been lit at the heart of the Giants' Dance? It almost certainly would have been part of a ritual, but whose ritual? Had the Wyrm wizards been involved?

Simon felt a light sprinkle of rain blow into his face. He looked up and saw that the cloudy sky had become even darker. Those looked like rain clouds.

Not far distant, Pellinor was conferring with his son Lamorak. Standing off to the side was the king's youngest warrior son—Torr.

"What news from the scouts?" the father asked his elder scion.

"Sire," Lamorak replied, "the scouts have found a causeway over the trench. There are two of them. The men at the horse camp are asking whether they should finish the encampment where they are, or build it inside the formation instead, given the safe crossing we now have."

"Have them build where they presently are," the war chief answered. "The druids don't want the ground trampled."

"Whatever happened here, they burned a lot of yew boughs," volunteered the boy Torr, holding up a branch of charred wood. "I didn't see yew growing anywhere along the way we've come."

Mog Ruith, being near enough to overhear the last remark, said, "Yew is favored for many ritual purposes, warriors. It's most often used to invoke demons from the underworld."

"Many a sorcerer calls up demons," said Pellinor. "That's still a far cry from summoning living dragons!"

"Maybe so, Laird. But the dragon business is part of your mission, not mine," Mog Ruith reminded him.

Simon, now catching up with his mentor, said, "I wonder why this place isn't being guarded by whoever is restoring it."

"What needs guarding?" asked the arch-druid. "What valuable items might intruders steal here? Friends, this place's vital essence resides within its stones and earth."

"What's so vital?" asked Lamorak.

"The stones are certainly aligned to resonate with the energy aura of the earth. The array must channel the power in the direction, or directions, that the builders wanted it to flow," answered Mog Ruith.

"And these energy flows send power along the dragon paths?" Simon asked.

"They add to it, certainly. The stones at the center ring are bluestones. I believe they are precisely placed upon nodes of power so that their resonation magnifies the current. In effect, this monument is an artificial lake of earth energy, and from it, streams of power flow."

"I don't understand that kind of talk," said Pellinor.

The Samaritan, disregarding the war chief, inquired of Mog Ruith, "Was the ancient work carried out by ordinary people?"

"If it was, I can't imagine how," said the Wren. "This array hails from the Dragon Age. Letting this work continue today presents an unacceptable danger. King Arto must be made to realize the menace that it represents."

Simon mused: "Maybe druids are planning to trick the Romans into helping them with their engineering. Wouldn't that speed up the work immensely?"

"It definitely would," the elder druid affirmed. "I imagine that the Wyrms will do their best to manipulate the Romans, but in attempting it, they play a dangerous game. If these powerful and brutal invaders realize they are being manipulated, they will not hesitate to massacre them all. And they will probably pursue any survivors to the ends of the earth."

Simon shook his head. "How can the Wyrms hope to control such a rebellious and turbulent race indefinitely?"

"I think they expect help from the Dragon Spirits. Brute told us that the spirits can corrupt and control the minds of men. Rome governs an empire with inherent weaknesses. Its power is entirely centralized. One man's will runs the entire system, and all other men are merely his functionaries.

"If the Dragon kind can achieve domination over the emperor and his inner cadre of supporters, all imperial resources would be instantly made available to the Wyrm Druids. But recall: Dragon Spirits, not druids, are behind this plan. I believe the rogue druids are merely carrying out their masters' instructions in fine detail."

"Like puppets? Are you saying that the druids are victims themselves?" asked Simon.

"Probably," said Ruith. "It is not possible for men—even skilled sorcerers—to safely link their mortal minds to a godlike mind. The Wyrm Druids, and many others besides, must labor as servile wretches, doing the bidding of the Dragon Spirits. Today's events must resemble those that led to the distant Age of Dragons."

"If that's the case," said Simon, "I can't see how we can attack the Dragon Spirits directly. Should we not focus on destroying their tools— the druids who are supporting them?"

Mog Ruith agreed, nodding. "That's likely the best way. I imagine that the Wyrms were too curious. Ambition made them go after secret knowledge like foolish children stepping into swift-flowing waters. Their probable fate will be death."

"It's all empty words!" broke in Pellinor. "Let me lay my eyes on a dragon if one truly exists! If I see it and believe it, I won't rest until I have made an end to the entire species—or until they have laid this body of mine dead on the ground!"

"A foolish oath, Warrior," warned the druid. "The gods scorn human pride, and often use thoughtless words to punish the speaker."

Old Pellinor made a scoffing sound and strode away, with his son Torr scurrying after him through the drizzle. Simon looked up again. The sky had grown darker and the raindrops were larger. With no tents in their gear and no natural cover on the plain, he thought they might all be in for a good soaking.

Mog Ruith stepped away and motioned for Simon to follow. The two of them left Lamorak standing alone. The pair had barely traveled over ten paces before there came a stentorian shout from Pellinor:

"To arms! Raiders!"

# THE FIGHT AMONG THE MENHIRS

## CHAPTER XIII

Lightning cracked overhead; rain rattled against the standing stones and blew into men's faces.

Riders, some leading horses, galloped from the horse camp, followed by running men. A mob of Pictish warriors—painted for war and heavily armed—were in pursuit a hundred feet back.

Pellinor at once plunged back into his element, shouting desperate orders—a man rejuvenated. He commanded his warriors back to the second ring of the Giants' Dance, where they made their stand shoulder-to-shoulder between the giant sarsens. Meanwhile, his horse-tenders hurriedly made a corral inside the central, horseshoe-shaped ring.

Simon ran to a thinly manned gap between menhirs. He was barely in place before a mass of savages rushed him with bladed weapons. His gladius in one hand and his *sica* in the other, the ex-gladiator defied their charge. He weaved, dodged, and stabbed his first foe in his exposed abdomen. With a shriek, the attacker stumbled rearward. Two more bullies barged into the vacated space, yowling war cries.

In the first minute, the battlefront became a chaos of clanking metal and furious shouting. The Picts were using massed numbers against the thin Brythonic line, determined to break the defensive ring and overwhelm the defenders with both front and rear attacks.

Simon fought bitterly to hold his ground while the cold rain fell, repelling one crazed primitive after another, while the young men on his flanks defended themselves manfully. Every defender fought his private fight, the shouting so intense that scarcely a man could hear the shouted orders of Pellinor or his son.

As if in frenzy, Simon intercepted and threw back one muscular Pict after another, his high-striking kicks shoving the foeman back, hurling them back against the pressing crowd of their fellows. Two tattooed warriors came at him with berserk fury and made Simon stagger backward. A third man supported them and the three tried to batter their way through his guard, but inadvertently narrowed the fighting front and cramped the free movement of their arms.

The arena-trained Simon jerked one of the Picts forward and threw him back into the faces of his cohorts. All three of them being in disarray, the ex-gladiator leaped like a panther, delivering cuts, slashes, and stabs. The blooded trio shrunk away like goats scattered by an enraged lion.

In the pandemonium, Simon maimed spearmen and swordsmen in rapid succession. Behind the front line, Mog Ruith and his druids were defending the horses. Savages had broken through the defensive perimeter at one point and rushed the band of druids like wolves. With his stout staff for a weapon, Ruith fought like the physically mighty man he was.

Simon continued battling where he was, punishing anyone who fought in his sector of the line. Close by, Lamorak struggled like a myrmidon, refusing to give up any inch of ground.

Despite the unrelenting pressure, the Britons refused to break. The wounded on both sides became detritus on the wet, trampled ground. Most of the fallen were savages, lacking both the effective armor and honed skill of their Brythonic adversaries. Simon suddenly realized the momentum had shifted. Many Picts stumbled backward, battle-weary with rain-diluted blood streaking their limbs.

"At them!" Pellinor bellowed. "Cut them down!"

Risking everything, the Picts charged forward and were unprepared to defend against the triumphant Brythonic assault. Although they outnumbered the opposition, confusion overtook them. As the slashing and stabbing Britons performed like avenging fiends, the Pictish warriors began showing their backs. A rout had begun.

Simon noticed two enemies observing the battle from a chariot on the far side of the trench, both dressed in druidic attire. The Samarian watched as they turned their ponies about and followed their spearmen in flight. Impulsively, the ex-gladiator dashed to the rear and commandeered one of the saddled horses.

The Samaritan, leading the beast to the outer ring of the Giants' Dance, saw Picts fleeing over a causeway. Springing into the saddle, he urged his gelding after the escaping leadership. He crossed the bridge while working his warhorse into a galloping pursuit after the fugitive chariot. Dense, wet gorse slowed the vehicle considerably.

The chariot was making for the low ground between two barrows, while Simon was urging ever more speed from his mount. When the enemy car abruptly bounced into the air and fell over on its side, its horses broke free and started running, dragging the broken pull pole behind them.

The two druids sprawled in the soaked grass where they had been thrown. They were going nowhere, so Simon slackened his forward rush. He didn't want to strike the same hidden obstruction that had upset the enemy vehicle.

Ignoring the fallen druid lying still in the grass, the ex-gladiator made after the man who had already gotten to his feet and was limping away.

Riding abreast of the lame fugitive, Simon swung from his saddle and started running after him on foot. The priest, glancing over his shoulder, saw no hope and dropped to his knees. He looked like a weaker beast supplicating to a dominant male. The wary adventurer slowed further in caution. Often, defeated opponents would feign exhaustion while being poised to defend themselves with a hidden knife.

"Druid, if you want to live, fall on your face with your hands behind your back," Simon commanded in Brythonic. When the green-robed man complied, Simon held him down while tying the man's wrists behind his back with a spare thong from his side pack. With the druid well-trussed, the Samaritan searched his robes for weapons.

Next, the adventurer compelled the enemy leader to stand. The fellow was a fifty-something Briton with a narrow beard and a stunned, lightly tanned face. "Start walking back to the Giants' Dance," Simon barked at him.

Despite a limp, the rain-soaked druid wasn't in great pain. "Where do you come from?" the ex-gladiator demanded. "Why did you lead those savages against us?"

The man's sole response was a backward glance, his face contorted by fiery hatred.


Since their meal in the grain field two days earlier, Broch and Voada failed to find much else to eat, and hunger beset them. A grove of walnut trees had provided nuts, but they had been raw nuts covered by a mushy hull, and handling them had dyed their fingers black. Using small stones as hammers, they found it hard to get at the unripe meat. The green nut meat proved unsavory, and they wondered if they were going to be made sick.

Still hungry, they continued southeast. Voada broke the silence, asking, "Do you think we should stop worrying about the coku catching us?"

"I don't know, but I'm not ready to let my guard down," he said. He looked from horizon to horizon. "I wonder how far south we are."

"It feels like we've walked a hundred miles."

"I wish it was a hundred miles. The faster we travel, the better off we are."

Voada shook her head. "If we're still in Glouchedon, why doesn't its king keep his roads safer?! His people call Estrangore backward, but they allow Picts to enslave people in broad daylight. And who knows if the Romans won't show up soon, too? Which do you think is worse, the Picts or the Romans?"

Broch faintly chuckled. "The Picts at least kill and move on, but the Romans will stay and treat everyone in Britannia as their slaves. And many

Roman masters are worse than cruel. They're degenerate. It's said that Cleopatra of Egypt preferred suicide to being taken to Rome."

"What would they have done to her in Rome?"

"I suppose they would have shown her to the crowds as a humiliated captive. After that, I'm not sure. After Vercingetorix was displayed that way, he was imprisoned for six years before being executed. I've never heard of captives of high rank being made slaves or fed to the lions."

"If they capture the kings of Britain, do you think they'll slay them, too?"

"Probably," sighed Broch.

"Do you suppose Eastland will capitulate to the Romans? They're very close to where the fighting is."

The harper answered thoughtfully. "Prince Prasutagos can't stand the Romans, but his father values the trade his kingdom does with Rome. He doesn't like this war."

"Is he friendly with the Romans, or is he afraid of them?"

"Both. Eastland is close to Gaul, and the Romans can make surprise landings anywhere on its coast. Also, I think the king is naïve. The Romans have given him gifts and flattery for years, trying to make him less loyal to Camelos. But taking sweet words from a Roman is like accepting a wooden horse from a Greek."

"Tell me, is Prince Prasutagos as bad as you've described, or were you only telling twisted jokes?"

"*Well...*" the young man said slowly, "I exaggerated his vices. Everyone has good days and bad. One thing I once overheard Prasutagos say is that the wife he'd most like to have would be patient, forgiving, and kind. He wants one that's pretty, but I don't think you'll have any problem in that category."

"But how pretty is he?"

Broch shrugged. "He's not as ugly as I've told you. He's not fat or bald, and he never had the pox."

"Oh, you! Did you tell me that just to make me miserable?"

"It was just a joke! I wanted to find out if you cared about who you married, or if you only wanted to be a queen."

"A house servant has no right testing his master's betrothed that way! By the gods! You *do* deserve a beating!"

"Guilty. I'm the impudent sort," said the youth. "It's in my blood and it's hard to control."

"You probably didn't get enough thrashings when you were small."

"No doubt. But I promise to answer your questions honestly from now on."

"I'll test you! Will Prasutagos make a patient, forgiving, and kind husband?" Voada asked.

"Once he gets to know you, I'm sure he'll be all those things to you."

"Few people make any effort to be kind. When I most needed kindness from my family, they could only think about politics. They were always pushing me to do things for political reasons, even things I didn't approve of."

"Like getting married?"

"No. I think wives live better lives than daughters or sisters. But I know that wives can be miserable if they have the wrong sort of husband."

"What's the right kind of husband?"

"If I had to name just one thing, I'd say I'd want a kind husband."

"What does the word kindness mean to you?" Broch asked.

"I keep thinking of those two servants who may have given up their lives for us—mostly for me. It makes me ashamed that I can't remember their names! What would make someone give up his life for someone else? Was it only because I was royalty? They didn't know me well enough to care about me as a person."

"They may have done it because you're so beautiful."

"Men! All they care about is beauty!"

"You need to understand men better. Beauty fascinates them. Remember the Greek story about the face that launched a thousand ships?"

Just then, the pair came to a steepening grade. The climb consumed all their breath and they stopped conversing. At the ridge's summit, they entered a grove of tall beech trees.

Broch made a suggestion. "If we climb one of these trees, we'll be able to see a long way. Do you feel up to it?"

"I've climbed trees before," she replied.

"You're a surprising girl, especially for a princess."

"As a child, I liked to climb trees. If a princess wants to climb trees, nobody should say that she can't."

"Princesses shouldn't risk their lives. Royalty needs to stay alive so that the people can have leadership."

"If you want me to lead, I'll say we should start climbing," Voada said.

To scale a tree while shackled was no simple proposition. With effort, the princess and the harper ascended to a good height. From their vantage point, they sighted something of very great interest.

"A palisade!" Voada exclaimed.

"I don't think Picts build stockaded villages. And there's a road running up to it."

"Is it a royal highway?"

"No; it's more of a cart road."

"Maybe friendly people are living there," Voada proposed.

"There might be. But if they're scoundrels, they'll grab us the moment we show ourselves."

"I'm hungry enough to take the chance," said the girl. At that, the youths descended as quickly as possible.

"The odds are that we're still in Dobunnian territory," Broch said. "That means you should tell the village people that you're Dobunnian. Only, don't speak too much. Someone might recognize your Brigantean accent."

"Will you be a Dobunnian, too?"

"I don't need to be. People are used to wandering harpers. We have to go where the work is. But you'll have to act like a village girl, not a lady brought up at court."

"Does that mean I should show bad manners?"

"No," he said, "that's something only princesses do."

"You!" she exclaimed and kicked him in the calf.

"Don't be so sensitive! If you don't like that advice, I have more. You should use a different name. Voada sounds too Brigantean."

"In some tribes, my name would be pronounced Boudica."

"I've heard that name. I didn't realize that Voada and Boudica were the same name in different dialects."

"But how do we explain this chain? Wouldn't it be best to tell people the truth?"

"It might be, but we still shouldn't tell anyone you're royalty. When politics become an issue, unfortunate things can happen."

"But if they believe we're slaves, what can we do to convince them otherwise?"

"I'm not at all sure. Maybe we can start speaking Latin," replied Broch.

"I can't speak Latin. But I speak Greek. Do you suppose that anyone in a Dobunnian village would know Greek?"

"Not unless they're from the noble class."


The couple climbed down, crossed between hills, and then had to climb again. Though they were drawing close to the stockaded town, the road and fields stayed empty. That made them wonder whether the people had taken shelter behind their palisades. That thought heightened their awareness.

The sight of a breached section in the town's wooden wall disheartened them. The hole was so wide that multiple attackers could have walked through it abreast.

"Do you suppose that the Romans attacked this place?" Voada asked perplexedly.

"No. They were hurt badly at the Medway, and need to be refit and reinforced. No reinforcements would be sent to Britannia with winter coming on."

"I certainly hope there isn't an army of Pictish raiders watching us!"

With caution, the puzzled couple approached the village's damaged fence. The town's interior had sustained severe damage, as if there had been rioting or looting. The destruction looked as though it could have been wrought by a wild stampede.

Voada whispered, "Maybe someone is alive around here and needs help. If we help someone, maybe we can make friends. And if everyone's run away, there are probably food and supplies left behind."

"Whatever happened here, the danger might still be near," Broch said.

"We needn't stay overnight, but we have to have something to eat. Also, the more we learn about what happened here, the safer we'll be."

"There's a feeling in the air that I don't like. Remember that old story about how curiosity killed the otter?"

"I'm going in, whether you come or not."

"Don't let anyone overhear you talking like royalty," Broch reminded her, "or they may sell you to the Romans."

She shook her head but didn't answer.

A short way beyond the stockade, they found dead bodies. The visible wounds suggested attacks from animals possessing powerful jaws. Oddly, some huts were crushed, as by battering rams! The young people mostly ignored human footprints in the mud, but drew up short at the sight of huge tracks with three toes forward and two spur-like toes facing back.

"What made that track?" the princess asked.

"I'm afraid to say."

"Oh, gods!" Voada declared. "You don't suppose it could be a dragon?"

"If the thing is gone, it probably won't return," supposed Broch.

"Probably?"

The youth shrugged. "Probably."

Hunger overrode their wariness, and their exploration devolved into a search for food. They entered one of the intact huts and rummaged through it. The domicile looked as though it had been hastily abandoned after a ransacking. Had the disorder been caused by looters, or by the family itself when it seized items needed for panicky flight?

Wanting to eat before darkness, the scroungers located some roots and vegetables inside a storage bin.

"Can you make a fire?" Voada asked.

The lad nodded. "I could, but who knows what the light could attract? Something wrecked this town today, and we don't want it coming back."

With the room darkening swiftly, they gnawed the raw aliments and drank from a water bucket left beside the hearth. As tasteless as their cold meal was, they welcomed every bite. It took little of such fare to kill their appetites. With the darkness growing dense, the chained couple appropriated the hut's largest sleeping shelf, hoping to get a good night's sleep.

# The Thing in the Brake

## CHAPTER XIV

"Strike me and you are a dead man!" the captive growled, discounting his bound condition.

Simon of Gitta had already sized up his druidic prisoner as a fanatic, and fanatics were the most difficult prisoners to question.

Laird Pellinor suddenly joined the novice druid, asking, "What did he say?"

"Nothing", Simon replied.

Mog Ruith arrived now as well. "It would not surprise me if the man's silence results from the Dragon Spirits' control over his mind."

"Pfft! Even the most stubborn men can be persuaded to talk," said the king of Avalon.

The arch-druid shook his head. "The Dragon Spirits will not care how severely a slave of theirs is tortured."

"I advise you druids to give the hot iron a chance," the war chief said.

"Since these men are dressed in Wyrm Druids' robes, the entire college is probably in rebellion. It behooves us to understand what that order is up to as soon as possible."

"You've already told me you want to go to Caer Draig," said King Pellinor. "But what can one man accomplish there? To go where the enemy is strongest is like thrusting one's arm down a wolf's throat."

"I will not be alone," Ruith answered. "Simon, are you still willing to accompany me to Caer Draig?"

The younger man nodded. "We'll learn more there than we can by dragon-hunting."

"I think we already have enough evidence to bring a charge of treason against the Wyrms," Pellinor objected. "I'm going to recommend that King Arto move against them with an army."

"We have to know for certain the aim of their treason," said Mog Ruith. "If their Master Wyrm is allowing attacks against men serving the kings of Britannia, he must be feeling very confident. We need to learn the source of that confidence so we can move against his college effectively. Laird, have you sent a message to King Arto concerning this battle?" asked Mog Ruith.

"Hardly! We haven't even had time to bind our wounded or bury our dead. But it's vital to draw support from Arto. If he takes my advice, he'll send us a few hundred more fighters."

"Until help arrives, what do you intend to do, Laird?" asked Simon.

Pellinor turned pensive. "Our scouts just told me that they encountered refugees from a fort settlement called Glew. They say that the Wyrm Druids raided them and took captives. I'm going to determine the cause. It will work against the Wyrms if we can get some direct accusations against them. We'll then catch up with you two at Caer Draig. If you like, I'll give you a few warriors for your escort. That will give the druids something to think about."

Mog Ruith shook his head. "I think stealth is better. But if we need warriors or want to reunite with you, knowing Glew's location is crucial."

"The scouts say Glew is a few hours' ride northwest of Caer Draig," said Pellinor.

"Very good," said the arch-druid. "Simon and I will take our rest early tonight and ride toward Caer Draig in the morning."


A poke in his ribs brought Broch wide awake in the dawn's gray light. Several faces were glowering down on him, and some were tonsured druids. One of them muttered. "Escaped slaves!"

The rough voice awakened Voada beside him. She protested before comprehending the situation. The intruders reacted by seizing both young individuals and dragging them out of bed.

"We're not escaped slaves!" declared Voada. "We were captured by Pictish bandits, but we slipped away from them!"

"Liars!" a lean druid with a strong Pictish facial cast declared, "There are no Pictish bandits. Take them!"

"Take us where?!" Broch demanded, but the answer was a backhand slap across his mouth.

A druid thereupon grasped Voada's hair and pulled. "What is your name, wench?"

"Boudica!" stated the princess. "And I'm not a wench!"

"A Brythonic name!" The Pictish-looking druid declared that no Briton was to be trusted.

Broch was perplexed. If a dragon had raided this village, why were these holy men behaving like raiders? Landless scavengers might behave this way, but druids?

Outside the hut stood two more men in druidic robes. "You Wyrms are bold," the priest in black said to the priest in green.

"In times like these, boldness is called for, friend Goddeu," said the green-clad druid—an older and uglier man. "But raiding is a poor application of our time. Hopefully, the Romans will soon be supplying our college with all the slaves it requires."

"Hopefully so," said the one called Goddeu.

"We need to collect the additional captives that our men have been out raiding for, then return to the temple," said the ugly one. "I feel uneasy leaving the Roman legate unwatched for all this time."

"I agree," said Goddeu. "If Romans are not kept under continual pressure, they start to assume they are the ones in command."

Broch and Voada, under pressure from the Picts, joined the captives on the other side of Glew, where men, women, and children milled about under guard. They looked like common villagers.


Asiaticus continued to have restless sleep since arriving at Caer Draig. He had awakened each morning feeling out of sorts and drained. He ate each breakfast indifferently. It required determination just to chew and swallow it. The legate had wondered whether the cold, dank ride from River's Mouth had brought on a malady of some sort. Disturbingly, his aides and servants had voiced similar complaints.

Since arriving, the Romans had repeatedly solicited a meeting with the Master Wyrm Bhort, but Bhort had left the fort shortly after the Romans' arrival, supposedly to make a tour of the region. Following that, the Romans lingered pointlessly in the dreary town.

The stockade walls offered little that was diverting, but he had learned during his listless peregrinations that the god honored by the Wyrms was named "Gatanothog." It—he could not call that monstrosity a "he"— was depicted as a knot of tree roots with their tubers splaying out in all directions. These strange roots, adorned with eyes and mouths by carvers, were made even more grotesque.

This morning, Asiaticus had taken his principal aides, Quintus and Sextus, into the forest for a hunt. He thought the odoriferous town might make people ill, and that fresh air and exercise could fortify them. The Romans had not become weak, after all, but depressed and apathetic. Accompanied by two senior aides, they soon found themselves at a brook called the Gagle. It wended its way along a snakelike course through marshy spots and wooded lowlands. Asiaticus hoped to find abundant game, but the muddy stream banks presented them with nothing worth shooting or spearing. Even rabbits seemed to be scarce.

The Romans encountered a party of Pictish warriors who searched the water's edge as if they were hunters. The Romans hailed the primitives to ask for hunting advice, and one savage answered in a broken dialect of

Brythonic. "There is scant game," he said. When asked what he and his companions were seeking, he laconically answered, "Stray goats."

Responding to the legate's query as to why soldiers hunted goats rather than shepherds, the man stated that shepherds had more important duties. The Picts ignored further inquiries and departed at a fast walk.

Subsequently, Asiaticus had Sextus accompany him into a denser part of the forest, while Quintus stayed with the horses. The Roman officers scouted out the backwaters armed with bows and boar spears. They soon found their way obstructed by a broad grove of blackthorns.

Asiaticus noted that the sloes hanging on the bushes were mushy and wrinkled, showing that their best time for harvesting was past. Blackthorn berries were used in Gallic religious rituals, though they were bitter and astringent. Asiaticus ate some of the sacred berries in respect of an ancient Druidic practice. He occasionally did such small observances to stay in touch with Gaul's vanishing traditions.

Suddenly, a crackling in the shrubs made the hunters perk up. They waited silently with arrows in their bows, watching for movement.

"Sextus," the legate murmured, "move around and flush out whatever's hiding there. I'll be ready to fire. Let's hope it's something more interesting than a lost goat."

The dispirited subaltern listlessly followed orders and was soon lost to sight. Asiaticus bided his time, ready to shoot.

Of a sudden, he heard a Latin yell and a thrashing in the blackthorns. Asiaticus dropped his bow, seized his spear, and hurried toward the disturbance, shouting, "Sextus!"

"Decimus Valerius!" came the young man's answering call.

The Roman officer fought through the shrubs and spotted Sextus lying under the shadow of the greenery, propped up on one elbow. Asiaticus looked about for any sign of an attacker, human or animal.

"It ran off when you shouted, Legate," the subaltern muttered.

"What was it? A boar?"

"I don't know. I only glimpsed it through the brush. I ran to take a closer look, but I stumbled on a root. I landed on my knee and it hurts like Tartarus!"

The officer did not appear to be seriously injured, except for his pride. "Good Heavens, man! If you're not disabled, get on your feet!"

Sextus struggled to rise. "I got a glance at it," he yammered. "It was pale—sickly pale, and looked like an obese man."

"It ran on two legs?"

"Yes, Decimus Valerius!"

"Only bears can walk on two legs, but they don't run that way. It had to be a man if it seemed white. A bandit, maybe?"

Sextus shook his head. "Whatever it was, it acted afraid of me. I saw its naked *mentula* jiggling."

"What about its face?"

The subaltern shrugged. "I didn't see it, but the strange thing had hands!"

"A naked wild man?" The Pictish warriors may have been hunting a runaway slave. But why hadn't they said so?

Asiaticus glanced back at Sextus. "Pull yourself together, soldier. You're an officer of the Second Augusta. Encountering an enemy should be nothing to you!" He was less angry than he sounded. He knew that neither he nor Sextus was feeling well that day.

"Pardon me, Decimus Valerius," the *decanus* replied smartly.

"Let's look for tracks. It may be inedible, yet we can find out what it was."

With the limping officer in his train, the legate circled the blackthorns watching for tracks.

Asiaticus noticed spots of blood on the decaying autumnal litter. "Did you cut the fellow, soldier?" he asked the decanus.

"I never touched him."

"Well, the stranger is dripping blood. Maybe it stepped on something sharp or was scratched by thorns. What wild beasts have skin so thin?"

They explored for only a few minutes longer before Sextus noticed prints in the mud and knelt to inspect them.

"It looks human," the younger officer observed.

"It appears to be a big, soft-looking human foot," said his commander.

"Perhaps the druids could tell us what's in these woods," the subaltern suggested.

"Possibly. But they're secretive devils. I've heard nothing interesting from them."


The sun was a pale vermilion spot behind a bank of wispy gray clouds when the three Romans returned to the hill of Brynymeir. Before reaching the turnoff to the hill-climbing track, they noticed a big man riding downhill. When he was closer, they saw he was a fair-haired Brythonic type garbed in a brown mantle and a straw hat.

Unfazed by their Roman attire, the stranger held their stare. He purposefully turned and rode towards them.

"You are Romans," the stranger stated in a deep, mellow voice when he came within earshot. He spoke exotically accented Latin. "Has Plautius' army reached this far? I have not heard."

"The army is nearby," Asiaticus said ingenuously while sizing up the rider. The stranger was broadly and solidly built, middle-aged, and intelligent-looking. He wore his confidence like a cloak while displaying a genial smile.

"I have met few Romans," the man said. "I hail from Erin, the island to the west. Our kings have friendly relations with the empire."

"I know where Erin lies," stated Asiaticus matter-of-factly. "We call it Hibernia. By the way, before this meeting, you're only the second Hibernian I've met. I made the acquaintance of an Irish gladiator at the Statilius Taurus amphitheater." The legate wished to start a friendly conversation. An unhurried conversation could yield valuable information.

"A trained Roman fighter, eh?" said the Irishman. "I'm not surprised! The Irish are famous for their prowess," said the stranger, his tone unabashedly prideful.

"Are you a druid or a merchant?" asked the legate.

"Primarily, I'm a scholar," the stranger stated.

"A scholar?"

"I read, write, and speak Latin and Greek," the wanderer said jovially. "But I own that we Irish have no writing of our own. Wisdom is a wild beast, and the gods wish wild beasts to remain uncaged. It is rude to imprison knowledge on a piece of leather or confine it to chiseled grooves on a piece of rock."

"Such a notion would confuse most Romans," the legate stated. "However, I've heard similar things. I had druids for kin and know how they look at life. Say, friend, you ride a fine mount. Is Ireland good horse country?"

"It provides fine pasturage, but we have fewer foreign breeds than the Britons. This one is nobly British, though it is descended from continental stock." The stranger casually drew off his hat and mopped his brow with his sleeve, displaying his druidic tonsure.

"Ah, you are a druid."

"Did I forget to mention that?" the stranger asked.

"You said you were a scholar. Do Hibernians frequently visit Britannia?"

"Some do. The islands are not far apart. By the way, despite your striking armor, Roman, I see you have Gallic features. *O bwy sir rydych chi'n dod?*"

Understanding the words, the Roman legate answered in his native language: "I'm from Narbonensis. Massilia is my city."

"I narrowly missed visiting that old Greek town."

"My name is Decimus Valerius Asiaticus, Senator of Rome," the legate said as he extended his hand. A Roman offering a hand clasp showed he was accepting another as a worthy companion.

The druid took his hand firmly, saying, "You may call me Atha Moir." The Irishman glanced up at the town. "The odd smell of that place didn't suit me and I came out for fresh air. Unfortunately, I will have to go back up all too soon. I dislike sleeping on open ground unless I am in good fellowship. Are you noble Romans just arriving? Have you introduced yourselves to the Wyrm brotherhood as yet?"

"We met them some days ago," said Asiaticus. "We have been billeted and boarded acceptably."

"Is this a healthy location?" Atha Moir asked. "Your men look unwell. I am a healer and would gladly brew a fortifying tonic for whoever needs it."

"In truth, I have questioned the health of this air myself. I had hoped that time spent hunting would benefit us, and to some extent, I think it has. I feel much better than I did this morning, when I arose very fatigued."

"Your game bags look empty. Bad hunting?" the brown-robed man asked.

"Indeed, we have had ill success. No doubt the local people have hunted the woods empty."

Atha Moir frowned thoughtfully. "That is regrettable. But regarding your indisposition, I would gladly place myself at your disposal. My specialty is restorative herbs and healing prayers."

Asiaticus smiled. "I will gladly call on you if necessary, Atha Moir. Are you lingering in this area, or is Caer Draig just a short pause on a lengthy trip?"

"I intend to remain at the caer some few days only. I have much to see before winter sends me home. Though I intended to take a ride, I've changed my mind. I have been tardy in requesting lodgings from the temple druids and, as I say, I don't care to sleep under the stars."

"Please accompany us," the Roman Senator said to Atha Moir. "I will request that the druidic clerks assign you fit lodgings."

"I would very much appreciate that courtesy."

Thereupon, the soldiers and the Irishman became one party riding up the cart road to the hilltop gatehouse.

# THE DOOR IN THE CLIFF

## CHAPTER XV

Pictish slavery now seemed preferable to Broch and Voada's current plight. The coku had been relatively careful in disciplining the princess in anticipation of her sale to the Romans. But their current captors, the corrupt priests, regarded her as a common captive from the countryside. Thus, Voada faced arbitrary violence. Despite the danger of the situation, they didn't dare improve her treatment by disclosing her status as a valuable political prisoner. As a hostage of the Romans, she could destabilize the entire Brythonic alliance. Estrangore, Clarents, and even Eastland would be affected. Additional bricks could fall once the affected kingdoms became loose bricks in King Arto's coalition against Rome. As for the fellow captives around them, they were plain, workaday people. The men were mainly middle-aged or older. Lothan's border town, Glew, had contributed its young men to the Roman war front in the east.

The Druids made their prisoners march back and forth, giving them barely enough food to survive. The Wyrms' prisoner count increased with captives taken from different areas—Pictish raiders, acting as mercenaries, were seizing them in the remote regions.

From whispered snatches of conversation, Broch and Boudica learned what happened at Glew. An enormous beast was seen lumbering toward the town, sending panicked harvesters racing up Glew Hill. The people scarcely believed what they heard, but closed the stockade gates while the town's leaders opened the storehouses to pass out spears and blades for the people's defense.

Men on the wall sighted the creature, while nearly everyone heard its echoing roar. The dragon came to the foot of the palisade and began throwing its scaly body against the pales. Its repeated strikes broke the wooden stakes, and the monster squeezed through the open gap it had made to invade the town proper.

It smashed through the lanes, tearing down huts, savagely mauling anyone it caught. Rather than engaging in serious fighting, the townspeople escaped through the hill fort's limited exits or climbed the palisades, resulting in injuries for some.

This dragon's size rivaled that of whales taken by fishermen from the sea, a gray-green lizard thing with snakelike scales. Using its great triangular head as a weapon, it battered structures right and left of it. Witnesses described the monster's eyes glowing like live coals inside its skull.

The dispossessed inhabitants fled across the countryside, especially families with children. Some braver souls stayed hidden close in to watch the beast's rampage. The destruction lasted an hour before they observed the dragon leaving the stockade. Even then, few of Glew's dispossessed had courage enough to reenter the town. The situation worsened when a band of druids barged into the village, followed by Pictish warriors.

Some hoped these mighty sorcerers had arrived to offer protection and aid. But when a group of townsmen greeted them, the warriors seized and bound them. Horrified onlookers belatedly understood: these were slave raiders!

None of these disheartening stories explained the outrageous behavior of the druids.

When the coffle was stopped to pick up new captives, the black-garbed druid named Goddeu stepped up behind the shackled couple.

"Whose slave are you, mudlark?" the arch-druid inquired of the blonde girl. His Gallic accent was distinct.

The princess looked back indignantly. "I am no slave! My name is Boudica. My father is a merchant of Gloucedon."

"I'm aware of the slave shackle you were wearing when discovered."

"I was with a group captured by Pictish bandits. We escaped."

The druid looked at Broch. "Who is this boy?"

"He's a harper employed by my brother."

Goddeu frowned. "Do Picts chain male and female slaves together?"

"We know very little about Pictish ways, Reverend One," Boudica replied.

"Are you two lovers?"

"No! But we have suffered together and have become friends."

"Would you like the chain removed?" asked the druid.

"Very much so, Revered One. Ransom us, I beseech you, Reverend One! My brother is the master of our house and a generous man!"

Goddeu shrugged. "Gold is important, but so is beauty."

Boudica looked away. "Will you not be merciful, Master?"

He responded vaguely, then left.

The young people looked at one another. "How do you interpret that?" Boudica asked in a whisper.

"It's all too plain!" Broch said irritably.

"I think he fancies me."

"Is that a surprise? What man would *not* fancy you?"

The maid shook her head. "This may be to our advantage."

"How?"

"He is an ally of our captors. If we act friendly with him, we may gain better treatment."

Her words left Broch incredulous. "He wants nothing of me. He's a lawless and ruthless renegade who would gladly separate my head from my body if he saw me as a rival. You can guess what his intentions are toward you! Or has he charmed you with that foolish goat's beard of his?"

Boudica frowned. "I'm not charmed, but think of our situation. The Glew people are afraid that the druids will slay them in human sacrifice. That could be our fate, too. We must use every opportunity to help ourselves."

Then her mood changed suddenly. "I must make things better because our awful condition could be the gods' judgment upon me."

"What do you mean?"

"Weeks ago, I prayed to Branwen to rescue me from marrying a man I didn't know and might not find appealing. Maybe this punishment has come upon me for disrespecting my king's decision."

"Don't blame yourself! You have not angered Branwen. You were on your way to Eastland to obey your king's commands, weren't you?" the harper reminded her.

She sighed. "Yes, but doubt and anger filled me."

"Shhh!" said Broch. He had seen guards looking their way. Prisoner conversation was forbidden, and the Pictish warriors had been generously doling out kicks and blows.

The princess glanced about and then whispered, "I will speak on your behalf." Abruptly, she winced. "I'm sorry. I know how foolish that sounds coming from someone in chains."

The guards forbade touching, too, but the harper unmindfully grasped her left with his right and squeezed it.


Each night, the druids' prisoners slept on the ground without blankets, huddled together for warmth. Each morning they were prodded awake, fed a little, and forced to their feet to march. Later on this day, the guards suddenly drove the captives off the royal road and made them follow a cart track leading into a woodland. Soon they reached a clearing by a cliff wall, where a large hut stood. Though it resembled a hunter's shelter, the nearby Pictish men carried themselves like guards, not hunters.

The coffle being halted, one druid strode up to the rock wall and thrust the end of his staff into what looked like a natural crevasse. There must have been a bell hidden within, for a jingle immediately sounded.

"Why have we halted?" Goddeu asked his collaborator, Bhort.

"A hidden door exists within that wall. It gives access to an underground slave pen. These caves are very useful, and our forebears established our stronghold here because of them. We hold our sacrificial captives within."

"I see. But I don't want the slave I spoke to you about earlier to be sacrificed!" the Black Goat stated.

"Why is the girl so important?"

"She interests me. Do you hold her in some great significance?"

"Is it only a matter of the flesh?" Bhort asked.

"All men are flesh," said Goddeu. "I do not see that the Wyrms are more dedicated to asceticism than we are. Or am I wrong? Does Gathanothog demand celibacy from his clergy?"

"The matter is not a simple one—" began Bhort, but then he shrugged. "Oh, I care not! You are a friend and an honored guest. Because ours is a hospitable order, you have my leave to take the creature for yourself. Do with her as you please."

"And the boy, too?"

Bhort's brows knitted. "Why should you want the boy?"

"Because he and the girl are friends. I do not wish to use force on my new slave. But if I hold the life of one whom she cares for in my hands, she will be motivated to behave well," Goddeu clarified.

"Why be so subtle? Just thrash her until she yields!"

"I care nothing for holding women by the threat of punishment. Mere prisoners make for tedious company."

The Wyrm Druid shook his head. "This inconsiderable matter is nothing worth quarreling about. Take both of them, if you must. You can hand them over for sacrifice to the gods when you are weary of them."

"Bhort is a gracious host," Goddeu responded. The green-clad druid, his expression still dour, looked away.

The black-robed man instructed his Gallic guards to take Broch and Boudica out of the coffle and keep them under guard.

After the Black Goats' Gallic bodyguards loosed the pair, they made them kneel at the feet of the Master Black Goat. "You are very fortunate, mudlark. You will fare better in my service than you would inside that rock. For my kindness, I shall expect gratitude and exemplary service."

Broch captured Boudica's glance, his eyes imploring her to reject the offer. But the maid looked away and stared at the ground, remaining discretely silent. Goddeu noted her behavior approvingly.

The creak of hasps drew everyone's attention to the rock wall. A hidden door on the bluff suddenly swung outward, having gone unnoticed up to a moment ago.

From the open door, the crowd of prisoners smelled a stockyard odor. Everyone realized that the hill's interior must be filthy. The harper was thankful he and the girl could avoid the foul darkness.

The guards began driving the other slaves into the cliff face using quirt blows. The prisoners bleated with fear, especially the children. Tears streaked Boudica's cheeks as she watched their departure, and Broch felt the ache of pity as well. Some of the Pictish guards accompanied the prisoners inside before the door was shut in their wake.

A much smaller crowd now remained with the Black Goats. Bhort instructed the coffle's carts to return the way they'd come, then led the remaining group along the base of the cliff, following a faint footpath. At some distance, the path intersected the royal highway, and they followed it to the front side of the hill of Brynymeir. Broch, looking up, sighted the stockade on its summit. He guessed that this must be the stronghold of the Wyrm Druids. Their fellow slaves called it Caer Draig and feared it.

Broch overheard Bhort and Goddeu speaking again. "The Romans will be demanding to meet with me," said the Master Wyrm. "The Great Ones' influence should improve their tractability. If not, I might have food drugged, making them too ill to depart. While they lay in their sickbeds, the spirits will have full play with them. The legate, once made to serve the Great Ones zealously, will be the first of many Roman leaders we recruit in that way."

Goddeu nodded. "Let them serve the Great Ones for now, but I look forward to the day when the true gods shall destroy the Roman race utterly."

"As do I," agreed Bhort. "Until that joyful day arrives, the Romans have the power to support the Great Ones' cause greatly."

Broch wondered. If the druid leaders plotted both against the kings and the Romans, how did they hope to carry out their scheme? He realized the Roman destruction of these corrupt druids might follow if the invaders saw the Black Goats and Wyrms as enemies.

But Broch couldn't imagine how he could contact the Romans. He and Boudica had to prioritize their immediate survival.


Mog Ruith stood musing at the mouth of a fetid alleyway. After a couple days at Caer Draig, he was growing frustrated. So far, he had gathered little useful information, other than confirming that the Wyrms were dealing with the Black Goat Druids and were in intimate communication with the Romans. He had tried to make friends with some of the Wyrm Druids, but they were reserved and cautious.

The Wren, not a seasoned spy, wondered how he could best carry out his mission. Passive observation was unproductive. He had to apply more aggressive measures, but remained unsure what he should so.

Because of Master Wyrm Bhort's absence, Ruith did not carry out the interview he wanted. The Wren's best hope was that the Wyrms might seek to recruit him as a collaborator. Brute thus gained considerable knowledge. The college by now probably knew that Brute had been a spy, leading to their decreased trust.

On the positive side, Ruith's early contact with the Roman Asiaticus had been fortuitous. Their cordial meeting could be expanded upon if he made inquiries regarding the state of their health.

The Irishman noticed a body of men entering the fort through the gatehouse. Some of them wore the robes of Wyrm and Black Goat Druids. Just then, he noted a pair of chained captives, two dirty, ragged young people.

The Wren recognized the boy as Broch, the young harper from the court of the Icenians. How had he gotten to this remote spot? Mog Ruith wondered whether his capture was related to the Master Merlin's prophecy.

Mog Ruith took a second look at the girl to whom Broch was chained, wondering if she was also from the wedding party. His jaw dropped upon recognizing the Princess Voada from Estrangore. She had been reduced to a pitiable condition.

He wondered whether the Wyrms knew that they had captured a very important political hostage. But if that were true, why would they also take the harper?

Ruith wondered whether Asiaticus' true mission to the fort might not be to take custody of the princess. Preventing the transfer was paramount. He needed to speak to the girl in secret, as difficult as that might be. As casually as he could, he followed the guarded captives to learn where they would be held.

# The Ferret

## CHAPTER XVI

With evening drawing nigh, Mog Ruith retired to his hut. Shortly afterwards, Wyrm servants arrived to serve him a bland supper consisting of a big bowl of cooked turnips, goat's flesh, and a little thin ale. They had no message to deliver regarding his requested interview with Master Bhort, but he considered that an unnecessary formality. The Irish mystic had a much more significant adventure planned for himself.

From his pack, the wizard plucked two leather pouches, one filled with dried ash leaves and the other filled with crushed catmint. The catmint particles he sprinkled upon the wood-plank floor to form a large circle and into this he seated himself, his legs folded. Mog Ruith then took from his bag an animal skin and set it on his knee. For the next element of his ritual, he poured ash leaf fragments into his palm and then crushed them even smaller. Holding this residue, he intoned a prayer: "Powers of the East, governors of Fire, gift me with my heart's desire." Thereupon, he cast a pinch of the ash leaf powder toward the eastern cardinal point.

Facing south, he said, "Fertile lords who grace the South, grant my prayers now being wrought." Then, looking west, he said, "Water lords who rule the West, lift my spirit, I request." Finally, addressing the boreal realms, he said, "Gusting currents from the North, draw my essence, call it forth." Last of all, with both hands raised, he declared: "To those gods who aid me now, my faithful service I avow. Come ye Powers, with thine aid, twixt man and god the pact is made!"

Ruith clutched the furry skin to his heart, concentrating intensely. After a minute, he lost awareness of his body, feeling light as thistledown drifting on the updrafts.

Suddenly, he felt like a leaf spinning in a whirlwind. The next thing Ruith knew, he opened his eyes to a new and different place.

Despite the darkness, his sight was extraordinarily keen, seeing such a plenitude of colors that he knew no name for the greater number of them.

His ears, too, had gained heightened sensitivity, receiving sounds from very far away. And his nose! It assailed him with repulsive odors—death and decay, rotting fungus, putrid flesh, worms, and moist soil.

His spell had worked!

He was an animal.

This was not Ruith's first transmigration, so the overwhelming range of sensations did not shock him. After a moment's disorientation, Mog Ruith gradually relaxed. He could see very little of himself except for his hands—his paws—but that was a small matter insofar as already knew what a ferret looked like. The lesser sorcerers of his order were mostly restricted to possessing only their sacred bird, the wren, but the arch-Druid had labored mightily to bind his spirit to several different species. Each separate creature possessed abilities that he had found useful at different times.

Knowing that he could maintain his transmigration only briefly, Ruith crawled, awkwardly at first, toward a trace of light. That beacon guided him out of the burrow that he presently occupied. The ferret emerged into a forest of grass. By the gods! How seductively sweet was the scented breeze.

An animal could spy upon human activities almost with impunity, but doing so was always dangerous. A small animal needed to be wary, for outside its burrow, danger was everywhere. Cats were forever a threat, but they were cowardly creatures; even a small adversary, if aggressive enough, could frighten one of them away. A more serious problem was the continual threat of the dog.

He struggled to clear his mind and focus on his task—which was to seek out the Princess Voada. But being only inches tall, he was handicapped by his stature. Even reared up on his hind legs, Ruith was not able to see very far. But what he did see was a wooden post. He scurried to it and climbed to its summit, at which point he gained a vantage point from which he could see from the perspective of a man. Ruith already knew where to look for the maiden; that afternoon, after the captives were marched past him, the Druid had surreptitiously followed behind the young peoples' captors until they arrived at their place of confinement.

The arch-Druid was able to confirm that he was still atop the hill of Brynymeir, having seen landmarks that gave him his bearing.

Ruith descended to the grass again and hurried on his way, like a man crossing through a breast-high brake. Despite the shortness of his legs, he had inherited the ferret's speed and the Druid swiftly arrived at the shed which housed the captives. It stood next to a larger structure, the lodge which he had already ascertained was occupied by a Black Goat Druid.

Ruith scurried to the lodge, a thatched and pitched-roofed affair constructed from fitted logs. The effluent rising from its rooftop smoke hole informed him that its occupant was currently inside. The spy very much wanted to make a surreptitious visit to that person.

Ferrets were natural climbers and the log-ends forming the corners of the lodge offered him a ready ladder for his ascend. Once on the eves, he ran up to the roof ridge to stand at the sooty edge of the smoke hole. Gazing down, he saw a dimly-lit room below.

Unfortunately, the twisting smoke rising from the brazier underneath made his eyes smart and he drew back. But Mog Ruith's brief look had beheld a bundle of robes piled onto a stool. More importantly, he had heard a muttered conversation and was determined to listen in on what was being said.

The transmigrated wizard took a deep breath and scurried back to the smoke hole. Marking his landing spot by means of a quick glance, he dived in, dropping several feet onto the soft robes. From there, he was able to make out spoken words.

"I'm not sure what you mean, Master Goddeu," said a Gallic speaker.

"I mean, these Wyrms have been keeping very much from us. If they trust us so little, caution demands that we be wary about what we say. I want you to carry my word to our senior people, reminding them to interact discreetly with the Wyrms, even while keeping their eyes and ears open."

"What is it that we should seek to learn?" asked the acolyte.

"I want our people to take note of anything that is strange or interesting. When a man comes upon an anomaly worth reporting, I want to know about it."

"I shall inform the brothers, Master," responded the young man.

"Good, lad. Now take some food out to the slaves before you go off on your errand. See to it that they have sufficient blankets. There are suitable ones in that chest against the wall. I want the girl to appreciate that she will be decently treated as long as she behaves, and her friend will benefit at the same time. When I am not so beset by urgent matters, I intend to have her cleaned up and given a proper bed."

"Yes, Mentor. Do you have any special instructions regarding the boy?"

Goddeu shrugged. "At present, there is no reason to make him any more uncomfortable than necessary. Now, get about your tasks. Take the two of them rations from that other chest, yonder, and see that they have plentiful water, too."

The acolyte made obeisance and set about gathering the bedclothes and provisions that his errand required. He dipped a small bucket into a larger clay vessel full of water and sank a clay drinking cup into it. When ready, he carried his awkward load toward the door.

"One more thing, Garym," Goddeu called after the youth, "send Erbin to me. My steward and I have weighty matters to discuss."

After the acolyte's departure, the Wren stayed where he was, wanting to overhear Goddeu's upcoming interview with the one called Erbin. He hoped that the two Black Goats might discuss matters of more weight than what he had told the acolyte.

Mog Ruith, in reflection, had noticed that Goddeu had not made any reference to Voada's royal status. Was it possible that he did not know her real identity? If not, the wizard reasoned, it was probably to the good.

Now that he was alone, Goddeu sank to his knees before a wall on which a wooden figure hung. It was an image of a flat-faced crone whose genitalia made up most of her torso. This was not any goddess honored in Erin, but Mog Ruith had seen other depictions of the unpleasant creature while in Gaul. It represented the dark goddess Sheila-na-gog.

Simon of Gitta had informed him that this goddess was worshiped by the Black Goat Druids. Furthermore, they believed that a certain amorphous abomination that existed in a sacred cave near to their stronghold was an earthly manifestation of the entity. Goddeu's carving was a small one, an image he could carry about in his baggage. The kneeling Druid commenced a low-toned orison.

The earnest manner in which the Black Goat prayed made Ruith wonder whether the man might actually be pious before his goddess, unlike many dark sorcerers who considered their gods to be mere sources of mystical power. But it mattered little to the Wren whether Goddeu was a hypocrite or the most pious man on Earth, not so long as the object of his worship was a blasphemy whose adoration should deservedly be stamped out.

Goddeu heard a tapping on his door and stood up. "Erbin?" he called out.

"Yes, Master!"

"Enter!"

A short, portly, and tonsured man entered. The steward wore a goat-beard, an affectation shared by all of the black-robed Druids that Mog Ruith had seen so far. The servant dropped to his knees. "How may I serve the Master Goddeu?"

"How are the Romans faring?" asked the arch-Druid. "What do they speak about?"

"I have made inquiries of their servants, as you asked me to do. The Romans appear to be of mixed health, Your Glory. But the legate is waxing very impatient at having been denied his interview with Master Bhort for so long."

"I know that Bhort is deliberately drawing the matter out, and for good reason. But the details of that small intrigue do not concern you." Then Goddeu added, "You may get off your knees."

Erbin obliged. "Does Master suppose that the Master Wyrm is wisely dealing with the Romans?" asked the steward.

Ruith noticed that Goddeu did not rebuke his subordinate for his inquisitiveness. From that omission, the Wren supposed that Erbin might be in confidence with the arch-Druid.

"I agree with his plan so far, but if his schemes go awry, he will realize how unwise his course of action has been," the Master Black Goat responded. "If Bhort mishandles the forging of the Roman alliance, it might force us onto byways that we should not want to travel."

"But surely no one is better prepared to enlighten the master Druid on matters involving the Romans than you are, Mentor."

"You're doing it again, Erbin! Do not annoy me with obvious flattery," Goddeu remarked with mild scorn. "I distrust clever men when they play the fool. If your former master Ferchobhar had not been content to take bad advice from sycophants, he might have acted more wisely and avoided the trap that eventually slew him!"

"I forget myself, Master. I do indeed prefer to speak plainly with His Glory. May I ask what terms are to be offered to the Romans?"

"The terms have not changed but, as you know, what we tell the Romans is only the bait for our trap. The Black Goats and the Wyrms wish to become the privileged religious orders in this land when it is conquered. The Romans must pledge to support our program of restoring the old worship sites. That should not be a difficult concession to wrest from them, as they have many excellent engineers. Furthermore, they are a spiritually dead race. They see all religions as false ones. To unbelievers, the devout are deluded people, and they treat faith as a merely political thing, a means of inducing obedience into the common people. Preserving Roman naivety on this point serves our ends—until they learn to their sorrow that the gods are indeed real."

"Surely Caesar must have advised his countrymen that the gods of Gaul are very powerful," said Erbin.

"Julius Caesar only did what served his own interests. He was cunning, I'll grant him that, and a capable war leader, too, when everything favored him. The Romans, fortunately, have no generals as effective as he was. I suspect it will take them decades just to subdue this small island."

"What if Rome sends a better general than Plautius?" asked Erbin.

"They certainly have better generals, but their pool of talent is small. That is what happens to a people in decline. The only political leaders they are able to find are like Tiberius, Caligula, and Claudius—dullards and madmen."

The lesser Druid grinned. "Let us hope that every Roman generation will grow duller and madder than the one before it."

Goddeu nodded. "And let us hope, also, that the downfall of Rome is not far away. Even now, the city is a worm-eaten apple ready to fall. They know how to wage war against men, but they will be blown away like the dust when they draw their pathetic swords against the resurrected dragons."

Mog Ruith had been taking all of this in. But would these minor Druidic brotherhoods be capable of raising sufficient creatures from the Otherwhere to win a war against Rome? What was the time frame of their scheming?

Erbin's head perked up. "Now that I think of it, the Roman servants reported something they overheard from the talk of the lesser officers."

"What?"

"Asiaticus and two of his aides went hunting this afternoon. They saw a thing."

Goddeu met his servant's glance. "Something to our detriment?"

"I don't think so."

"Well, what was it?"

"They saw an animal in the bottoms. Or maybe it wasn't an animal."

"Not a dragon!"

"No, it was a man, or something very like a man."

"Yes?"

"The important thing is that he was no common sort of man. He—or it—impressed them as being deformed."

"Might he have been one of the spawn, such as the goddess Sheila-na-gog creates within her cavern in Regio Averonium?"

"Holy One, if that were so, it would mean that there is an avatar of the goddess here in Britain, also. And if it is not our goddess, what other god could be responsible?"

Goddeu frowned. "I cannot say, not with Bhort and his underlings holding back so much information."

"If the Wyrms are telling us so little, should they not be considered too dangerous for us to keep as allies?"

Goddeu shook his head, not in disagreement, but uncertainty. "Many times allies prove to be more dangerous than one's declared enemies. Think how close our order came to dissolution because Ferchobhar had been dealing so recklessly with Aelius Scaevola."

Erbin nodded.

From this point, their conversation drifted into matters of little concern to Mog Ruith. At the end of their discussion, Goddeu reminded Erbin that he should continue to heed everything that the Romans were saying or doing. Then, following his aide's departure, the arch-Druid returned to his prayer spot to complete his devotions.


Mog Ruith was not yet feeling the sensation that told him his time was running out. He climbed a wooden pillar, ran along the rafters and leaped to the smoke hole, whose tarry edge he caught. Once having climbed down to the grass outside, he made for the nearby shed. Prowling along its foundations, he came upon a gap between boards through which voices were issuing.

"—belaboring this, Broch," a girl said. "I think it makes sense for me to offer my compliance in exchange for your freedom. So long as Goddeu is interested in me, it may be possible to mollify him. If I can persuade him to set you free, you'll be able to gain an audience with King Caratacos Pendragon. He is likely to send an army and seize this treacherous caer. But if politics tie his hand, he might still be willing to ransom me from Goddeu, or at the least alert my brother about my location and my need for ransom."

"If the Druids suspect me, they'll never let me get away alive!"

"He won't suspect you of planning to start a war against them, not so long as he doesn't know who I am. My situation will not be improved until four kings are informed and start insisting upon my release!"

"You must not start thinking of Goddeu as an ordinary bad man," admonished the youth. "He is a Druid who uses black magic. I have heard of the abominable acts committed by sorcerers who traffic with evil spirits."

"What else would you have me do?"

"Tell him who you really are. After that he may be wise enough to start treating you as a valuable political pawn, not as a slave to be abused."

"No! He'll immediately sell me to the invaders. They will turn me into a weapon to use against both Eastland, Clarents and Estrangore."

"Isn't that better than being an abused slave, one who could be murdered on a whim?"

"You said it yourself. Those who are royalty don't have the privilege of thinking only about their own welfare. If I let myself be politically used, it will hurt all the tribes, not just my own. Give me a better plan and I'll listen."

"If I don't have to leave, I'll do everything that I humanly can to make this situation better."

"What can you do? It's easy for a person to imagine himself brilliant or heroic, but if we go on defying Goddeu what will my treatment be—or your treatment? You know that if I anger him, he will punish you before he punishes me."

"If you try to please such a man, it will lead very quickly to your defilement. You'll be an outcast in the eyes of every tribe. You'll be scorned personally as well as politically. Are you willing to risk that?"

"He's able to rape me whether I'm willing or not. The only positive good we can get out of this situation depends on you being set free. As you've already said, he probably sees you as a rival to be rid of. Won't it be better if he frees you instead of kills you? As long as he thinks that I'm only a merchant's daughter, he should have no strong reason to either slay or hold you. Listen, here's something I could try: Once you're well away, I'll tell Goddeu who I really am, for whatever good that can do."

"You'd have to be quiet for days because as soon as you speak, he'll have a hundred men out seeking for my life! As long as you don't protest, he will feel at liberty to do anything he likes with you. If you refuse him on even the smallest whim, he might shove you through that stinking door in the cliff!"

"Don't you see that it is time for the both of us to take risks? We're only about three or four days' walk away from Camelos. I think he wants me for a cooperative concubine, so maybe I can stall him long enough for King Caratacos to demand my release."

"What if you can't stall him?"

"That will still leave me the option of confessing my identity rather than give in to him. Maybe he won't have enough time to hand me over to the Romans before he has an army outside his gates."

"The whole idea is horrifying!"

"I hope it's horrifying enough to motivate you to travel quickly as soon as you get out of this despicable fort."

# THE ROMAN AND THE IRISHMAN

## CHAPTER XVII

Mog Ruith, in his ferret form, had no means to warn Broch and Voada against taking dangerous risks. The best he could do would be to send a message to King Arto, alerting him of the princess' peril.

But ever since arriving at the shed, the Wren had felt the tugging of the Silver Cord—that mystical link binding a soul to its living body. When a magician transmigrated, the Cord gave him a limited time before it called him back. The soul-traveler had to magically counter the force, consuming his *mana* to withstand the pull.

It was always a losing battle because resistance could delay the soul shift for a short term only. But the druid had learned what he needed to know and saw no reason to continue resisting the pull, not if he expected to keep his stock of *mana* high.

In the blink of an eye, the non-resisting wizard awoke on the floor of his hut, still in the seated position he had assumed earlier. He had become his clumsy old self again—large, heavy, weak-eyed, weak-eared, and with a dull sense of smell. Naturally, he preferred not to have a sharp sense of smell near Caer Draig.

Ruith struggled to stand up on his cramped legs. Though wobbly and groggy, he was more or less fit. He still remembered why he needed to contact Simon of Gitta. One of them needed to intercept Pellinor and ensure the Laird dispatched a rider to Camelos before Goddeu could harm the princess.

But he was in no condition to leave the fort immediately. Because of the after-effects of the spell, he wanted to drop into bed. He fought it; sleep held peril. The caer was haunted by the Dragon Spirits. He had seen their deleterious effect on the Romans and Brute. Fortunately, Ruith had a means of self-defense.

Lying on his cot, Mog Ruith gathered his mana and his strength of will to enter a meditative state. For centuries, this meditation had been used by druids to resist spiritual possession. Fortunately, meditation would be almost as refreshing to a body as natural sleep.

He awakened with the sun's warm rays in his eyes. Even before he could roll out of bed, a doorknock sounded. It turned out the caller was a Wyrm acolyte. The youth delivered a message that the Master Wyrm would be most pleased to receive Atha Moir at the temple of Gathanothog in the seventh hour. The mage affirmed his willingness to attend the meeting, and the boy withdrew.

Alone again, the Wren prepared to leave. Before his excursion, he ate a simple breakfast from the contents of his traveling pack, mainly hard bread and dried meat. But chewing the rough fare, he heard another knock. This time, the caller was one of Asiaticus' Roman subalterns. The arch-druid unsurprisingly found the young officer's demeanor discomposed.

"Atha Moir," the officer said, "I am *Decanus* Jovan. The legate is unwell and gratefully solicits your services as a healer. I will immediately escort you to his quarters if you have no objections."

Mog Ruith nodded. "I would be most pleased to assist the legate. Are you feeling fit, Decanus?"

"I've been better. We've found this area unhealthy. Might there be an impurity in the water, Healer?" the Roman asked.

"That is one possibility," Mog Ruith replied ingenuously.

Following the soldier, he entered a hut built up against the palisade wall in the village. The soldier and the druid found the Roman legate still bed-bound.

"Decimus Valerius?" said Mog Ruith softly, not wishing to startle the man should he be drowsing.

Asiaticus turned his head, saying. "Forgive my present humor, druid. My hunting excursions haven't revitalized me as I'd hoped."

The Irishman stepped closer. "What are your symptoms, Legate?"

"The symptoms are… vague. It's mostly a weariness of spirit—but I do not find bed rest either restful or enjoyable."

Mog Ruith carefully asked his next question: "Might you be feeling as though your life essence has been *drained* from you?"

The Roman assumed an odd expression. "That is a very apt description."

"May we speak alone?" suggested the Wren.

Asiaticus blinked. "Why? Is my disease a humiliating one?"

"It's not a disease, but it *is* an affliction. You may or may not prefer to discuss it in private."

Decimus Valerius Asiaticus was briefly silent and then said to Jovan, "Search him for weapons, and if he is unarmed, wait just outside the door."

"Are you certain, Commander?" asked the officer. "I have heard that druids can kill with the mere touch of a finger. And they are also notorious poisoners."

"If the man assassinates me, I expect my officers to swiftly repay the courtesy," said the Roman.

The decanus searched for weapons and then withdrew.

"Speak now," said Asiaticus. "What is this need for discretion?"

"I have seen people borne down by your present condition before."

"What condition?"

"You are the victim of an evil spirit—and likely more than one."

Asiaticus looked away disdainfully. "Priests! With priests, everything is the fault of evil spirits!"

"Are you a skeptic, Decimus Valerius?"

"I know demons are real! But it's always the worst of physicians who blame every ailment on demons."

"Not every illness is inflicted by spirits, I own, but your infirmity may be an unfortunate exception."

"Tell me what you're hinting at," the Roman said.

"I have something to ask first. Rome's Wyrm allies no doubt have healers, so why did you summon me instead of one of them, especially since you've suspected me from the very start?"

"I never accused you of anything."

"You haven't needed to. I've noticed your watchful glances, the tightness of your smiles."

"To answer your question, I'm here to parley with the Wyrms, not to trust them. I positively distrust them."

"I understand you arrived here with the Black Goats."

"If anything, I distrust them even more than I do the Wyrms."

"I commend your caution, Legate. These are treacherous times, abounding with treacherous men. It may make me sound like a spy, but I've come upon valuable information that could benefit you."

"So you *are* a spy!"

"Not professionally, but I hear things."

"Are you saying that you have information to sell?" asked the legate.

The big druid shrugged. "I had not thought about selling information for profit, but the idea is intriguing."

"In that case, what price are you asking?"

"I propose a trade—information for your friendship."

The Roman made a scoffing sound. "It is usually easy to pay off a spy, but friendship is expensive. It takes trust to purchase it."

"Let us build trust, then. Let me begin by saying that your allies are playing you falsely."

"Of course they are! That's the nature of allies."

"On that point, I'm inclined to agree."

"Enough banter!" said the legate. "What do you factually know?"

Mog Ruith sighed. "These Druids intend to make use of Rome to weaken their enemies, the kings of Britannia. They are maneuvering to betray and expel the Romans, as well. They intend to rule this island, and their ambitions extend even farther afield than that."

Asiaticus scowled. "What details do you have regarding their ambitions? I strongly doubt that a handful of priests will find Rome easy to expel."

"No doubt, but if I tell you everything I know at the very outset, what is my leverage to gain my payment?"

"Are you speaking of friendship or of coins? In either case, I will need details if I'm to take you seriously."

"I lack readily believable details. But as for your illness, I believe it to be a spiritual affliction. Have you heard of the Dragon Spirits?"

"No, not by that name."

"In divers lands, these wraiths are frequently called otherwise. But wherever they haunt a vicinity, they inflict sickness and madness, making a region a place to be shunned."

"Are you referring to some sort of malevolent *genius loci?*"

"That term is not familiar to me. By my Latin, I assume it means something like 'the guardian deity of a place,' " replied Ruith.

"That's a cautious way of describing the vile entities. The term 'genius loci' almost always refers to trouble-making and afflicting spirits."

"I know another term by which they're known. The Dragon Spirits have been called the *Loigon* by the Greeks."

"The 'teachers'?"

"That translation seems incorrect. It is more likely that the name comes from some foreign word. Erin's legends depict phantoms manifesting as dragons."

"A dragon!" Asiaticus echoed incredulously.

"Bear with me. In the lore of these islands, these creatures once ruled this island, Erin, and vast portions of the mainland, even unto Syria. This was long before my people's ancestors came to this land. A revolt of the inhabitants banished them, but they are truly spirits and unkillable by the means available to mortals. They have been biding their time, waiting for a chance to return. I think the Black Goats and the Wyrms are jointly laboring to assist the Dragons' restoration."

Asiaticus sighed. "I don't see why I should believe a word you say. Why would mortal men seek to be ruled by evil spirits—much less rampaging dragons? Usually, when men do mad things, their goal is self-aggrandizement, wealth, and power. What reward do the Druids expect to gain from their mad scheme?"

"Their most immediate aim is to use Rome's power to subdue their enemies, the Brythonic kings and the uncorrupted druidic colleges. Afterward, I'm sure that they intend to unleash the incarnate Loigon to overwhelm your empire and the world beyond it by main force."

Asiaticus shook his head. "Perhaps your true aim, Atha Moir, is to deceive me. One who sympathizes with the Britons would like to create a dissension between Rome and its allies."

"If you prefer to carry on with your present course, I wish you good luck."

"You need to sharpen your powers of persuasion and deceit," the Roman told his visitor. "Try being more forceful in your arguments. A trickster cannot prosper if he offers nothing but vague warnings and weak lies."

"If deceit were my aim, why do you suppose I would concoct a lie that sounds so preposterous?"

Asiaticus smiled ironically. "Because you are a clever man. Big lies convince unwary men more easily than do small ones."

"That's possible, but further details exist."

Asiaticus tossed his hand. "Speak up if you have something to say."

The Wren Druid recounted in simple terms everything he supposed to be true about dragons and Dragon Spirits while avoiding the subject of Voada's identity or the fact that he was indeed a Brythonic ally engaged in espionage. The legate listened, frequently asking questions and arguing. Each man recognized their parley as a meeting of enemies, yet each understood that enemies could share common goals.

"If you know so much about demons, I have a demon story for you," remarked the Roman suddenly.

"And what demon is that?"

"I think there is a mysterious creature roaming the valley. My aide saw it in the woods. I didn't catch sight of it myself, but I saw its tracks." Asiaticus then described the encounter as minutely as he could. "How would such a bogie fit into this convoluted tale of yours?"

Mog Ruith shrugged. "I do not know. Can you share more details on this matter?"

"I've told it all. Is there a night creature in Brythonic spirit lore like that one?"

"Not really."

"So, you're no great fount of information, after all, druid. Where is your peculiar dissertation on mythic lore leading us, my friend?"

Mog Ruith shrugged. "I cannot say. But I came here to give fair warning, and that I have done. As for your illness, I recommend you leave this vicinity as soon as possible. If the Wyrms argue for you to stay, don't listen. And be careful of what you eat or drink. If they want you to stay against your will, I would not put it past them to feed you a debilitating drug to make you too ill to leave."

"Is that all?"

"This haunted castle is not a welcoming place for humans. Remember, Decimus Valerius, many people around us show the same symptoms as you."

"How can the druids exist here if that is true? Why haven't they all left or died by this time?"

"That's a complex question. But I do not think that the spirits seek to slay everyone. They wish to subject them to possession. Wyrms seem possessed; that the Black Goats are possessed also is questionable. Under the influence of the spirits, the Wyrms could easily induce you to commit treason, such as giving your commanding general information that will help the druids but will do injury to Rome."

Asiaticus sighed heavily. "Even if I believed you, how could I convince my superiors to take seriously a tale about spirits?"

"If you believe what I'm saying, you'll find the words you need."

"Show me how wise you are, druid. Offer me something to improve my depleted condition."

"I would most gladly assist you, Legate. I have protected myself from spiritual assault by an ancient technique. Hopefully, it will benefit you as well. Tell me, do you have mystical training enough to enter a trance state?"

"My druidic grandfather taught me some meditative techniques."

"Hopefully, then, you'll be able to apply the methods I will describe. Most importantly, do not give in to natural sleep while you are in this area."

"How does a man go without sleep?" the Roman asked incredulously.

"There's sleep, and then there's proper *sleep*. Listen to what I have to say." Asiaticus paid heed while Mog Ruith described the means he used to enter a defensive trance state.

"Does Goddeu know about these Dragon Spirits?" Asiaticus asked abruptly.

The Druid shook his head. "I'm unaware of what the Black Goats know. I believe, however, that Goddeu is strongly motivated to support Bhort. Using one against the other will be difficult. Though distinct individuals, the druids are two of a kind. It would be unwise for you to reveal your doubts about the Wyrms to Goddeu. He would probably inform against you to Bhort."

When the Roman made no reply, the druid inquired, "Am I free to leave?"

Asiaticus settled his head back against his bolster. "I'll take your advice seriously," he said. "I've lived long enough to know that opponents are not always enemies, nor are allies always friends. Travel well, druid, and may our gods be generous to us both."

*     *     *

That afternoon, Mog Ruith met with Master Wyrm Bhort in his study. The Wren arrived with little hope that the meeting would lead to anything beneficial, yet it would look odd if a visitor did not show due courtesy to a host. A display of respect would shore up his assumed persona of a harmless and not-too-bright wayfaring scholar.

The Wren found the proximity of the arch-Druid disquieting. His ugliness was an intimidating factor. Bhort proved to be an aggressive interrogator, questioning Ruith on diverse subjects. Ruith praised the hospitality that he had received during his stay with the Wyrms and vowed to commend Caer Draig to his college at home.

The Master Wyrm continued to press him with questions. He especially wanted to know where the Irish savant was next bound.

Ruith stayed close to the truth and freely admitted that he intended to visit Camelos, ostensibly to learn the character of the new high king. He also wanted firsthand accounts of the war from veterans. His colleagues in Ireland would be especially eager to hear every detail.

Mog Ruith, however, sought to mislead Bhort on one important subject. He inferred he had lately been afflicted by an infirmity that had left him tired, listless, and depressed. Because he felt unfit to resume his arduous journey, he claimed he would tarry at the caer longer than planned and carry out a program of self-treatment. Ruith told the Wyrm he planned to spend the afternoon searching nearby fields and woods for medicinal herbs. He hoped that tea and broths brewed from nature's bounty might prove restorative.

Bhort, apparently wearied by the conversation, offered Atha Moir his best wishes for a swift recovery. Then, excusing himself, he withdrew on the excuse of a heavy workload.

The Wren exited the temple primed to act. Because of his distrust of the Wyrms, he thought it prudent to leave Caer Draig as soon as possible and without advanced warning. The plight of Princess Voada was paramount in his mind, and it was high time he rejoined Simon of Gitta to compare his discoveries with the Samaritan's.

# THE LABYRINTH

## CHAPTER XVIII

The first day that Simon prowled the marshes and forests around Brynymeir Hill, he caught sight of three Roman officers out hunting. They impressed him as unimportant; if he had simply killed them, he would have learned nothing. So, instead, Simon shadowed them. With time passing, he discovered nothing from the invaders' activities except that they were poor hunters. He kept on their track until they were approached and intercepted by Mog Ruith, who was already at Caer Draig.

The Samaritan returned to camp, believing his capable associate could uncover the reason behind the Wyrm Druids' hospitality toward Roman agents. Simon and his druid companion split up upon reaching the hill. Mog Ruith would enter the caer as a wandering druid, while the adventurer would survey the activities of the countryside.

He had observed Pictish workers harvesting turnips, but little else. On the third day of scouting, however, he observed something that aroused his curiosity.

Ten turnip-loaded carts had inexplicably turned off the royal highway a little short of Caer Draig and traveled down a dirt track into a wooded quarter. Simon had traveled this path, finding only woodland and pasture. He followed the wagons until they stopped behind the hill of Brynymeir. There the cart road ended, having gone nowhere.

At the foot of the barren cliff stood a single large hut serving as a barracks for several Pictish men. Neither storage sheds for turnips nor herd beasts were in sight. Bringing so much fodder to this empty spot seemed without purpose.

Simon marked the harvesters at their tasks, filling wicker baskets from the stopped turnip carts and toting them into the cliff through a wide, yawning door. Because he was familiar with the area, someone must have deliberately hidden the portal for him to miss it.

Because a hidden door implied secret activities, he had to expose the Wyrm Druids' plotting. Instinct told him that he needed to discover what was happening inside that cliff.

The hill could not contain an ordinary root cellar. The Caer Draig community's other crop-storage huts had been left quite visible. Maybe hungry animals were inside, yet why hide a simple stable so carefully?

The area showed no sign of animal activity and no dung or animal tracks were seen. Donkey apples peppered the cart track, but there were none where beasts might have grazed.

Was the door perhaps the entrance to a slave pen or prison?

But if so, why the extreme secrecy? These elements added up to a mystery, and Simon believed he needed to discover the solution.

It all came down to whether the risk was justifiable.

After a moment, Simon's gambler's instinct won out over his caution.

While the Samaritan watched, one of the field workers strayed away from his team. Stealthily, the adventurer followed the worker to a secluded spot behind the hut, concealed behind the bushes. The Pict, believing himself alone, dropped his baggy pants and squatted. Simon, as silent as a shadow, took the harvester from behind. A thumb jab to a pressure point on the man's neck knocked him out cold.

Simon's mentor, Daramos, had taught his pupils this Indian technique. It temporarily subdued an enemy without seriously injuring him. The magus disdained to kill and schooled his trainees to preserve life as much as possible.

That was the admonishment that Simon had often had trouble following.

Simon stripped the Pict and donned his garments. Afterward, he set to work, altering his appearance through the application of the hair and waxen prosthetics he routinely carried in his pack.

At Persepolis, Daramos' pupils had learned to swiftly create credible disguises without the benefit of a mirror. The Samaritan aimed at looking Pictish. Fortunately, he'd been going clean-shaven of late, and by the application of pieces of dyed, uncarded wool and body paint, he gave himself a convincing Pictish face. He even smeared streaks of blue pigment on his wrists to suggest tattooing.

Finally, the Samaritan donned the man's straw hat, pulling it down to his brows to cover his tonsure. He returned to the carts quickly, intending to join the workers seamlessly. He expected the guards to assume he had arrived with the carts, and the harvesters to think he had just left the hut.

With a full basket of turnips balanced on his right shoulder, Simon walked through the cliff door behind a pair of fellow workers. The faint odor of urine and manure that tainted the air near the cliff-side suddenly became very strong, as one found in a badly kept prison. Several lamps illuminated the cliff tunnel ahead. He walked slowly, letting his eyes adjust to the darkness. On either side of the entryway stood a Pictish guard, but the careless fellows paid scant heed to mere field workers.

Once Simon had advanced beyond their line of sight, he paused. He could no longer see the harvesters, and choosing a tunnel proved difficult. An additional guard accosted him with a frown. "What are you dawdling for?" he demanded in Pictish.

The Samaritan excelled at language acquisition, yet knew few Pictish words. He muttered, "Sorry," in the Pictish tongue and, projecting subservient body language, bustled ahead. A returning laborer carrying a basket showed him the route to take.

Simon followed a passage into a dug-out chamber lit by only one lamp. It was mostly filled with mounds of turnips, some of which smelled fresh, while others oozed the tang of decay.

The spy emptied his basket on a pile of turnips and then lingered there contemplating his next move. To move freely, he assumed the persona of a guard. He put his hat into the basket, which he had concealed behind a mound of vegetables. Following that, he covered his give-away tonsure by tying the rag around his neck to resemble the headcloth some Picts wore. The infiltrator then investigated another direction.

He walked with a bully-like swagger, like a guard would. His impersonation conveyed the illusion of authority. Indeed, most of whom he passed declined to look him in the face.

At a tunnel fork, Simon heard the sounds of people in distress and hesitated. Because he believed he would be safer among prisoners than guards, he approached the noise.

The adventurer trailed into an ill-lighted tunnel, outfitted with a row of holding cells cut from the living rock. Within each cell were huddled prisoners who looked like ordinary Brythonic villagers. His guard disguise alarmed the captives, who averted their glances from him.

These individuals resembled farm laborers: elderly men, women, and children. He assumed they were slaves, perhaps newly captured, but wondered why they had to be kept in a hidden pen. Were the Wyrms running an illegal slave-trading operation, seizing country people lawlessly? The captives did not look like prisoners of war or confined criminals.

A sharp-eyed old man caught the Samaritan's attention; he went to the bars facing him. He whispered: "Come up, grandfather. We need to speak."

When the elder looked perplexed, Simon coaxed, "Fear not. I am no friend of the people keeping you captive."

Warily, the elder edged closer, like a timid beast of the night.

"I am not a guard," explained Simon hushedly. "I have been sent by King Arto—Caratacos—to learn about lawlessness happening in the countryside. Why are you locked up?"

"I-I'm from the village of Glew," the man stammered. "We don't know why we were brought here."

"I heard Glew was attacked. Attacked by what?"

"The gods alone know! A dragon appeared from nowhere—"

"A dragon?"

"Aye! We fled to the forest and stayed hidden until druids arrived with warriors. A few of us hurried over to inform them about the attack, but their servants seized us. We were forced to walk in chains for days. Then we were brought here. The air is so bad that it's making many of us sick!"

"What are the druids demanding of you?"

"Nothing—except obedience. They give us water and turnips to eat. Otherwise, they ignore us. But other prisoners say that a monster ran past this spot."

"A monster?"

"A deformed man, maybe. No one was sure!"

"Are you certain of this?"

"I only know what people say."

"What have seen yourself?"

"Each day, more bodies leave these cells."

Simon recalled what Brute had said—that Dragon Spirits haunted Caer Draig, sapping men of their life essence and hastening their deaths.

The prisoner continued, mentioning how living individuals were occasionally removed from these cells. His emotive voice was growing weaker.

"Taken where?"

He pointed into the dark. "That way. They want the younger women especially. We fear they are being slain for sacrifice."

"If I'm able to help you, I will. But I'm alone here and must summon the warriors I serve. I will urge them to free your people."

Just then, he heard faint, echoing footsteps. Simon left the incarceration area to pursue them. A short distance on was an ascending passage chiseled from the bedrock. Since he heard no more footfalls, the Samaritan chose to ascend the ramp to observe his surroundings.

The incline brought him into a huge cavern—broad and high-ceilinged. A weak light filtered in through holes cut into one wall. The penetrations also admitted enough ventilation to make the air less rank. On the same level, he discerned shadowy structures. Some structures were stone; others, lath and thatch. He searched the area, very soon coming to a sheer drop-off some fifteen feet above a different level. It amounted to a rough-hewn mezzanine overlooking an open area where standing stones were arranged in a formation of monoliths. He guessed that the site probably served for festival celebrations or worship ceremonies.

It seemed strange that the Wyrms would worship their gods in a place so offensive. Most priestly colleges favored fresh forests.

He heard footsteps, looked, and saw figures emerging from the shadows.

Simon ducked into a hut and hid behind its doorpost. A powerful smell filled that confined space. He recognized the stench of stale blood and rotten meat.

While watching through the door crack, he saw two guards passing by and overheard their grumbling. Simon felt empathy. Their daily labor had to be odious.

The Samaritan waited until the malcontents' voices faded away and then opted to explore the foul hut. To aid him, Simon worked a simple spell he knew. It caused his right hand to glow, but he kept the light dim, lest it give away his hiding place.

The adventurer saw behind him a cluttered, glistening plank table. He touched an object on it and felt its coat of slime. He drew back his hand, sniffed his fingertips, and winced at the smell. He had just stroked a butcher's block—an especially befouled one.

If this was a butcher shop, what kind of meat did it prepare? Could the Wyrms be depraved enough to engage in ritual cannibalism?

In disgust, he quelled his magical light and departed the hut, eager to breathe some less vile air. He was hearing a distant gibbering sound—not speech, but something like a human voice mouthing gibberish. He tracked the sound; a wall, taller than himself, stopped him. He pulled himself up to look over the cornice. What he beheld made his eyes open wide and his jaw drop.

The old man had been right!

There *were* monsters in these accursed caverns!

Man-sized creatures milled about an enclosed area, jostling against one another like swines at a wallow. But these were not swine; they were something much worse. Despite poor lighting and distance, the figures impressed him with their obesity and filthiness. Mud- and dung-smeared, flabby of body, the creatures—the beings—both appalled the adventurer and aroused his pity. Whatever they were, they had been penned in intolerably degrading conditions! It wasn't possible to see them clearly, but the creatures looked deformed. They moved about in the filth of their pen like quadrupeds would, their very long, fat arms used as front legs. The gibbering was issuing from them. Did they lack the voices—or the minds—to utter anything but meaningless sounds?

Simon squinted, trying to make out the entities' faces, but only captured an impression of idiocy and brutishness.

Simon dropped from the wall, profoundly disturbed. What were these pathetic creatures? Had they descended from abused men and women forced to live like ill-tended beasts? Had generations of progeny degenerated to the level of herd animals? A weaker mind would have faltered.

The word *cannibalism* again came to mind. Were the creatures being used as swine for meat? What scene in the Greek Tartarus could have been more shocking? Whatever was happening inside this hellish cave system, it had to be stopped! There needed to be a powerful intervention of authority against this evil. He knew Brynymeir Hill existed in Lothan and would be under the scepter of King Arto. The Samaritan couldn't help but believe that a man like Pendragon would eliminate the evil practices happening under Caer Draig.

Simon felt ready to leave this dreadful place. He retraced his path with confidence. A less trained man might have become lost in such a confusion of tunnels, but Daramos had trained his pupils extensively. Below the fallen Persepolis ran many miles of twisting tunnels, and the magus had often sent his young trainees underground with instructions to race their peers to the surface. Eventually, they would be expected to make their victorious escape blindfolded. The adventurer was tempted to believe what Mog Ruith suggested—that the gods intervened in the lives of certain individuals to prepare them to face extraordinary challenges in life. Quickly and quietly, Simon made his way back to the open door by the cliff. But he had arrived only to see his way of escape closing!

To dash through the door before it closed would surely lead to a challenge from the guards. His identity and behavior would be demanded and his inability to speak Pictish would expose him as a spy. Despite there being only two door sentries, extra guards could be summoned from nearby tunnels and the hut. Though he was trapped, he held firm. Daramos had trained his followers to control the fear reaction. Any student who failed so crucial a test had been sent away. But Simon had learned well and his mastery over emotion had often saved his life.

Simon, in hiding, stifled his animal fear and entered a self-aware meditative state.

He watched the guards seal the portal. To his relief, the exit would be locked with nothing more than a sturdy crossbeam supported by iron fixtures. That posed no challenge, given his strength.

Simon intended to hide until things settled down, until the guards lolled at rest, unsupported and alone. The two men could not possibly impede his escape.

Suddenly, two muscular males came lumbering out of the darkness behind him. They saw him crouching and one spoke.

"*Eir klu ymdei?*"

Simon guessed that the guard was demanding to know what he was doing.

"Nothing," was one of the few Pictish words he knew.

"*Veur mul n'prog?*" the same bully asked. The Easterner didn't comprehend his words, and so simply shook his head and looked thoughtful.

The improper reply caused the guards to spring at him. Simon's hands flashed like blades and one Pict was knocked senseless to the stone floor. The second fellow leaped away nimbly, only to trip over a dropped turnip and fall sprawling to the stones. Simon threw himself on the man and beat him with calloused fists. But the hard-headed scoundrel kept bellowing a word that probably meant "intruder!"

Another Pict ran out of the tunnel but stopped short at seeing the husky Simon overwhelming two men single-handedly. The worker spun about and stampeded down the dark tunnel with the adventurer giving chase. The fugitive ran into the arms of two more Picts—either workers or guards. The frightened man pointed frantically back at Simon, jabbering Pictish words.

The Samaritan snatched his hidden sica from its scabbard and attacked like a Thracian gladiator fighting for his life. His first strike delivered a killing blow to the one informing against him, while his leap simultaneously bowled over the other two men. He would have needed only seconds to kill them, but two additional Picts stomped out of a passage, drawn by the shouting. While this pair made no attack, they started yelling for help.

Simon dashed between them and plunged back into the labyrinth. His survival hinged on discovering either an alternative route to the surface or a hiding place.

He inaudibly cursed his luck as he plunged into full darkness.

# Reunion

## CHAPTER XIX

Simon fled down the tunnel where the cell row was. Just beyond it, he heard voices, which made him veer in another direction. A hundred feet farther on, he entered a room with torches and a set of stone-cut stairs leading upward.

Running up the steps, the adventurer tried a door on a higher landing, only to realize it was locked. He heard men climbing after him, giving him the choice of standing and fighting or climbing higher.

He did not overly fear his pursuers. The best men would not be given sty duty. The guards would probably be only toughs and bullies who would lose their nerve if he went at them violently enough.

But after that, what?

He again remembered his mentor Dositheus saying, "One thing at a time."

The stairs were slightly curved and so Simon waited with his sica tightly gripped until his adversaries rounded the bend. He sprang at them, shrieking an arena-spawned battle cry. They stopped in alarm and he sprang into their midst, dealing out slashes and leg-breaking kicks. Thrown into confusion, they barely defended themselves.

In seconds, they were stumbling backward in terror of his fast-striking blade. They fought to be first in the retreat. Men fell down the stairs in a bouncing avalanche of human bodies. The ex-Thracian kept pace with them, wounding one after another.

With the landing floor awash in a terrified crowd, Simon skillfully maneuvered around them. But he saw two late-comers ahead, bracing to meet him. One wielded a knife and the other's bow was drawn. At the bowstring's twang, the adventurer dodged and closed with the archer before he could fit another arrow. The sica made strings of his blood splash hotly over Simon's face and tunic.

The knife man broke away and ran, but the ex-gladiator pursued and brought him down with a sica strike. Only now did Simon feel a definite burning in his thigh. He touched the injury but found that the arrow had only scratched his flesh.

Ignoring the blood and discomfort, he raced down the tunnel, leaving behind the men he had defeated. Finding an alternative escape route would require the Samaritan to search extensively. The cliff door was the sensible destination. While numerous guards searched, the exit's sentries weren't likely to anticipate his return.

His searchers spread out in the caverns, encountering little resistance as he returned to the cliff door. He took his few adversaries by surprise and left few of them uninjured. Breathing heavily and sweating profusely, the Samaritan staggered toward the exit. He thought his intense effort and the foul air had worn him out.

Hope remained: only two men guarded the exit. He burst from the shadows, instantly disabling a man. The other guard dived for the alarm bell, but Simon's sica cut his desperate act short. The ex-Thracian lifted the portal's crossbeam from its hardware with a grunt, so heavy it was.

The Levantine warrior stumbled out the door into the clean, cold air. A gift from heaven greeted him. A pony, tied to a post before the hunters' hut, lacked visible guards. Despite his unsteadiness, his fumbling hands loosed the beast, and he struggled to mount its bare back. With a heel jab, he started the beast backing away from the hut.

Suddenly, stomping feet drummed behind him; a guard was rushing after him. He kicked the pony's flanks to start it running. The guard, apparently unarmed, caught up and grabbed at Simon's garments, trying to pull him down. Simon slashed with his sica and the Pict stumbled away. Then Simon reeled in his saddle, sick and woozy; his only thought was to break away and reach his hidden camp.

He realized that there was something wrong with him. His leg had been cut by an arrow, and the Picts were notorious for poisoning their arrowheads. If cut by such an arrow, he realized that he might never end this ride alive.


Simon of Gitta, coming to, found himself slung over a strong man's shoulder. His captor's walk bounced him rhythmically. His weak and trembling right hand groped for his sica, but touched an empty scabbard. He bunched a fist, intending to break the stranger's back with a blow, but instinct halted him. He needed to know his target before taking a life.

"Simon," said a booming voice. "Don't get skittish. I've brought to you to a new camping place."

The Samaritan dimly recognized Mog Ruith's voice. But was this moment real? He couldn't think clearly, and couldn't put two reasoning thoughts together.

The muscular druid now sank to his knees to lower his living burden carefully to the ground.

"What... what..." the Samaritan murmured.

"You're not well, Simon," said the Wren. "Don't move. I'll bring you a tonic. Maybe it will clear your mind."

The next thing he knew, Ruith was gone. The injured warrior lay on the grass, forgetful of where he was, until the druid returned. Simon felt his friend's hand lifting his shoulders high enough to accept a cup containing a warm, bitter beverage.

He next awoke under a black, starlit sky. Though he couldn't see, he heard movement. He had to hope that it was Mog Ruith. "F-Friend, where are we?" he asked.

"Feeling better now, are we?" the Wren Druid inquired.

"I-I've… been poisoned," Simon stammered.

"I suspected that. Your only real wound is a shallow cut on your thigh. I've heard about Pictish poisoned weapons. I don't think you were greatly affected by the bane," remarked the Irishman. "Or, more likely, you were hit by a capture arrow, which makes its prey helpless temporarily. I lack knowledge of the toxin; blood cleansing is my only option."

"How… how did you…?"

"How did I bring you here? I folded you over your pony's back and led it by a tether to our camp. There might have been searchers after you, so I moved us farther from Caer Draig. I salvaged our necessary gear, however, and moved us farther up the road."

"W-Was I pursued?"

"Oh, yes, and the Picts captured you, too," said the priest.

"*Captured?*"

"I met three tribesmen along the highway bringing you bound across a pony's back. I suppose they were taking you to the Wyrms."

"What did you do?"

"I asked them to turn you over to me and then run like the *Dullahan* was chasing them. Otherwise, I promised to kill them all."

"So?"

"They accepted my second option. A pity. Now I feel obligated to save some additional lives to make up for the lives I've taken. How did they snare you? Did they bring you down with a poison arrow?"

Simon shook his head, trying to remember. "I don't recall being captured. I was escaping from a cave, almost too sick to ride. I remember nothing after that."

"The Picts probably found you unconscious. By the way, one of them had looted your sica. I took it back from him."

"Thanks…" he said in a strained whisper.

"Beginning at dawn, I'll scrounge the woods for medicinal herbs," said Ruith. "Hopefully, there will be something useful to augment my packed stock. By the way, I chose this spot because it's near a clean stream. You should drink as much as you can bear until you're better. Plentiful water is considered a treatment for poison in the bloodstream."

"How did you find my horse?" the adventurer asked.

"It remained where you left it, near the old camp. It's a better animal than the pony. Releasing the little one, I hoped that its tracks leading in the opposite direction would throw off any trackers who may come across that spot."

"Where exactly are we now?"

"We're northeast of Caer Draig, beside the royal road that Laird Pellinor should be taking. With luck, the general's band will pass this way one of these days. I'm going to be watching the road so we won't miss him."

"Why don't we ride north and meet his band?"

"Because I don't know how serious your condition is. You aren't fit to ride; I'd have to haul you like baggage."

Simon tried to speak, but couldn't.

"I've already squeezed out all the blood I could from around your cut and covered it with salve," Mog Ruith continued. "I saved our blankets and I'm getting a fire started. I'll keep it going all night so you won't suffer from chills. Sleep if you're able to. I don't think Pellinor will travel by night, but if anyone comes along in the dark, I'll be monitoring the road traffic."

With Simon only half conscious, Ruith went to add more sticks to the fire.


The Samaritan awakened to an overcast morning. He rolled over and pushed himself up to his knees. Trying to stand, his face flushed hot, and he fell to his belly.

Mog Ruith showed up to resettle him atop the mossy sleeping mat that he'd scraped together for a cushion.

"You seem to get stronger," he said to Simon. "Either my herbal broth is helping, or the bane is naturally wearing off."

"However I get rid of it, I want to be rid of it."

"Aye to that," said the druid.

"How near are we to the Wyrms?" asked the adventurer.

"The distance is considerable, however, we shouldn't be careless."

"I think I'll be able to travel soon," the Samaritan said.

"I disagree."

"You haven't told me what you found out," the Samaritan said.

"I learned a bit," said Ruith. He filled Simon in on his conversation with Asiaticus, and what he'd overheard at Goddeu's lodge. Finally, he let Simon know that the Brigantean princess Voada had become Goddeu's slave.

"We have to get her away from him," said Simon. "Tell me about the Wyrms' defenses. Can Pellinor achieve anything?"

"Pellinor will need to be careful. The Pictish warriors hereabouts are very many. But the tribesmen might be in poor fighting trim. They're almost certainly being sapped by the Dragon Spirits like everyone else is."

"If Pellinor can't attack head-on, maybe he can strike at the flank."

"What do you mean?"

"The best way to injure the druids is by killing Bhort and Goddeu. But I'm not sure how to reach them." Simon then expressed his need for a solid meal to help him generate good ideas.

"Hunger is a sign that your body is restoring itself."

"Fine. I could use a positive sign."

Mog Ruith departed and came back with a clay cup containing spit-roasted pieces of hare. Simon ate cautiously, his stomach feeling unsettled.

After this small repast, Simon drank copious water.

"I took enormous risks gathering the information I came across," the younger man said afterward. "It didn't go well, and I barely escaped alive."

"So it seems. What did you learn?"

"The Wyrms are attacking area villages and capturing whoever they find. They're imprisoning their captives in filthy underground cells beneath the hill of Brynymeir."

"Why? For slaves? For sacrifices?"

"For food!"

"Food?" Mog Ruith repeated perplexedly.

# ON THE ROAD FROM GLEW

## CHAPTER XX

"I mean food for the Dragon Spirits. The druids will need more captives soon, considering the death rate. However, I believe there is real cannibalism happening as well."

"And you are serious?"

"Have you ever heard me joking before?"

"I can't say that I have. If you were more inclined to laughter, you might live longer."

"I'll laugh when the world is no longer horrifying."

"Well, it *is* that, I suppose," said Mog Ruith. "Legends claim that dragon servants practiced cannibalism. The dementia that the dragon spirits inflict on the human spirit may rob a victim of his moral taboos, including those against cannibalism."

"Did you eat any suspicious meat at the caer?"

"Human meat, do you mean? The hospitality was not effusive. Mostly, I ate from my rations and am pretty sure the little meat they offered was goat."

"I wouldn't be surprised if human flesh is being reserved for the Wyrm elites. I wonder if this wasn't what drove Brute out of his mind. He could have discovered what sort of meat he'd been dining on."

"Possibly, the poor fellow. I think the Wyrms are extending the Romans' stay at the caer to subject them to the Dragon Spirits' mental subjugation. Their plan to defeat the Roman army must heavily rely on that."

"I won't wish any Roman well, but I also wouldn't want their army to be controlled by dragon-worshiping druids." Simon paused and looked uncomfortable. "There's something I haven't mentioned yet, something I wish I could forget."

"How bad can it be?" asked Mog Ruith.

"It's unbelievable. They have animals down there. Only, they may not be animals. I fear that they're human, or at least partly human. They seem to be people confined like beasts for generations and raised for slaughter. Probably the Dragon Spirits instigated their creation."

"Do they look like animals?"

"They looked like human beings degenerated to the level of domestic swine. I saw a pen filled with them. The Wyrms' devotion to turnip planting suggests a large population of degraded creatures."

"What else can you tell me about these... swine?"

In a weary, halting voice, Simon recounted every repellant detail he'd observed.

Mog Ruith grimaced. "Maybe a Roman saw an escaped beastman near the river. If these beings still desire freedom, they may still have human spirits."

"Don't read too much into that," cautioned Simon. "Any caged beast wishes for escape. But imagine! Those penned creatures represent a part of the new world that the Wyrm Druids seek to bring into existence. Do you suppose that the Black Goats are cooperating in this madness? They're bad, but I saw no insane depravity like this in Gaul."

"I had no direct contact with any Black Goat at the fort," replied Ruith.

"If they are aware of the Wyrm's secret diet and support it, they should be eradicated from the planet. I only wish the Romans had done a better job on them," said Simon.

The arch-druid sighed and shook his head.

"How much do you suppose the Romans know of this craziness?" asked the adventurer.

"They don't seem to know very much. I did my best to help Asiaticus understand that the Romans should cast off the renegade druids."

"No demon-worshiper is sane," said Simon. "The lot of them have to be exposed and destroyed."

Mog Ruith sighed and nodded.


In the morning, Simon was still unfit for hard travel, so they remained encamped. Mog Ruith maintained his watch on the road until mid-afternoon, when he came running into camp. "I see horsemen! They could very well be Laird Pellinor and his band."

Simon wobbled to his feet, still unsteady but able to manage a shuffling walk. "Help me to the road," he said.

The two of them crouched behind a tall growth of dry weeds. Three men rode ahead of the primary group. When these were passing the hidden men by, Mog Ruith stood up, stepped onto the roadway, and shouted. The trio of horsemen reigned in and looked back.

"You're the Wren!" one man stated.

Now the Samaritan joined Mog Ruith out in the open.

"And you're the Merlin!" the same warrior declared.

"Yes," said the adventurer. "We have a dangerous situation here. We must speak with Pellinor immediately."

The two outriders signaled to the warriors and druids following at a distance. When the troop drew near, Simon estimated that Pellinor still had over a hundred fit men, plus Mog Ruith's druids.

"*Here* you are, finally!" old war chief declared. "Did you two discover anything of interest?"

"What's happening here is beyond the bounds of sanity. It's going to take some explaining," Simon yelled back. "How have you fared, Laird?"

Pellinor dismounted and walked up to the pair.

"What happened at Glew?" Ruith asked him.

"They told the same story that the refugees told at the Giants' Dance. A dragon attacked Glew, and the druids abducted every villager they could capture. But tell me, what have you been up to?" the old warrior asked.

The first secret Mog Ruith revealed concerned the capture of Princess Voada.

"So *that's* what happened to her!" the king of Avalon shouted.

"What do you mean?" Mog Ruith asked.

"We spoke with a few Glouchedonian warriors along the roadway south. They had some interesting news."

"About the princess?" asked Simon.

"Yes," said Pellinor. "Several days ago, a small party of Belgaen warriors encountered a suspicious group of Pictish slavers. Because the Belgaens were badly outnumbered, they decided not to provoke hostilities. After pretending to be deceived, they alerted the nearest Glouchedonian war camp. The war chief there sent a couple hundred men to uncover the truth. The Britons they met along the way directed them to a large Pictish village off the main road.

"When the Glouchedonians got there, human sacrifices were being carried out. Glouchedon forbids such rites to the Picts. The warriors broke up the orgy and took many villagers for questioning.

"Some freed slaves at the settlement were from the Estrangorean wedding party. It had been ambushed and massacred by Picts. The captives taken had included Princess Voada, but she had already escaped before the Gouchedonians arrived.

"They learned that most of the slavers were still off pursuing the escaped slaves. Dobunnian horsemen were dispatched to find her, but slavers ambushed them, and they were forced to retreat to the village. The entire force of warriors went into the forest after the slavers and sent them scattering.

"Now, damn it, you tell us that the princess went on to be captured by the Wyrm Druids! These outrages have to stop! Might the Wyrms have orchestrated the initial wedding party attack?"

"I doubt they did, Laird," said Mog Ruith. "What I overheard made it sound like the druids at Caer Draig don't know about Voada's true identity."

"Curse every one of those renegades! I'll send what you've told me back to Arto. We need a large force to level Caer Draig to the ground!"

"It will take time for Arto to send the men we need," warned Simon. "Do you suppose that his vassal, King Loth, can provide you with more immediate support?"

"Take help from Loth?!" the war chief fairly shouted. "Look at what he allows in his kingdom! The man is either too stupid to depend on, or he's collaborating with the Wyrms—and I'd bet on the latter! We don't need a couple hundred of Loth's hand-picked men lurking at our rear while we're facing off with hundreds of wild Picts!"

"I propose we meet with Bhort," said Mog Ruith. "Once he knows he is being investigated, it might disrupt his activities until Arto himself intervenes."

"I'll consider your advice," Pellinor stated. However, his tone informed Simon that the man was all too ready to charge like an aurochs bull into a dangerous situation.


Simon and Mog Ruith joined the war band, but with evening coming on, Pellinor called a halt to establish a night camp. As the cook fires blazed, the two spies shared the details of their investigation with the men of Logres.

"Cannibalism?!" Pellinor echoed. "Are you certain, Merlin, or did that poison arrow give you nightmares? If it's true, I hope neither of you ate anything you shouldn't have."

"I've been entirely living on dry rations and hare flesh," Simon said firmly. "Mog Ruith swears he's innocent, too."

Pellinor shook his head in incredulity. "Princess Voada needs rescuing from those maniacs. And such a rescue is exactly what Arto needs for leverage in dealing with weak allies like Clarants, Estrangore, and Eastland."

"She's in danger," agreed Simon. "It's crucial that the girl doesn't stay captive for very much longer. And we have to prevent the Romans from getting their hands on her."

"The handful of Romans you describe won't be a problem," returned Pellinor.

"The Wyrms, and the Romans, are well supported by Pictish warriors," said Mog Ruith. "And warriors have to tread carefully when facing off against a druidic order. If the other religious orders take offense, they'll hold Arto accountable. Such risks have to be avoided during a crisis."

The Samaritan spoke up again. "We must thwart the druids' plot until royal reinforcements arrive. One way is to assassinate Bhort and Goddeu in some fast, clean way. Otherwise, we need to make a show of force at Caer Draig. When Bhort realizes a royal intervention is on the way, he'll have to retrench. If he does something stupid, we can move against him."

"Are you saying that I should parley with those filthy cannibals?!" the old warrior thundered. "The man will either fight or flee. When we're fighting off his warriors, he'll slip away to continue with his plans. Maybe that will be behind Roman lines!

"Worse, once the Wyrms are known to be in open rebellion, their example might encourage other uprisings. There's Roman bribe money all over Britannia!"

That was possible, Simon admitted to himself. Britannia's ongoing weakness was its incomprehensible system of tribal rule.

# The Black Goat and the Lamb

## CHAPTER XXI

The prisoners looked up when Goddeu's young acolyte, accompanied by a rugged-looking Pict man and three tribeswomen, entered the shed. As soon as they fixed their interest on Boudica, Broch shifted his body in front of her. The result was a kick in the ribs from the big Pict.

The hostile intruders seized both the princess and Broch, then yanked them to their feet. Once outside, they were forced to walk to a sooty hut in the nearby village.

A strong-looking, tattooed tribesman wearing a leather apron stood inside with his arms crossed. Beside him was a rude table holding an array of smithing tools.

The Pict controlled Broch with a neck lock while two of the women held onto Boudica's arms. The smith placed the girl's cuffed wrist against a cold, rusty anvil. Then he brought up a hammer and chisel to strike at the cuff's rivet. The rivet broke after just two blows.

With a wrench, the metal worker opened the cuff, freeing Boudica's hand. The women urged the girl from the anvil. Glancing back, the princess saw that Broch's shackle was also being removed.

Boudica had to walk ahead of the women into a simple open-fronted bathhouse. The tribal women stripped the prisoner of her filthy shift and held her nude while the third woman climbed onto a wooden bench holding a pot of cold water. She poured the contents over the girl's head and shoulders. The Brigantean reacted with a yowl as she was drenched. The other women scrubbed her skin with rags, but that did not end Boudica's ordeal. She had to endure two more cold pots and two more scrubbings.

Next, the women took towels from a stack and wiped the shivering maiden dry. Afterward, they ran a crude comb through her hair.

The women broke her snarls with hard pulls, but had to cut the worst snags with small, sharp knives. Then the Pictish females made their prisoner sit on the bench and brought up a tray holding primitive women's cosmetics. Using paint held in tiny clay vessels, they colored the maid's face in the manner favored by Pictish brides.

When she was made up, one woman took a red linen shawl from her shoulders and draped it around Boudica's waist as a hip wrap. Last, the girl was given a better pair of clean sandals for her feet. When taken outside again, Boudica made hand signs to tell them she wanted her breasts covered. The Picts only laughed as they dragged her into the night.

They arrived at the door of Goddeu's lodge. A Gallic warrior, his long sword hanging scabbarded at his waist, stood sentry. The serving women pushed Boudica's face against the closed door. When the guard shouted an announcement of the princess' arrival, a mumbled reply from indoors bade them to enter. A Black Goat serving boy drew the door open and the Pictish women nudged their half-dressed charge across the threshold.

Goddeu, in a dark house robe, stood in the center of the room observing the girl's entry. He used a right-hand motion to dismiss both his servant and the Pictish women. These exited the lodge with swift steps and the door guard pulled the portal closed, affording privacy to the Black Goat and his slave.

"Well, my fair one, you clean up very well," said the tall, goat-bearded druid. His eyes were lively and his smile smug.

Boudica, holding her hands over her bare breasts, searched the room for something with which to cover herself.

"No," Goddeu said. "Do not be modest. Modesty and beauty have no common ground. Take your hands away so I may feast my eyes on your loveliness."

Boudica's face flushed hot and she made a dry swallow, but didn't obey his words.

"You blush," Goddeu observed, "but bashfulness is a symptom of vanity." Goddeu, stepping closer, touched her slender hands. He drew her wrists apart as she stood with her teeth clenched. Boudica wanted to strike him, but for Broch's sake, she couldn't risk provoking his anger.

The Estrangorean maiden noticed an ornate dagger resting on a shelf next to a bed. Part of her urged her to seize it and slay the man, but an inner voice warned her to forebear. The blade in plain sight could be a test, and if she failed it, Goddeu might punish both her and Broch. She was trained to fight like a man, but here she could only fight as a woman.

Stepping back, the druid admired her beauty. The girl's head swam with mortification.

Goddeu retrieved a sizable towel from a small table. Re-approaching Boudica, he draped it over her shoulders. "I know you speak the truth about being freeborn," he said. "A slave your age would not be so shy."

"I-I *am* freeborn, sire," she affirmed.

"Many people become slaves," Goddeu said. "It is no disgrace. Such things occur and one must deal with them."

"My laird—" Boudica began.

"Call me 'master,' " he instructed her.

She swallowed hard. "Master—m-may…"

"Shhhh," he said. "Have you watched how slave girls behave?"

"Y-Yes, master."

"How so?"

"There are slave women in my father's home."

"I'm pleased to hear that. All you need to do is behave like your father's servant girls do."

Her glance became a dazed stare.

"In your father's house, do not the pretty slave girls look at the floor when they address their master?"

Swallowing hard, Boudica dropped her anxious gaze. After a moment of quiet, she said, "Master, may I ask a question?"

"Not immediately. First, tell me, lovely, what should I call you? I wish not to call you 'Mudlark' any longer. You are too lovely for that. Is there any slave name that you'd prefer to assume?" he asked.

"My name is Boudica," she stated, her gaze still fixed on her toes.

"That means 'victory,' which is a fine name for a free woman. But is it appropriate for a slave?"

Another quiet moment passed.

"*Oen!*" he pronounced. Boudica knew the word meant "lamb." "Would that name suit you?"

The princess flinched but did not wish to start a dispute. "Yes, Master; it is a good name."

"Very well then, Oen, you may ask the question you have."

Boudica drew in a nervous breath. "Master, the boy who was captured with me… What will… happen to him?"

"If you want to discuss him, he must be important to you. Do you have a special interest in the boy?"

"No," she replied. "I have no special feelings for the boy."

"Are you so indifferent, then, that his death would not upset you?"

She looked up, blurting: "No! Please, Master!"

Goddeu smiled once more in his superior way and placed his left hand on her right shoulder. "Because you are young and afraid, I wish to be gentle with you," he said. "A slave must never refuse a free man, especially not her master."

"Forgive me, Master," Boudica said.

"That's better, except that you must cease to use the term 'I.' It is an improper word on the lips of a slave. Only free people may refer to themselves as 'I.' Or was it different in your father's house?"

Boudica glanced down again. "No, it was not—Master."

"It is custom. A slave has no human identity. The world prefers it this way, sadly. Should you not say, 'Oen apologizes, Master'?"

Boudica almost shouted in indignation, but fighting down the impulse she said, "Oen apologizes, Master."

"Oen is forgiven," Goddeu said. "Now, tell me your concern about the young man."

"It is…" Boudica paused, trying to speak as he wanted her to speak. "Oen wishes to ensure the boy's happiness because he is a friend. Though I couldn't compel respect, he was respectful. I had no reward to offer, but he was always kind. When we found food, he shared it with… Oen… He did not keep most of it for himself."

"The harper seems to be a fine lad. How else was he kind to you?"

"He… he often spoke to Oen. He kept her from always being sad and afraid."

"Does this matter?" asked the priest. "Should not a servant always see to the needs of a master—even a free servant working on hire?"

"Yes, Master. But it is important because, though he was a servant, he became Oen's friend."

"Should he have done that? Is it not impudent for a low person to treat his master's daughter like a friend?"

"No, Master. A friend's company is better than a servant's."

"That may be so. I am glad he could be your friend when you needed a friend. I might be very well disposed to him, given his kindness toward my lamb. I will happily treat him well if Oen desires to be my devoted servant. Does she wish that?"

"Yes, Master," Boudica said. She avoided asking what being a 'devoted servant' meant. If he told her, and she agreed to it, her promise would become a trap for her. She believed a promise should be kept, but honoring such a promise would make her less free.

"Tell me, what is making your friend sad or uncomfortable?" Goddeu asked.

Boudica inhaled and exhaled. "He is kept in chains. He went from free to captive. Oen begs her master to set him free. If my master is kind to the harper, Oen will be his good slave."

"And what is a good slave?"

"My master will instruct me on the qualities of a good slave."

"That's true," the druid acknowledged. "But your request is large. Suppose I refuse his release? Will Oen then behave like a poor slave?"

"No, master!"

"Then what difference does it make whether I treat your friend well or badly if Oen will be a good slave either way?"

"I don't know, master." No, that was not a useful answer, Boudica realized. She tried again. "Oen asks this because knowing she has a kind master would make her happy."

"If I released the fellow, would my lamb miss him and seek to run away and join him?"

"No, Oen would not!" she declared.

"What is the harper's name?"

"Broch, Master."

"Why is he called a badger?"

"Oen does not know. She has never asked."

"How is Broch feeling at this moment?"

"He is well, but no one can be happy chained in a cold shed."

"We can treat Oen's friend better than that. But first, we must see if Oen is truly sweet-natured and gentle. The more my fondness for Oen grows, the more I shall wish to make her smile."

"Yes, Master," Boudica whispered. She lacked a counterargument. Goddeu had given her his answer, and no master would suffer a slave who nagged or argued. She feared for Broch's safety, but also her own.

At that silent moment, Goddeu began stroking his lamb's warm breasts. She had to accept his touch and wondered what he would require of her next.

The druid suggested moving Broch to a warmer place if he didn't like the cold shed. "We might even unchain the lad and permit him to walk around. Would Oen care for that?"

"Yes, Master!"

"Fine. But for the moment, I am thirsty." The arch-druid crossed to a chair and sat down. He pointed to a wine pot on the table. "Pour one of those cups full, dear one, and then serve me as your father liked to be served by his favorite slave."

"Yes, Master."

"Begin."

Boudica crossed to the pot, a roundish vessel of glazed clay decorated with unattractive stick-like images. The maid stood close to the dagger, but her instinct warned against looking at it.

The degree of her enslavement went beyond a single man's desire to control her; his will was supported by a system. Even if she could strike and kill Goddeu, it would only lead to her death by torture. The druid's followers might also take out their wrath on Broch. The wisest choice was to be obedient and bide her time.

Boudica carried the cup to Goddeu, imitating the walk and mannerisms of a Brythonic slave girl. She sank to her knees before the seated man, holding her elbows in an appropriate position and keeping her glance low. The druid took the cup from her and put it to his lips.

"You serve well," he said, wiping his lips with the back of his hand. "What other skills does my Oen possess? The art of the loom, perhaps?"

"A little, Master," she admitted. She chose not to mention her sword and knife proficiency.

"Are merchants' daughters in Britain taught to dance?" Goddeu asked. "Most free Gallic women dance."

"Yes, Master, Oen dances," the princess replied. Court women danced before guests. All of Britain knew that Igraine, the high king Caratacos' mother, was admired for her dancing skill.

"Oen likes to dance, Master," she said. "At home, she often wished that she had a better teacher than the one provided."

"Delightful! We shall find a fine dance teacher for you," the arch-Druid promised. "Arise now and show me a dance that you know."

Nodding, the girl got to her feet and took the towel from around her shoulders to use in her dance. Stepping to the center of the room, she asked, "May Oen begin?"

The seated man nodded.

Boudica raised her arms and stepped into her dance, using the towel as dancers used veils to emphasize their flowing movements. Goddeu began clapping his hands, providing her with a rhythm akin to a drummer's beat.

After a few minutes, he said, "Enough. Your grace pleases me very much. I seldom find tall girls attractive, but you are the exception. I know a Roman of high dignity. If I invited him to dine with us some evening and you entertained him, I think he would be charmed. Because your friend is a musician, he can no doubt provide us with a melody. Would Oen care for that?"

"Yes, very much so!" Boudica said. The maid forced a smile, calculating that a smile would please Goddeu.

It occurred to the Brigantean girl that life was like a dance. One worked one's way through a dance one step at a time, its many small parts gradually creating a whole.

Also, no matter how long it lasted, it had an ultimate ending.


Pellinor's desire to attack Caer Draig seemed to harden in the face of dissuasion. Simon opposed the idea—though, ironically, Pellinor's plan resembled Simon's. The old soldier proposed strategies for taking down the druid leaders at the outset of the fight. But no one put forward any good idea for creating an assassination trap.

Simon was not in a suitable position to argue for an alternate victory strategy. The Britons saw him as an outsider, in both his origin and outlook. Mog Ruith backed most of his opinions, but the druid was himself a foreigner. As for the young bravos around Pellinor, they were spoiling for a fight, as was usual with young warriors.

Instead of ruling out the plan, which would only annoy Pellinor, the Samaritan did the next best thing. He offered ideas about improving the strategy for attack. By degrees, Simon's primary idea became central to Pellinor's battle plan.

The dragon hunters remained encamped for a full day, working out an evolving stratagem. The lost hours benefited Simon, affording him additional time to regain his full health and vigor.

Rising before the sun, Pellinor's warriors and Mog Ruith's druids mounted up and stole in closer to Caer Draig. Near Brynymeir Hill, they concealed a horse camp. The attack plan did not call for mounted men.

In darkness, Simon and fifteen others crept close to the cliff-door entrance into the labyrinth, awaiting the hour to begin.

It was a clear night. While the warriors observed the stars for the appointed hour, a disconcerting event occurred.

A dozen large wagons clattered toward them from the hill. Despite the moon's dimness, the men discerned canvas-covered wagon boxes. The warriors asked Lamorak for permission to attack, but he denied them. Any digression from the agreed plan would make carrying it out more risky. The ruckus of a fight might eliminate the element of surprise later on. Realizing that their flank was vulnerable, the defenders would strengthen it, forcing the attack to be abandoned.

Hidden, the men watched the wagons vanish into the night. Lamorak ordered an advance on the cliffside hut once the hour had come. The guards inside, taken unawares, offered only a confused defense and were subdued.

Unfortunately, the captured Picts refused to yield any useful information. Lamorak, not at all a patient man, started putting them to death one at a time, expecting someone to become an informer. None spoke, and all died. Simon was opposed to killing prisoners, but the stakes were high. The attack plan was short-handed already, and soldiers could not be spared to guard prisoners. The Samaritan had no choice but to accept the harsh judgment of his group commander.

Simon saw war like a gladiator fight. The question of success and failure, life or death, made even good men do evil things. Simon of Gitta had hated gladiatorial servitude, and likewise disliked military procedure.

For now, the battle was looming. The Samaritan knew that the worst still lay ahead.

# Night Attack

## CHAPTER XXII

Two Britons were left behind to observe the cliff door and keep it barricaded to prevent enemies from escaping. Lamorak gave Simon of Gitta the go-ahead. It was time for the plan to be carried out.

Simon's tactics involved scaling the cliff above the door and gaining access to the fort through its lightly watched rear side. Simon's role in the plan was to lead the volunteers in scaling the treacherous rock face. The Samaritan's rock-climbing skills exceeded those of anyone else present. The cliffs that Simon exhaustively practiced upon high above Persepolis' ruins had been formidable indeed.

The Samaritan's intended aim was not far removed from the Greek ploy at Troy. This time, however, the heroes would not enter the walled city inside a wooden horse. Instead, they would invade the guarded town by the daunting climb up a backside cliff. Mog Ruith had cited this as a weakly defended point.

With the man from the East in the lead, the thirteen bravos began their perilous ascent. After climbing for an hour, Simon heard the last scream of a falling man. Simon sighed and continued climbing.

After another half hour, Simon saw a weedy rock edge above him. The wooden stockade wall rose above it. The five- and six-inch diameter tree trunks were narrowly set back from the drop-off. The builders had deliberately made the edge incredibly narrow. It offered a rock climber only a precarious ledge to stand on. The slightest misstep or a mild onset of vertigo would betray a man to death.

Simon heard no sound to show the wall above was heavily guarded. He heard no footsteps, sneezes, wind-breaking, shuffling noises, nor the low whispers of a conversation. It was a section of the wall that could be easily defended from within. The Logresians' success depended on it having almost no defenders at all.

As climb leader, Simon had to loop a rope over one or more of the pointed stakes composing the stockade wall. But he couldn't do it while clinging to an almost vertical rock wall. He didn't think it could be brought off by anyone not standing on that appallingly narrow ledge above.

Simon took the piece of rope he had been carrying and tied it around his waist. He knotted its other end around a jutting boulder, in case he should fall. A final, short climb allowed him to put his strong fingers between the wooden pales. His hold enabled him to draw himself up so he could place his knees on the narrow ledge. Still holding on, he used his arms' strength to draw himself into an upright position.

Balancing on a ledge just over a foot wide, he leaned against the log wall. In such a position, even turning around was dangerous. With the utmost care, the adventurer pivoted, forced to release his steadying hold on the stakes. The rock climber now stood rigidly erect, looking across a valley so intensely dark that there seemed to be nothing in the world except the dim stars of a misted sky.

Simon didn't have the rope he needed to finish scaling the stockade barrier. Another man was carrying the cord—and that warrior was Torr, Pellinor's youngest son.

The boy understood his responsibility. He swung the end of his rope high for the dexterous Simon to catch.

The Samaritan snatched the cord out of mid-air. Now that he had it, he had to perform a difficult maneuver. He had to throw the looped rope backward over his head. If it caught on something, he would be able to climb it to the top of the wall. Any wrong shifting of his weight, or an unusually strong puff of wind, might topple him from the narrow ledge. The safety rope he wore around his waist might save him, or it might not. One man had already died on this climb; he might become the second.

Simon whispered a Baal prayer and made his cast. The line found no purchase and dropped back, its bristles raking his face as it fell. Slowly, tensely, Simon regathered the cord. After meditation and several deep breaths, the trained mountaineer attempted his second toss.

Again it failed.

The frustrated man now rested, trying to focus on his concentration, his balance, and his nerves. If any of those failed, his effort would fail, and he might die. Finally, with the utmost focus, Simon made his third try. This time the line caught and stayed up. It was supported by something, but from his viewpoint, it wasn't possible to determine if it could bear a person's weight.

"Don't climb yet, Merlin!" warned Torr. "I can tug the rope and snap it to see if it'll stay in place!"

"Do it, boy!" Simon said. "Send a wave through it, but be careful not to lose your balance and fall."

"I'll try."

The boy put some weight on the rope. When it wouldn't budge, he snapped it to send a wave along its length. The lifeline still held firm. Simon was encouraged.

"Stand fast, wizard," the young Briton said, "I want to give it an even harder snap!"

"Yes, boy, try that!"

Torr repeated his action, but this time the hemp line fell loose. The disappointed Samaritan grimaced. The high-stakes gamble was yielding no results.

His fourth toss again hooked on something.

Torr, as before, tested the rope. After multiple hard pulls and shakes, the line held firm.

"Torr, what do you think?" the adventurer asked.

"It feels pretty good, Merlin," the lad said with little conviction.

"How good is 'pretty good'?" Simon gambled.

"I don't know. It's too dark to see what it looks like."

Simon gambled. He jerked on the rope he held, tentatively at first. When it stayed in place, he repeated the effort more forcefully. But this time, his move made him lose his balance. His foot slipped into the open air, but the hemp line he held arrested his fall. By grappling it, he got back into place.

"Boy," whispered Simon, "if I slip and fall on top of you, it could be bad. I want you to lash yourself to something firm."

"There's a rock knob here. I'll wrap my arms around it."

"Good," the adventurer said. "If the line holds me, I'll climb to the top. Don't let anyone climb up until I signal it's safe. Listen for the snipe's call I'll make when I think the rope is secure. The call will sound like this…"

Simon did a staccato imitation of the night bird's clucking song. "When you hear that," he stated, "the men should come up one by one."

Simon climbed the rope hand over hand. Grabbing the wall, he released the rope and then clutched the wall with both hands. Maintaining a two-handed grasp, he swung his legs to the other side of the wall and hung there, suspended. Simon could see almost nothing of the dark village. He could only hope there was solid ground below him.

The climber ran his hands over the rope, trying to discover how firmly it was held. Just to be sure, he added more knots to ensure it was safe for the climbers to use.

That done, he let himself drop to the ground. The solid ground felt reassuring. To signal the men, he filled his lungs with air and produced the snipe's call that Torr needed to hear.

Simon stood firm at the foot of the wall until Torr clambered over it. After him came a man named Ivor. The Samaritan ordered the two warriors to stay put and assist their fellow warriors in scaling the stockade.

Simon walked swiftly into the darkness, smelling the unpleasant odor of the town. He knew it was the diluted stench leaking from the labyrinth.

He saw the village huts, close together, ahead of him. The alleys between them were so narrow that a broad-shouldered man would have to walk sideways.

Simon was navigating the tight passage when he heard sounds behind him. "Who's there?" he whispered into the dark. Torr answered.

"I told you to help the others!" Simon said.

"I know. But I asked Morfran to stay and help Ivor. Merlin, what's next?" the boy asked.

"Go back to the others. Wait for your brother and then follow his orders."

"He's always ordering me. I'd rather help you!" the young warrior said.

This was no time to argue. Simon resumed his advance and came to the end of the alleyway. Once on open ground, he saw more huts and walls. The few people then abroad were, he assumed, night sentries.

Continuing along behind the huts, he entered an open area where he could see the gatehouse, illuminated with several torches.

Pictish warriors were pacing backward and forward in front of it, while some sat atop its roof, surveying the outer walls and the dark hill road beyond.

Pellinor's plan required Lamorak and his men to enter Caer Draig and take command of the gatehouse. They were then to hold the gates open until Pellinor's forces entered.

Simon told Torr, "Lad, go tell the men to hurry. If we move in a mass, we'll outnumber the sentries posted at the gatehouse!"

The youth nodded and darted away. As Simon waited for the other men to catch up, a hue and cry arose. He guessed the Britons had been spotted, and the battle was going to start at any moment!

He heard running and then saw his men emerge from between huts. He also heard every Pictish voice in the fort yowling alarms. Simon yelled: "I'm going to the gate! Follow me!"

Simon launched himself at a dead run, his naked gladius leading the way.

The ex-gladiator slammed into the defending sentries like a fox leaping into a cluster of hens. His surprise attack wounded two men, but he could scarcely draw a breath before their Pictish comrades were on him like a wave. While he hacked, dodged, and parried, his Brythonic followers took the battling tribesmen from the flank. The clangor of iron weapons rang on every side.

The Pictish shouting continued. Those on the gatehouse roof resisted by throwing spears at the invaders. Once they had disarmed themselves, they climbed to the ground and joined in the combat.

Simon battled the enemy with ferocious intensity. The Picts gave way, and he broke into the gatehouse's interior. An oaken bar, holding the double-leafed gate shut, was guarded by two spear-wielding savages. The

Levantine warrior dodged the attack and defended himself while urging the Britons onward. "Open the gates!" he cried.

The Logresians shouldered their way into the gatehouse. The outnumbered Picts who couldn't flee were killed. Then the situation was reversed. The Britons deployed to defend the gatehouse against a mob of hastily armed Picts arriving one by one from their beds.

With the foe tenuously held back, Simon lifted the gate doors' pivot-held crossbeam. Once he had shoved the gate leaves open with his braced shoulder, he snatched a torch from the wall. Under the cloak of night, he signaled Pellinor with the flames of a brand.

Without waiting for a response, the former Thracian gladiator plunged back into the melee. The Britons fiercely defended Pellinor's entryway, yet the opposition's strength was bearing them down.

Amid the wild fight, Simon caught the sound of running boots, but couldn't afford to glance back. With the suddenness of a lightning strike, a strong flash came from behind. The burst dazzled the Pictish warriors. They staggered backward under the weight of Pellinor's howling reinforcements.

The Samaritan chose to dart away and search for the kidnapped princess. He slashed through the Picts' broken line and, once on clear ground, he ran pell-mell into the darkness ahead.


A group of Black Goats beat on Goddeu's lodge door shouting about the Brythonic incursion. Their master let them in and threw on a cloak. Oen was sitting up on her bedroll with an excited expression. The arch-druid took her by the arm and dragged her outside.

Because of her protests and struggles, the Master Black Goat pushed her into the arms of his underling Erbin. "Ow!" the steward cried out as the princess kicked his shins and bit him.

"To the temple!" Goddeu commanded. Erbin did his best to make the balky girl keep up with the group, controlling her by twisting her right arm behind her back while holding a handful of her light blonde hair.

The Black Goats encountered no enemies on their way to the temple. Once there, Goddeu fist-pounded the fane's double doors, demanding admission in a cult language. The portal swung open before the priests.

"Bhort!" Goddeu called past the Wyrm servants into the interior gloom. "Where in Harag Kolathos are you!?"

An excited Wyrm druid of a lesser rank answered him. "Master Goddeu! Take heart! The leader is speaking a great incantation against the enemy. He will subdue them! Fear not!"

"I'm angry, not afraid!" the Gaul said sharply. "Lead me to your master! I can add my power to his."

The agitated priest agreed. "Yes, Master, but make no sound. It may break our brothers' trance state."

"I know how incantations are done!" Goddeu declared. "Show us the way!"

Boudica continued her struggle with Erbin. "Warriors! Here we are!" she cried out. Goddeu marked her and raised his voice. "Gag the minx, Erbin, and don't let her slip away."

The Black Goats walked at speed after the Wyrm guide, who led them into a large chamber crowded with Wyrm Druids.

Goddeu, though angry at Bhort's failure to protect the village, knew he dared not interrupt the arch-wizard. The spell-shouting Master Wyrm and his senior druids circled a hazy incense burner. Above them loomed a grotesque idol of Gathanothog depicted like a mass of tree roots.

"I call upon you, gods of the Fomorog, Sacred Masters, givers of power and guidance!" Bhort called out. "Succor your obedient slaves! Guide us through this perilous night! Help us, masters, so we may complete the labors you've given us! Empower us in the name of your eternal glory! *Nenalmy htys ny h'cwe!*"

Bhort's face streamed with sweat. He reeled, almost ready to fall—a circumstance that the magic-wise Goddeu did not wonder at. Finally, the Wyrm sorcerers stopped howling their incantations.

"What will happen?" asked Goddeu.

"You will see," the Master Wyrm said breathlessly. "But mark me, we must stay hidden until the invaders are obliterated. Trapped men are dangerous men!"

"Hide where?!" Goddeu asked impatiently.

"We have a place. Follow us!" said the Master Wyrm.

Bhort and his underlings led them through a door to a hallway leading to the far side of the temple. They entered a large room decorated with mystical symbols. At its center was an altar maide from rough-dressed stone and standing on a large dais. It took the united strength of two Wyrms to open a decorative wall shield mounted on hinges. Behind the shield was a narrow recess where a lever was concealed. The priests pulled it in unison.

The group heard a creaking mechanism come to life inside the wall. The altar and its dais began to travel over a concealed track. The displacement revealed a flight of stairs descending into darkness. From it, warm air gushed, odious air that the Black Goats were not prepared for. Goddeu recoiled and covered his offended nose.

"Let us go down," said Bhort.

"Down into what?" the Gallic arch-druid asked.

# The Dragon at the Gate

## CHAPTER XXIII

Simon navigated the shadowy, perplexing village until he arrived at the park Mog Ruith had mentioned. After spotting the arch-druid's lodge, he deemed killing Goddeu his immediate responsibility. He'd never met Goddeu in Gaul, but supposed the Master Black Goat was likely much like the loathsome Ferchobhar, his predecessor.

The adventurer discovered the lodge door was open and unlocked. He opened the door with a swift kick and his gladius raised, but the large room was empty. Simon searched the premises but found nothing of interest. A pool of spilled wine on the floor showed that the house had not been empty for long. Frustrated, the swordsman returned outdoors and crossed to the adjacent shed.

Pounding on its pinewood door, he shouted, "Is anyone in there?!"

"Who is it?" answered a young man.

Simon remembered the voice. "*Broch!* Is that you?! I'm Simon of the Merlins! Who else is in there?"

"No one!" the boy answered. "The druid has taken Boudica!"

Simon didn't know the name "Boudica" and wasn't curious. Asking no questions, he examined the padlock and decided the mechanism would give him no trouble. His bodkin, applied to the keyhole, made the mechanism click.

As the Samaritan pushed the door open, the youth called to him out of the dark, "I'm chained to this timber!"

Simon conjured a luminous hand and approached the man. Unlocking the shackle was easier than unlocking the door. The boy groaned in pain as he stood, his knees stiff and sore.

"Thank the gods, Merlin!" Broch declared.

"Where is Voada?" the Easterner demanded.

"The druid took her. I heard her protesting. He was compelling her to go with him."

"They must have gone to the temple," Simon guessed.

"I'll go with you."

"It's dangerous."

"Once I get a weapon, I'll be dangerous, too!" said the harper.

*Why do young people never listen?* Simon thought. He exited the shed, but Broch kept up with him, despite his limp.

Flames engulfed the village. Simon thought Pellinor was using the fires as a distraction; most defenders had families and homes at stake.

While seeking the temple Mog Ruith described, Simon stayed away from the fighting. He was as determined as ever to get rid of Goddeu and Bhort.

Torr staggered out of the billowing smoke, coughing hard. One hand covered his mouth and nose, while the other clutched his blade.

"Never surprise an armed man, boy," Simon warned the lad, "not unless you want a panicky fool to run a sword through your guts."

"Merlin!" cried the young warrior. "Lamorak needs you! There's a dragon at the gate!"

A dragon?

Simon hadn't seen this coming.


Amid the strangling billows, Simon saw both Britons and Picts scattering in fear. From behind them came an ominous roar, like a Nile crocodile's. The Samaritan saw an enormous lizard's tail disappearing behind a cloud of smoke.

"Stay back!" he bawled to his young companions and darted after the unnatural thing. The ex-gladiator's smoke-teared eyes glimpsed the outline of an enormous head swaying. The ground before him was littered with dead and injured, most of them Pictish warriors.

Simon heard timbers cracking behind the screen of smoke. The rampaging monster's strength and weight must have been tremendous. Facing even one dragon presented a daunting fight.

The Samaritan sighted men sheltering in the mouth of an alleyway, and one of them was helmless, smoke-stained Pellinor. The old war chief was leaning his weary bones back against a hut wall and coughing.

"Pellinor!" Simon shouted.

"Merlin!" the breathless warrior called back. We can't defeat both the creature and Picts at the same time."

"The Picts are running, too!" said the ex-gladiator. "The demon can't tell friend from foe, or it doesn't care!"

"Merlin!" Torr yelled. The giant lizard was veering in their direction. The Britons with Pellinor jammed themselves through the narrow alleyways to evade certain death. Simon and his companions absconded likewise.

The fugitives entered a wider spot between the huts and rallied there. Some Brythonic warriors jammed their spear butts into the ground to form a barbed hedge against the dragon. Simon doubted material weapons could fend off an entity that was materialized from spiritual energy.

Torr, at the Samaritan's side, threw his iron-tipped spear. It struck the beast's scaly thigh but bounced off, doing no visible harm. As the warriors braced for the clash, the creature glided away in another direction.

Simon said to Torr, "I have an idea!"

"Will you use your spells?" asked Pellinor's youngest.

Simon shook his head. "No, listen…"

Laird Pellinor's rasping voice broke in: "By the gods! Use magic, Merlin! That thing has harder armor than a Roman legionary!"

"I'm only half-trained in magic!" confessed Simon. "We need real druids to vie with that thing."

"Where are they?" the old warrior shouted back. "The Wren was leading them against the Picts. They may not know there's a dragon!"

"I've got an idea!" said Simon. "The Wyrm leaders must be holed up in the temple; if we can make the dragon follow us there, maybe we provoke it to bring the fane crashing down."

"I think I can find the temple!" declared Broch. "They dragged us past it when they brought us in." He described its location.

"Good!" said Simon. "Pellinor, I want you to divide your men into two different groups. Have one group enrage the beast and make it chase them toward the temple." After adding a few additional details, he said, "I could use a man who's quick on his feet."

"I'm quick!" said Torr.

"No!" Pellinor exclaimed. To Simon, the hard old soldier sounded like a protective father.

"It's your call, Pellinor," said the adventurer. "But we need your best warriors for the most dangerous work. I vow I'll protect the boy as best I can."

"Say yes, Father!" Torr implored.

"Do it then, damn it!" Pellinor answered through clenched teeth.

Following Simon's plan, the war chief sent out his warriors. The first group set off to hunt the beast as soon as they got their orders. The second group followed Broch toward the temple.

Simon and Torr raced along on the flank of the first group. When the Britons found the dragon amid the smoke, they cast a spear volley at it. Many of the throws struck true, but none inflicted noticeable damage.

The incited creature lumbered toward the offending detachment, which turned and ran. Simon and Torr continued after the dragon while keeping out of its line of sight.

When fleeing Britons led the abomination past the established ambush point, Samaritan shouted, "Now!" and the second column burst from cover. Their volley of missiles redoubled the monster's fury, and it veered after these new antagonists. The assailed warriors made for the temple, with Broch leading the way. Meanwhile, Simon and Torr continued the chase.

Houses crumbled, and villagers fled out of the way of the dragon's path. Simon shouted, "Now!" and he and Torr sprinted into the creature's field of vision.

Torr made the monster's right eye his mark, hoping it to be a vulnerable point. But the javelin struck its jowl instead, wresting another roar from the dragon.

The smoke thinned as they neared the temple, and Simon could see the palisade wall that ran behind it. An alternate idea flashed into the Samaritan's mind.

"Fall back!" he shouted to Pellinor's son while Simon let the behemoth catch a good look at him, waving his arms and making meaningless ejaculations at the top of his lungs.

The roaring beast followed like a rampaging elephant, slowed by obstructions. At the last possible moment, the arena-trained fighter sprang out of the abomination's trajectory as it lurched past him.

The dragon slammed into the wooden wall, shattering its pales like rotten wood. That section of the stockade fell outward, to be left hanging over the cliff edge like a wooden ramp leading nowhere.

But the dragon stopped just in time. While its hind claws maintained a secure grip on the solid ground, the creature sought to pull itself away from the drop.

Simon took up a broken pale and shoved it under the beast's rear left foot, manipulating it like a lever. With all his strength he was trying to break the saving grip of one of the dragon's hind feet. "Help me!" the Samaritan yelled to those around him.

Torr leaped in, adding his youthful strength to Simon's. The beast's thrashing tail flailed like a slaver's whip, forcing both man and boy to duck away. Unable to approach the monster, they faced it with swords only. The monster held on to a post that was still sturdy and inched its way back toward safety. Simon looked on, unsure how to save the situation.

But the Samaritan's call had summoned Pellinor's warriors out of the darkness, with Broch hurrying on ahead of them. The harper lad snatched up a piece of wreckage and attacked the dragon. The next thing he knew, Pellinor's men were on both sides of him. But for all the warriors could do, they might as well have fled away. The dragon's strength exceeded that of all its determined opponents combined.

A brilliant flash of light, followed by a tremendous crash, impacted the post with immense force. Wood chips filled the air like a locust swarm. Men sprang away as the energy bolt destroyed the beast's essential support structure.

With nothing to hold on to, the dragon pitched forward. The supporting spikes were ripped out of the flimsy wreckage. With a yowl, the dragon toppled forward over the cliff edge amid a shower of broken wall pieces.

Above, the men saw little through the dark, yet they heard the creature's body bouncing off the rocks and ledges as it fell down the cliff. With bated breaths, they waited to hear the dragon's body thump against the rocks below.

But that sound was never heard.


Mog Ruith caught up with Simon.

"Was that your magical bolt?" the breathless Samaritan asked the big druid.

"It was a quick shot, but a lucky one," Ruith stated. "The spell drained me dry. But do you suppose a materialized spirit can be killed by a physical fall?"

"I don't know," Simon said. "We came here to slay men, not dragons. If we don't kill the arch-druids, the Picts will not give up. There's too many of them and we can't fend them off forever!"

"So where are the cannibal druid leaders?" Pellinor demanded from across the alley.

Mog Ruith gestured toward the temple. "If they're not inside the fane, your guess is as good as mine!"

Simon raised his sword. "Let's peer inside their box!" The adventurer knew that the immediate elimination of the Wyrm leadership was essential to the success of the mission. Otherwise, the Picts would celebrate a victory.

# THE FLIGHT IN THE DARK

## CHAPTER XXIV

With the dragon fight raging, the senior druids of Caer Draig remained closeted underground. Goddeu and his Gauls felt nauseous, waiting under the Hill of the Dead for news of the dragon attack.

"What is this grotto?" the Master Black Goat asked the Master Wyrm. "Is it your sewer?"

"It is the glory of our cult! We conduct some of our most sacrosanct rites in this place," said Bhort.

"It smells worse than an outhouse!" Goddeu complained. "What do you keep in these tunnels?"

"Reserve such questions for a moment less perilous than this one. If the village warriors fail, we shall be compelled to abandon the hill."

The foul air was giving Goddeu a headache. Every part of him craved an explanation for this underground's purpose, yet he, a cautious man, understood power dynamics well. He distrusted Bhort's wisdom, yet this wasn't the moment to begin a quarrel.

"So why are we just standing here?" he finally asked the Master Wyrm, keeping his tone mild.

"If the situation goes poorly, we can retreat from this sanctuary and regroup. We will be able to rebuild our forces at a different location."

"You have a safe spot to retreat to?"

"Most assuredly," said the Master Wyrm.

An echoing shout came from the stairwell. "Master!" a youthful voice was calling. "The holy beast has been thrown over the cliff!"

"Impossible!" Bhort reacted. "A Great One cannot be conquered by any feeble human weapon or spell!"

A rapidly descending acolyte from the temple descended into view. "It is true, Master! We watched it happen from the balcony."

"How did they overcome the dragon?!" Bhort demanded.

"A magical bolt caused it to plunge over the cliff. The attackers now batter at the temple doors. What should we do?"

"How goes the fight?"

"We can't tell. It is all smoke and confusion."

"A thousand curses!" declared the Master Wyrm. "We must leave here before the enemy finds his way down! We have several well-concealed refuges in the surrounding forests. We must wait out this battle hidden inside one of those! Friends, follow me!"

Goddeu grimaced, being against running and hiding. Perhaps Bhort had become despondent after exhausting his mana on the summoning spell, but what the fighting men most needed was leadership. Unfortunately, Bhort did not seem to be open to sensible arguments. It might ignite a row that the outnumbered Black Goats were not well situated to win. Bhort was in his power base with many defenders to call upon.

The Master Wyrm waved for his companions to follow him, and he began walking. Goddeu directed his followers to keep up with the Wyrms. The Gallic Druids were led along subterranean galleries, down stone-cut steps, and across a multiplicity of ramps. In a tunnel chiseled from the living rock, they found sickly people confined behind bars.

"These serve as food for the Dragon-Spirits," Bhort hastily explained. "They do not live long when fed upon by the Great Ones. It is because of the death loss that our warriors must continually raid for replacements."

Goddeu set his teeth. If Bhort was sacrificing lavishly, why had the gods allowed him to be attacked successfully? The Gaul wondered if the Wyrms had deceitfully enticed his Black Goats into an impending disaster.

"The outdoors are ahead," the Master Wyrm stated, continuing his fast-paced walk. Bhort brought the group to an exit door, which he ordered the posted guards to unbrace. The Picts attempted to follow the order, but the portal could not be budged.

"Open it!" Bhort shouted.

"We cannot, Master," said one sentry. "Something's obstructing the door."

"I can guess what's happened!" the Master Wyrm declared, scowling. "A spy entered and escaped from our labyrinth four days ago. It was he who brought back enemy warriors to attack us. No doubt a score of armed men wait to strike us dead now that our mana is depleted!"

"I disagree!" stated Goddeu. "If the attackers arrived in a large group, they would likely have left the door open to ambush us when we came out. There might be no guards. This would be the best exit for us if that's true! Let's use magic to break this door down!"

"That is only guesswork," protested Bhort. " 'Tis prudent to leave the labyrinth by a safer route, one that the spy couldn't have learned about." He used coaxing hand motions to urge those around him to follow. "We must move swiftly!"

Just then, Erbin yowled. Goddeu, wheeling about, saw his steward fall to his knees, clutching his breast. Everyone could see that Erbin's dagger was now clutched in Boudica's hand.

"You'll wish you hadn't done that, girl!" the Master Wyrm declared.

"And you'll wish you'd never been born, dog!" the princess answered back, holding up the blood-stained blade like a knife-fighter would hold it.

From Goddeu's palm, a glowing miasma flowed. It struck the Brigantean maid and knocked her off her feet. Two men immediately grabbed the maid, disarming her.

"Arrogant rebel!" Bhort exclaimed. "You will die slowly!"

"Nay!" said Goddeu. "Oen is my slave, and the man she's wounded is my servant. It stands with me to decide her fate."

Bhort scowled. "So, how will you punish her?"

"Punishment can wait! If you can lead us out of this ghastly excavation, you must do so swiftly," said the Master Black Goat.

Bhort didn't like to be defied, but he held his temper in check. "As you will," the Master Wyrm said through gritted teeth. "You are, of course, right about the girl's punishment. Follow and I will lead us all to safety!"


The Temple of Gathanothog was now under Simon and his companions' control. With swords drawn, they searched its rooms but found only a few cowering acolytes. Despite the invaders' demands, these young, green captives refused to divulge any information. Pellinor told his son Lamorak to make them speak. The two most defiant acolytes were subjected to beating immediately. One of the onlooking Wyrm youths yelped for mercy. Seizing the acolyte by his cowl, Lamorak subjected him to interrogation.

Simon was distracted by talking from an adjacent chamber. Supposing that newcomers had brought news of the battle outside, he followed the sounds into the antechamber. Several disarmed Roman officers were under guard there, and Mog Ruith was speaking.

"Be gracious with the prisoners," the druid was saying. "Let us extend courtesy to the honorably vanquished."

Lamorak entered the room behind Simon. "What information have these Roman dogs yielded?" he asked.

A smoke-stained Brythonic warrior answered. "We caught this Roman offal trying to flee through the front gate."

"If they displayed cowardice, why be angry with them?" advised Mog Ruith. "Are legionaries with no taste for fighting not our favorite type of Roman?"

Laughter erupted all around.

Ruith addressed Asiaticus directly: "Do you vow to submit yourselves to the authority of High King Arto?"

The senator grimaced. "We have no choice on that matter."

"In truth, you do not, Decimus Valerius. I thought you would have put up a stronger fight," remarked the druid.

"Oh, we can fight," Asiaticus answered, "but we find no stakes in this vile place worth fighting for."

"I would agree with you on that one," said the arch-druid.

Pellinor entered the room by its second door. Ruith suggested the high king should receive the surrendered men for justice, and they ought to be treated courteously until then.

Pellinor tossed his shoulders. "The old one can be pampered, I believe. We can probably gain a large ransom for his carcass."

"We're here on a diplomatic mission," Asiaticus informed the king of Avalon.

Pellinor looked unimpressed. "We know very well what you are. You're emissaries colluding with Brythonic traitors. You may have even lured them into treason. Arto will probably deal with you better than you deserve!"

"Please!" stated Broch. "Insulting prisoners is a waste of time! These insane Druids hold Princess Voada; we must rescue her!"

"Keep in your place, boy," warned Lamorak.

"You little know my place, warrior!" Broch declared fiercely. "Though I have been traveling in disguise, I am Prasutagos, son of Antedios, king of the Icenians of Eastland."

The crowd stopped muttering and listened.

"If true, why pretend to be a harper?" Simon asked pointedly.

A strange look on his face, the young man looked away. "Should we discuss such a minor matter now?"

Ruith smiled. "Word is, you've grown attached to the princess. I believe I smell wedding flowers in the air!"

"You will certainly smell them if I have my way," said Prasutagos.

"First Romans and now lovers!" snorted Pellinor. "Let's stop talking and start doing something!"

"How is the fight going outside, Garel?" Lamorak asked a warrior next to him.

"The Picts are many!" the Briton answered. "We've taken many losses. Most of our warriors have had to barricade themselves inside houses and huts. The enemy controls the gatehouse, and they face capture or death."

That started men talking, but Simon shouted over the mutter: "It will discourage the Picts if we kill or capturing Bhort."

"So where is Bhort?" demanded Lamorak.

Torr spoke up. "I heard the acolyte saying that the senior druids are seeking escape through the labyrinth, the one the Merlin told us about."

Simon nodded. "We've blocked one exit, yet other escape routes likely exist. We've accomplished nothing if they escape. These tunnels might provide the safest escape from this hill."

"Good! Let's do it!" said Pellinor. "Lamorak, take enough men and hunt down those scoundrels. I'll take the rest of our strength and give succor to as many of our men outside as possible. We'll join you below afterward!"

Pellinor and Lamorak quickly divided the manpower, and they parted ways. Simon followed Lamorak back to the talkative Wyrm acolyte. Simon demanded that the boy show them the way through the caverns, and to do it quickly.


More than a dozen men followed Lamorak into the fetid pits. With him were some Merlin druids, Simon, Mog Ruith, Prasutagos, and several Brythonic swordsmen.

The deeper the search party descended, the more repulsive the odor. They encountered no formidable defenders. The cowards they encountered were sty workers, not warriors.

Along the way, the Britons caught sight of the penned man-beasts and halted in astonishment.

"What are these creatures, exactly?" Simon demanded of his prisoner.

"We call them *bwyd y duwiau*," said the boy.

This translated as "the gods' food" in Brythonic.

"Are you saying that you Wyrms *eat* these appalling wretches?" Simon demanded.

The youth trembled. "Their flesh is favored by the Great Ones. They allow their faithful to partake of the divine food as well."

Simon considered stabbing the young cannibal in the heart, yet he harbored more contempt for these people than rage. He had seen what charismatic leaders could do to induce otherwise normal men and women to commit insane acts. And a cult controlled by demonic spirits was probably the hardest of all to resist. He wondered what portion of the Wyrms' following enjoyed "god-food."

"How did these degraded brutes come to be?" the adventurer demanded of the acolyte.

"T-The Great Ones created them thousands of years ago!" the boy stammered. "The cult preserves the breed in anticipation of the gods' return."

Simon had heard enough. "Hurry along," he said, trying to check an impulse to give the boy a beating. Shrill echoes sounded in the distance: "Help! We're…!"

"It's Voada!" exclaimed Prasutagos.

"Faster!" shouted Lamorak. "We have to overtake them!"

The Samaritan pushed their guide along ahead of himself. The youth was ably navigating the poorly lighted tunnel system. Simon remained wary. This fanatic boy might seek to lead them all into a trap.

Simon made out distant figures illuminated by blinking torches. Unlike the sty workers, these wore robes. No doubt they had seen Lamorak's warriors, too, since their pace suddenly quickened.

The acolyte suddenly halted. "They must not know I betrayed them!" he exclaimed. Simon, unsympathetic, gave him a hard shove forward.


Bhort had only seldom gone down into the further reaches of the pit, so he had commanded a sty servant to act as guide. Erbin was keeping up despite his wound, helped along by Black Goat servants.

Goddeu held fast to Boudica's wrist, despite her foot-dragging. Her defiance disappointed him. She had captivated him from the start. He thought he could eventually quell her hostility, if this day didn't crush them with disaster.

The Master Wyrm had been sending whatever guards and workers they had encountered so far to fight and delay the Brythonic warriors. But he'd given them no leaders from his entourage. Goddeu's estimation of Bhort himself as a leader had plunged very low. The Gallic druid could only hope that the Wyrms possessed an alternate power base somewhere, as he claimed. The Master Black Goat's optimism was sagging.

The Gaul had been unaware of the *bwyd y duwiau's* existence and found the idea difficult to stomach. In fairness, however, rumors had always reached the Black Goats that the Wyrms practiced ritual cannibalism. The Black Goats could not be choosy. They needed new allies since the Romans could not be trusted. The Wyrms appeared to be strongest among their limited choices. Distastefully, Goddeu's thoughts turned to the meat the Wyrms had been serving the Black Goats since they'd arrived at Caer Draig.

Bhort paused before a vaguely illuminated wooden door ahead. Goddeu wondered if it offered escape into the clean air of the night.

Of a sudden, the druids heard a reverberating echo in Brythonic: "Surrender, dogs, if you want to live past this hour!"

Goddeu gritted his teeth. Faced with the warriors' rage, surrender would be the same as suicide. Trials wouldn't spare any of them from condemnation.

"Get that door open!" the Master Wyrm bellowed to his servants. "Wyrms! Stand your ground! Protect your leaders! Protect the sacred mission!"

The Master Black Goat could only wonder how hard these Wyrm Druids would fight. They had shown no stomach for fighting the Britons above ground.

The next thing he knew, the dim tunnel flashed with a dazzling light and shuddered from a deafening thunderclap. The cavern walls shook and stalactites fell from the ceiling. Those druids and servants struck by the enemy-cast bolt lay strewn across the rock floor. Goddeu was himself staggered. He had received a painful shock from the bolt's backwash. He could only see spots.

Boudica, in front of him, had been shielded from the worst of the blast. She turned and struck her captor's groin. With Goddeu doubled up on the floor, the girl spun on her heels and dashed toward the Britons.

The infuriated Gallic wizard raised his hand, pointed at her back, and forced his mana to rise.

But the Black Goat Druid stopped himself from uttering the kill word. He didn't want to slay the girl he had found so damnably alluring.

The unsteady arch-druid got up and stumbled into the chill night. How sweet was the outside air! With his vision slowly clearing, he saw Bhort and his servants running away. He and his Black Goats dared not lose sight of them if they hoped to avoid a battle with the enraged enemy.

"Master!" one of his senior druids called to him, "Hurry!"

Before taking that advice, Goddeu stopped the two servants nearest him. "Help Erbin!" the arch-druid said. "Then follow us!"


Lamorak and his warriors bypassed the enemies littering the floor and followed the druids out into the night. By moonlight, the prince saw two black-robed men dragging away a wounded companion.

"Warriors!" Pellinor's son yelled. "Bring back those renegades!"

Simon pushed away the acolyte guide that his party no longer needed. He suddenly realized that Prasutagos was no longer behind him. The Samaritan, glancing back, noticed the Eastland prince had reclaimed his Estrangorean princess.

"Prince Prasutagos! This way!" he shouted. Turning away then, the adventurer charged out into the November night. Victory depended upon killing or capturing the fleeing enemy.

But Boudica had comprehended the Samaritan's words and pushed herself out of Prasutagos' embrace. "Why did he call you Prince Prasutagos?" she demanded.

When the young man could not immediately reply, she backed away from him with clenched fists.

"Well?" she said.

The false harper sighed and looked perplexed.

# A Match Made in Hell

## CHAPTER XXV

"Well, I'm waiting," said Prasutagos' would-be bride.

"It's true," the young man stammered, "I am the son of Antedios, the king of Eastland."

"You've been making a fool of me all this time!" the Brigantean princess accused.

"I didn't enjoy tricking you, but I was no more at liberty to reveal my real identity than you were."

"Why did you lie to me from the start?!"

"It was a joke at first. But suddenly I had to keep it up to protect you. The more people who knew my secret, the harder it would be to keep it."

"So you thought I'd betray you!"

"Not intentionally. But if any of our enemies suspected you knew something important, they would have forced you to give it up. They could have used torture."

"When you entered our camp at the Fountain of Nimue, you pretended to be someone else, for no reason at all."

"I had a good reason for it," he said.

"What reason?"

"I was being asked to marry a stranger, but only if I liked her. I quickly wanted to know your character. It had to be done before you reached Eastland, because you'd be humiliated if I rejected you with the whole kingdom watching.

"I thought that if you didn't react well to me as a supposed common person, you wouldn't like me as a husband. You might have hidden your true feelings for a while if you met me as a prince, but high-born women show their worst nature when they interact with simple people."

"And if I didn't pass your test, you would have rejected me?"

"It would have ruined both our lives if I married you, with neither of us liking the other. My wish was for a wife possessing genuine virtue, not simply royal status."

"And what do you think is genuine virtue?"

"To me, the perfect wife is someone who is both pleasant and fun to be around."

"You were only fishing for excuses to not marry me! I'm glad you did, because now I know you for who you are! Naming yourself Broch and telling me you were a harper was an outrageous lie!"

"None of it was a lie. I've been called Broch ever since I was a child. My closest friends still call me Broch. And I play the harp. Can't a person who plays the harp call himself a harper?"

"I've never heard you playing the harp. I bet you're not good at it!"

"There are better harpers than me, I grant. If you had been lively and welcoming at the fountain, I would have been honest with you from the beginning. Being initially unsure about you, I decided to play my role for a little longer."

"When we rode together, you said terrible things about yourself and your own family!"

"It was a test. I want to know if you would willingly marry into an unhappy family. If you didn't care if your new family was a bad one, it might mean you only cared about being a queen. I suppose I did go a little too far. It's just that you're always so serious and easy to tease!"

"Oh, you scoundrel!"

"I saw a whole different side to you when you surrendered to the slavers to save a house servant. That made me understand your kindness. Ever since that moment, I have wanted you to be my wife."

"That decision took you quite a while!" she said sourly.

"Quite a while? Within a day, I knew I wanted to marry you."

"You're insane!" She turned her back and crossed her arms.

Prasutagos circled to her front side. "What's wrong about wanting a happy marriage? I wanted a good personal marriage, not just a good political one. Our diplomatic people came back telling us that Princess Voada was proud and angry. That sounded unpleasant; however, I wouldn't reject you based on scanty evidence. I wanted to meet you and decide for myself."

"Why *shouldn't* I feel pride and anger?"

The youth met her glance. "What kind of person wants to be proud and angry?"

"I'm not proud! But I have many reasons to be angry!"

"I know. You told me about some of them. The strange part is that you were dearest to me not when we were having fun, but when we were hungry and sharing, when we were in danger and I feared I would lose you. That was when I cherished you the most.

"Going through all the trouble together, I witnessed your bravery and how level-headed you were about solving problems. Should trouble arise, you're the person I want to be with. I'd marry you now, regardless of royalty."

Instead of answering, she stomped toward the cavern exit.

"Where are you going?" her suitor called.

"I refuse to remain here due to the odor."

"It's cold outside, and you're still dressed for bed!"

"I don't care about the cold!" she said over her shoulder. "I come from a cold home and I'm used to it!"


Simon, Mog Ruith, and the warriors searched doggedly for the renegade druids. The searchers were flummoxed by how they had disappeared so quickly.

Suddenly, the Samaritan heard the Wren Druid cry out in pain. He glanced back and saw Mog Ruith lying on the grass.

"Ruith! What's wrong?" he called back.

"I tripped over a piece of deadwood."

Simon hurried to help him rise. When the big man put weight on his left leg, he moaned again. The Samaritan checked the limb for injuries. "Ahhh!" the Irishman exclaimed. "You touched a burning spot," the Irishman said.

"You may have twisted your ankle or broken it."

"How is it possible for me to get wounded from walking on grass, considering I emerged unharmed from two battles?"

"Stranger things have happened," commiserated Simon. He called to a nearby Merlin Druid. "Tend to our friend," he told the man. "I have to help Lamorak run down those black wizards."

"Aye, Simon!" the druid said, nodding. "Go! Do not let those madmen get away!"


"Stop following me!" Boudica told her persistent admirer.

The youth took off his mantle, which he had taken from a corpse during the battle.

She pushed it away. "I want nothing from you. I have to go."

"Where do you intend to go?" Prasutagos asked.

"To catch up with the Logresians. I think you Icenians are all crazy!"

"The Catuvellaunians care about you only because you're politically important."

"I don't care!"

"For how much longer will you remain angry?" Prasutagos asked.

"Forever!"

"Watch out," he cautioned. "Constantly angry people always suffer from sour stomachs."

"Go away! Why do you want me when I don't want you?"

"Because I want to marry you."

"I've already told you I won't marry you."

"Why?"

"Because you lied to me!"

"I've explained it was only a little joke."

"I don't like your sense of humor!"

"What will your brothers say if you refuse to marry the person they picked for you?"

"Oh, I see, you view this to be a political matter!"

"I don't care so much about politics, but your brothers do. When you tell them how awful I am, they'll only scold you and send you back to Eastland. When they learn how well I looked after you in the wilderness, they'll see me as the perfect brother-in-law."

"You braggart! Whenever I was with you, I was constantly cold and hungry."

"Well, I was cold and hungry, too. You don't hear me blaming you for that, do you?"

The princess stopped and turned fiercely. "Even if my insane brothers force me to marry you, I won't ever love you!"

"Did you love me before? I heard something wonderful in your voice when you spoke to that untalented harper."

"I aimed to show kindness to the harper due to his lack of talent and future opportunities. I thought if someone didn't help him, he would die a beggar."

"That's wonderful! I like girls who are kind to poor people."

"Then marry some poor girl!"

"Marrying you will be like marrying a poor girl. Remember, I fell in love with a slave girl wearing a dirty shift."

"You badger! I'm not, repeat *not*, a slave, despite what some varlets claim."

"Why don't you, as a proud princess, welcome the opportunity to marry a prince?"

"Some prince you are! You watched our friends die at the bridge and didn't raise a finger to defend them!"

"I fought back; you just didn't notice. I killed that Pict who was about to hit you with his axe. I was the one who sent that spear through his body!"

She paused. "That was you?"

He nodded smugly.

"How dare you throw a spear at someone standing so close to me! You could have killed me instead!"

"Give me some credit. I'm rather apt at throwing javelins."

"You're apt at being conceited!" she said. "What good is your kind of love? You just stood there when the slavers hit me and chained me."

"They hit me and chained me, too. Any vainglory on my part wouldn't help you. Anyway, he had to turn you over the Romans in good health.

But if I'd fought or insulted him, he'd have killed me straight out. Who would you have kept you company or helped you after that?"

"He wouldn't have killed you if you admitted you were a king's son who could also be sold to the Romans!"

"Probably not, but my country might have had to surrender its freedom to Rome to make me free. I couldn't let that happen."

"So, your country is more important than I was?"

"You're both important to me. I hope nothing ever forces me to choose between you."

She turned away, but Prasutagos continued to speak: "Did you never suspect that I wasn't just a simple musician? Poor old Synhwyrol almost gave it away with his careless jabbering."

Boudica whirled, her fists balled. "You could fool me because you have the manners of a beggar's son! You never acted like a prince, and you still don't! Anyway…" She seemed to grope for words.

"Anyway, what?"

"I don't want to say it."

"Why not?"

"Because if I say anything that sounds nice to you, it will make your ego bigger!"

"Not true. If you say nice things, I'll simply smile and love you all the more."

"Oh, you! I was easy to fool because…" her words trailed off.

"Because of what?"

She took a deep breath. "I didn't guess you were a prince because—"

"Becaaaause…?" he teased.

"Because the gods never show me kindness! How could I suppose they would give me a suitor whom I could like?"

"Are you saying that you liked Broch the harper a lot?"

"Please, no! Neither of you would make a good husband!"

"You're not making sense. Are you turning me down because there's someone else you want to marry?"

"No!"

"Face the facts, Boudica. If you don't marry me, your brothers are going to make you marry somebody else. And do you suppose you can find a better match than ours? If we're fated to be married, the gods might punish you for defying fate. They might find some perfectly awful person for you to marry!"

"I'll refuse to marry anyone I don't love!"

"Why aren't you already married?"

"Because I haven't met the right person yet."

"Maybe you have."

"It's not you! I can't marry anyone short."

"I'm not short. I'm just as tall as you are."

"But I'm a woman, and that makes you short."

Prasutagos took her hand, and she didn't yank it away. She said, "You're so… conceited."

He wrapped his mantle around her bare shoulders, and this time, she accepted it. "Yes. I'm conceited. I'm conceited enough to think that if I took you into my arms and kissed the daylights out of you, you'd enjoy it."

Her glance seemed to challenge him to prove it. Holding her glance with his, he carefully wrapped his arms around her. When she didn't pull away, he pressed his lips to hers. Their initial kiss would forever be etched in their memories.


Simon and the Britons had run out of places to search. They could not wait for dawn to search the ground for spoor, but being outnumbered, they could not stay close to Caer Draig. At daybreak, hundreds of armed Picts with spears and poisoned arrows would pour out of the hillfort to attack them.

Captured Picts and Wyrms yielded no information regarding the druids' whereabouts. Pellinor and his men rescued some men from the battle. They led them, along with the prisoners, down into the Labyrinth. One prisoner, hating the underworld, willingly guided them to an exit door.

To Pellinor's prisoners, Lamorak could add some wounded sorcerers and low-level Black Goat prisoners. They drew no information from the former, and the Gallic captives knew none of the Wyrm secrets.

The reunited detachments hurried to the horse camp and rode out before dawn. They retreated toward Camelos until the sun was up. When Pellinor thought it prudent, they left the road, camped, and slept in shifts. During a night council, the warriors and druids discussed their successes and failures.

Pellinor's high-risk attack had cost many lives, but deciding the wisdom of his actions would have to be decided by King Caratacos.

Nonetheless, the dragon-questers had taken important Roman prisoners, as well as rescued the prince of Eastland and the princess of Estrangore. Also, they had good reason to think that their efforts had temporarily upset the schemes of the renegade druids. Simon argued his opinion that the traitors would abandon Caer Draig as soon as possible. A small military attack would warn them that a powerful military attack would soon be coming.

To Simon, the raid's greatest failure was the escape of the enemy leaders. In the countryside, new treasonous schemes would be taking shape.

By morning, the king of Avalon had decided what must be done. Pellinor sent scouting parties back to Caer Draig to keep watch on what the Wyrm Druids were doing. When King Arto arrived, Pellinor wanted to have good information to give him. By day's end, returning scouts were bringing back information that many savages and druids were leaving the stronghold with a train of carts, pack animals, women, and children. Pellinor increased the number of scouts, instructing them to follow the departing enemy and find out where they were going. With the passing days, several of these scouts failed to come back with updates. Pursuing the retreating Druids had turned out to be hazardous duty. The old warrior had to abandon the scouting venture to save lives.

He also sent a messenger to inform King Arto about the developing situation. He led his group back to the caer. The only people still in the town were the old, wounded, and sick—persons whom the druids had abandoned to their fate. Most were Picts; questioning them proved unproductive.

The returned Britons confronted the question of what to do with the hundreds of *bwyd y duwiau* languishing in the caves, unfed and unwatered. Lamorak suggested killing the creatures, however, Simon and Mog Ruith countered. They argued that only the high king could decide the fate of innocents.

Pellinor decided to tend to the miserable creatures' basic needs. There was no lack of water and turnips near Caer Draig.

News from the south brought welcome relief; King Arto, leading his soldiers, was near.

# THE JUDGMENT OF ARTO

## CHAPTER XXVI

King Arto soon arrived at Caer Draig, with a warrior escort much smaller than the one that had started from Camelos. While traveling northwest, Laird Pellinor's messenger intercepted the king to inform him that his warrior band had taken control of the abandoned Wyrm stronghold. Arto chose to return most of his army to the Roman front and proceed forward with only one hundred elite soldiers.

Pellinor and Mog Ruith briefed the king when he arrived. He asked to inspect the underground pens housing the creatures he had just been told existed. Arto returned from the labyrinth with profound concern writ large on his face.

An emergency council assembled the following day, held in the Wyrm's former Temple of Gathanothog, and Arto addressed the crisis he had just discovered. His speaking voice sometimes cracked with emotion.

"What was the purpose of these druids' actions?" he asked his counselors. "Were the Wyrms and their allies out of their minds?!"

His men gave answer. "Of course they were mad, Majesty," said Simon the Merlin. "We believe the proximity of the demonic Dragon Spirits suffices to madden and corrupt a man."

The king looked at his senior chiefs. "What say you, friends? Ought we to consider these pathetic creatures to be men and women still? Or should we regard them as an odious form of domestic stock?"

Getting no consistent reply from the warriors, he addressed the druids. "Men of expert knowledge, can you enlighten us on how the human body can be so distorted? Did this occur over many generations, or was it a physical degradation resulting from horrific magic, such as we hear about in our hero legends?"

Mog Ruith, still suffering from his fall, stood up with the aid of a crutch. "I think it is likely that the creature's ancestors were degenerated by using sorcery," he said. "I believe that the sorcery originated from the Dragon Spirits, ghostly entities born in a realm of evil. I believe this perversion of nature may have occurred many centuries ago during the almost forgotten Age of the Dragons.

"I suppose the physical and mental corruption may also have been brought about by forcing human beings to mate with inferior creatures of an unknown type."

Balin, the senior war chief present, spoke hard words. "We should not trouble ourselves with questions about what happened in ancient days. We face the problem that man-beasts exist. Their very existence is an affront to all true-born men. Getting rid of them needs a ruthless application of the Logresian confederacy's power."

Arto glanced at Simon again. "And you, Merlin? What have you to say?"

"It is a bitter question, Laird King," the Samaritan replied. "These creatures were created to feed the dragons. In the madness of those days, men who were possessed by a demon-inspired madness also fed upon their flesh. Had we not intervened, the ongoing slaughter would have continued.

"Knowing of their existence now raises a serious and very sad question for civilized men. Can we say that an injury imposed upon innocent people by demons and depraved men robs them of their God-created spirit?

"That is the vital question we face, Majesty. It is a profound moral question. It is also a question that has no answer in established law. The decision Your Majesty needs to make regarding these... people... forces upon us another pertinent question. How should fairness apply here?

"Whatever decision His Majesty comes to, it will be a statement about the character of this nation. It will bind Britannia to live with the outcome, be it glorious or shameful."

"Should the fate of these men not be decided by law, but by moral doctrine instead?" Arto asked. "I see your perspective. We must include men of faith in this discussion. What say you, Merlin? You are a priest. What insights can you offer about this painful issue?"

Simon shifted uncomfortably. Part of him wanted the creatures to be removed from the world, hoping their destruction would erase them from his memories of the labyrinth.

But he could not see them as mere animals to be destroyed. His wish was for a judgment on "the gods' food" that would be fair not just to the people of Britannia, but to the entire world.

He decided to remain silent. Most of the Merlin Druids present disliked him for the favor Emrys had showered upon him. He believed that however he advised the king, it would incite his enemies to argue for the exact opposite course. That was the wrong way to decide the fate of living beings.

For such reasons, Simon thought it best to step away from the matter. He couldn't interfere; a Brythonic judgment had to come from the Brythonic heart.

Simon said to the monarch, "Liege, I am a novice who is imperfectly schooled in the druidic faith. Further, your people consider me a foreigner with foreign opinions. The decision His Majesty makes in the name of the Brythonic people must reflect Brythonic values in every way. I am therefore very disinclined to advise the king with specifics."

Arto declared, "I'm no priest either, yet I require guidance from upright individuals. Let me hear your sage advice, learned savants."

The priests glanced about, but none rose to speak.

"Fear not! Nothing you say will place any onus upon you. While I would be happy to hand these sad matters over to others, my acceptance of the crown makes me responsible for all laws given to our kingdom. I seek wise counsel, but final accountability is mine.

"During moments like these, I realize that ruling during days of hardship brings no joy. Men's envy of kings baffles me. That being said, I urge one and all to speak with bold conviction. I value moral opinions above all."

This began a long conversation. Despite the many stated opinions, no simple answers were placed on the table.

After much listening and much debating, High King Arto, wearing a face of woe, announced his decision. He stated his decree that those called the *bwyd y duwiau* should be put to the sword, swiftly and with every mercy.

A deathly pall fell over the room. Even those who were most vehement about slaying the beast-men did not smile upon realizing that what they asked for would be accomplished. That included even the fierce and judgmental Laird Balin.

"I need to say one more thing," pronounced the king. "Everyone here must vow never to discuss this again. That Britannia's subjects should remain unaware of our decision is our Royal intention. No innocent person of this green land should be forced to share in our shame."

But a matter so complex could not be simply settled. Prisoners and villagers had testified that the Wyrm's carts had removed many *bwyd y duwiau* from Caer Draig before the fort underwent attack.

Simon had already discussed this matter with others. The consensus held that because a spy had entered the labyrinth, Master Wyrm Bhort had taken action. To safeguard the *bwyd y duwiau* breed in the event of a military raid, he had sent the best breeding stock away from Caer Draig. It had been his wish that future generations of the cult could carry on with their degenerate practices.

Mog Ruith offered Arto advice: "Bhort would not have sent the men-beasts away unless he could sustain them. The Wyrms have been feeding the *bwyd y duwiau* with a staple diet of turnips. Master Bhort will continue this custom. I, therefore, propose that inquiries be made in all parts of Britannia, north, south, east, and west. We must discover whether any subject of any kingdom knows of any large plantings of turnips. The pathetic creatures will be confined near such locations."

"A wise opinion," Arto stated. "We need to hunt down and slay these tragic beings. This ongoing destruction must be carried out under the cloak of secrecy. Our small group's shame must not be allowed to disgrace all of Britannia."

With that ruling, the matter of the *bwyd y duwiau* was finally, and mercifully, brought to a close.

# THE DARKNESS DESCENDING



The next most important issue was addressing the matter of the Roman prisoners taken at Caer Draig. The Britons already held many captured Roman soldiers, but this case was special. These Romans had been taken in the backcountry while abetting traitors engaged in black magic.

Mog Ruith required the aid of a crutch to rise from his chair. He had volunteered to advocate for the Roman prisoners.

"Based on my knowledge," he said, "I believe that none of the Romans now in custody had prior information regarding the evil doings enacted at Caer Draig. Yes, they certainly and knowingly encouraged the treasonous activities of the Brythonic renegades, but such activity is, sadly, a commonplace occurrence in wartime. I hold these officers deceived by the Wyrm Druids and kept ignorant of the cult's true intentions.

"Majesty, in my estimation, Asiaticus is as decent an individual as Britannica is ever likely to encounter among the ranks of the Roman enemy. He is an unusual Roman in that he honors his Gallic heritage and the sacred knowledge passed down from his druidic ancestors. Therefore, I urge our liege to treat the man and his associates with correctness and due honor."

After Mog Ruith completed his defense, Arto looked to the chiefs gathered about him. "Friends, do you have answers to the issues our ally from Ireland has raised?"

Balin stood up and argued that the Romans should be "persuaded" to reveal everything known to them regarding their army's deployments and plans for making war. If they refused to cooperate, he held that they should be shown no mercy.

Other opinions were offered, and in due course, Arto pronounced his ruling. "We shall inform Aulus Plautius of his subordinates' capture. His envoy and company will be treated the same way his own Brythonic prisoners were being treated.

"We shall aim for a courteous agreement with the general, facilitating prompt prisoner exchanges between Britain and Rome. We shall propose that the manner of these exchanges should be established through good-faith negotiations conducted between the representatives of the kingdom of Logres and the appointed representatives of the Roman army."

With the major issue having been agreed to, the Samaritan left the temple. Part of him clung to the hope that some modicum of decency might prevail between two races engaged in a bitter war.

But Simon considered the probability unlikely. As with Balin, the Samaritan's gorge rose when he thought about the oppressive system of tyranny the empire offered.

How long could King Arto hold this throne in the face of Rome's attack? Simon felt compassion for the idealistic young king. So early in his reign, he found himself making difficult decisions impacting the lives of many. Truly, leadership—if performed honorably—amounted to a terrible burden.


At the edge of the park, music lured Simon toward what had formerly been Goddeu's lodge. Inside, Brythonic warriors were filling their cups from a vat of strong wine. Their levity offered the adventurer relief from the sober deliberations of the council of druids and chiefs. One story, especially, was inciting the warriors to laughter.

After Plautius' defeat on the Medway, the emperor announced that his general had won a brilliant victory. Claudius' subjects were being told how German auxiliaries had swum across the flooded river while wearing full armor. They supposedly attacked the enemy on the far side, sending them running. This victory had allowed the Roman army to cross the river without loss, achieving every aim.

Guffawing rang the rafters. A warrior named Hueil merrily declared, "The only German miracle I saw at the Medway was how fast those little German boys could run! By the gods! They outran the noble Romans, even though the legionaries have a long history of running from lost battles!"

With darkness descending, Simon quietly departed the lodge. Though the wine had been ample, it had not lightened his melancholy one wit.

False stories about Rome's successes might make honest men laugh, but recent information provided by Arto's spies sounded disconcerting.

The Roman emperor had declared that he would arrive in Britain come spring, bringing with him a great host of reinforcements. Simon believed that if Claudius continued with his warlike program, the islands' prospects were bleak. The invasion, if pressed long enough and hard enough, would surely wear down the Britons.

Despite, or perhaps because of, the pessimistic outlook, Simon felt reluctant to leave Britannia. Mog Ruith's words rang true for him: one must fight evil, no matter how unlikely victory might be.

As the darkness became full, the Samaritan continued to wander through the battered, broken, and ill-smelling hillfort.

Questions continued to nag at the mystical scholar, especially one question he had been asking himself, and Heaven, all through his adult life. The question was a simple one: "What is the meaning of my life?"

But had anyone, would anyone, ever discover a satisfying answer?

# About the Authors

**Glenn A. Rahman**, in the '70s and '80s, was a frequent pre-computer era contributor to the semi-pro scene, such as *Fantasy Crosswinds*, *Eldritch Tales*, and *Crypt of Cthulhu*. His first professional publication came with the release of the fantasy board game *Divine Right*, published by TSR, Inc. in 1979. This was followed by *Knights of Camelot* (1980, TSR), the *Trojan War* (1980, Metagaming), and *Down with the King* (1980, Avalon Hill). During this time, Glenn Rahman and his brother Philip (founder of the still-extant Fedogan & Bremer book company, specializing in Cthulhu Mythos and supernaturally-themed literature) created a two-part article for *Sorcerer's Apprentice*, *The Lovecraft Variant* and *The Monsters of the Cthulhu Mythos* which amounted to the first successful transference of H.P. Lovecraft's style of supernatural literature into a modern role-playing format. In addition, Mr. Rahman has continued to publish board gaming and fantasy role-playing articles and supplements widely. His first book-length fictional work was serialized in *Dragon Magazine* (beginning in 1980), entitled *The Minarian Legends*, which keyed off his original *Divine Right* universe. *Minarian Legends* has lately been reissued as a paperback book. In 2001, Sidecar Books of Minneapolis, MN published his *Gardens of Lucullus*, a Cthulhu Mythos novel in collaboration with Richard L. Tierney. In 2023, DMR Books published *A Feast of Ambrosia*, featuring his two Dark Age sword and sorcery heroes, Bingor and Donalbain.

# ABOUT THE AUTHORS

**Richard L. Tierney** (1936 - 2022) was a poet, author, and editor of adventure fiction, mainly in the realm of dark fantasy. Since his mid-teens, he has been both a fan and scholar of H.P. Lovecraft, Robert E. Howard, Clark Ashton Smith, and other great names from the pulp fiction era. In 2010, he was nominated for the Science Fiction Poetry Association's Grandmaster Award.

In 1961, Tierney earned a degree in entomological science (Iowa State College) and served for many years with the U.S. Forest Service in several of the western states and Alaska. An archaeological tourist by instinct, he has traveled widely, especially in Mexico, Central, and South America. Many of the ideas and images that he has employed in his stories have been inspired by his extensive travels.

His major fiction works include *The Winds of Zarr* (1975, Silver Scarab Press), the *Red Sonia* series with David C. Smith (1981-1983, Ace Books), *The House of the Toad* (1993, Fedogan and Bremer), and *The Drums of Chaos* (2008, Mythos Books). His poetry collections include *Collected Poems: Nightmares and Visions* (1981, Arkham House), and *Savage Menace and Other Poems of Horror* (2010, reprint 2021, P'rea Press).

After many years enjoying his retirement in his house, "the hermitage," in the Corn Steppes of northern Iowa, Richard passed away in 2022.

# MORE BOOKS FROM PICKMAN'S PRESS

## SORCERY AGAINST CAESAR

Simon of Gitta, escaped slave turned magician, roves the Roman Empire battling dark magic and demons, all while pursued by Caesar's soldiers in sixteen stories by Richard L. Tierney and others that combine historical fiction, sword & sorcery, and Lovecraftian Horror.

## THE DRUMS OF CHAOS

In the Holy Lands, Simon becomes entangled in an occult plot call down a monstrous alien entity to herald a new aeon on Earth. Simon and his allies race against time to prevent the extinction of all life on Earth—but can they really thwart a covert scheme backed by the power of the Roman Empire?

## HEIR OF DARKNESS

The Romans have stolen the Ring of the Gods, which could save or destroy the earth. Osric, a German barbarian, must steal the ring back from the Roman Emperor Caligula—and before a witch from the evil Cult of Heid can, and uses it to bring about *Götterdämmerung* and end the world.

## REASSURING TALES

Creatures sinister but unseen. Madmen who may not be so mad. Realities that twist into astonishing patterns. Insidious new technologies beyond our understanding or control. Welcome to the existential weird fiction of master storyteller T.E.D. Klein, author of bestselling novel *The Ceremonies* and award-winning collection *Dark Gods*.

## THE GLASS MARINES

Marine Sergeant Christopher receives a bizarre order: Make 185 Malacan aliens into US Marines. With only three Drill Instructors, century-old weapons and equipment, and only eighteen weeks for Boot Camp, can Sgt. Christopher teach the meek and passive aliens what it means to be one of the few and the proud?

## THE AVEROIGNE ARCHIVES

All of Clark Ashton Smith's weird tales of Averoigne—the sinister, monster-haunted province of medieval France—are collected into one volume. Werewolves and satyrs stalk dark forests, witches and necromancers lurk in swamps, and giants terrorize the cathedral city of Vyônes in the heart of Averoigne.

## THE AVEROIGNE LEGACY

Over two dozen tribute tales and poems set in Clark Ashton Smith's world of Averoigne. Revisit Vyônes and Périgon, meet Luc le Chaudronnier and Azédarac once again, as tales of harpies and vampires, ogres and giants, changelings and cockatrices await you!

## CORPORATE CTHULHU

Just like the Great Old Ones, corporations are powerful but unseen entities we have no control over, yet subtly manipulate our lives and our world—and we don't even realize it. Endure twenty-five Mythos tales of bureaucratic nightmare, but remember: it's nothing personal—just business.